THE SHADOW RULE

THE STARS AND GREEN MAGICS
BOOK 2

NOVAE CAELUM

Robot Dinosaur Press

https://robotdinosaurpress.com

Robot Dinosaur Press is a trademark of Chipped Cup Collective.

The Shadow Rule

Copyright © 2022 by Novae Caelum

All rights reserved.

No part of this publication may be reproduced, stored in a retrieval system, or transmitted, in any form or by any means, electronic, mechanical, magical, photocopying, or otherwise, without the prior written permission of the copyright holder.

This is a work of fiction. Names, characters, organizations, places, and events portrayed in this work are either products of the author's or authors' imagination or are used fictitiously. Any resemblance to actual persons, living or dead, business establishments, events, or locales is entirely coincidental.

Ebook ISBN 978-1-958696-09-5

Paperback ISBN 978-1-958696-11-8

Cover art and book design by Novae Caelum

Author photo credit Novae Caelum

https://novaecaelum.com

AUTHOR'S NOTE

The Shadow Rule was originally published as season two of the ongoing serial *The Stars and Green Magics*, covering episodes 37-93.

I made some minor editing changes from the original serial version, most notably that Rhys's last name is now Delor.

This book features several characters who use gender neutral pronouns (they/them/their, fae/faer/faerself, e/em/eir, or other neopronouns).

This book, barring the occasional and inspired burst of strong language, is a solid PG-13.

For detailed content notes, please see:
https://novaecaelum.com/content-notes

1

NOT YOUR ENEMY

> *A love match isn't always a thing to be desired. Why tie yourself down when a good seduction will get the same result?*
>
> — LORD ESARA TEOH MÉRON BRINT IN *A GUIDE TO ETIQUETTE AT THE PALACE RHIALDEN COURT*

Dressa came out of her Change trance slowly, gradually aware of her surroundings. Under the covers, her body held its usual shape, and she sighed deeply, feeling its familiar bounds.

The scent of ocean juniper turned her head to find Lesander, just rolling over to face her.

She blinked several times. Had Lesander stayed there the whole hour it had taken her to Change? No, it had to have been more than an hour. Her mouth was dry and thick, more than a Change would account for. She'd—Adeius, she hadn't just Changed, she'd slept, too.

Dressa pushed up. The lamp on the end table was on dim, but the room had no windows, no clocks. "What time—"

"Early morning," Lesander said. "Shh. The Truthspeaker said the Adeium is guarded, and she guarantees the Seritarchus won't disturb us. She said she spoke with him last night. Came to me after. She said to let you sleep, and to sleep myself." Lesander yawned wide. "Which I did."

Dressa's breath hitched. "What did my father say?"

"You'll have to ask the Truthspeaker."

Lesander groaned and buried her face back in her pillow. "Would you mind sleeping a few more hours?"

Dressa wasn't anything like tired now, knowing her father had been to see Ceorre. She had to know how that had gone. She had to know just how deep in the shit she was. In the courtyard the day before, he'd nodded to her. What had that meant? He couldn't have approved of what she was doing, not after she'd flat-out defied him and gone over his head to Ceorre.

She looked down at herself, at her own self. Now that she wasn't Arianna anymore, her mind was not reconciling the urgent fact that she was the Heir—she, Dressa, not Arianna. She herself was the Truthspoken Heir, as herself.

Lesander shifted, pushed up to sit, too. "Are you all right?"

Dressa nodded, her mouth compressed.

Lesander tilted her head, bit her lip. Dressa's gaze went right there, white teeth on pink lips.

"Am I freaking you out?" Lesander asked.

"What? No! No, it's—" Dressa pushed her hair out of her eyes. She'd look a mess. Her dark hair in tight tangles, no makeup. Absolutely un-sexy. "I'm surprised I'm not freaking you out."

"Oh, you are. I'm absolutely freaking out." But Lesander's tone was sardonic, the corners of her mouth quirking up.

Lesander studied her, and Dressa, arrested by the growing heat of the look, stared back.

"So, am I your type?" Lesander asked.

Adeius, Lesander didn't mince words, did she?

"Uh—" Heat. She was being flooded with heat, and she debated the merits of trying to enter a light trance right now to calm it all down. Would Lesander notice either way? Should she tell Lesander she had a crush on her?

Well, but why the hell not? Lesander was her wife.

"Yes. Yeah. You're gorgeous. And so poised, and—"

Lesander's lips met hers, hot and full, her hand slipping around the back of Dressa's neck.

Dressa froze for one heart-stopping moment, hardly daring to believe this was happening.

Then she leaned in and hungrily kissed Lesander back.

Fingers tangling in Lesander's flame-red, bed-mussed hair.

She tasted earthy, she tasted like morning breath, and Dressa didn't care.

Lesander pulled back just long enough to breathe against her mouth, "You're my type, too."

Dressa knew she should slow down and think a minute, think about what she was doing, about the politics and the consequences, but she was hungry, in so many more ways than one, and Lesander was a goddess and willing and Adeius the soft skin of her neck tasted just as good as Dressa had imagined.

And then they were struggling out of their inconvenient clothes. Sheets were tangled. Skin to skin.

And—Adeius.

Dressa lay beside Lesander, their shoulders touching. She stared wide-eyed at the ceiling, her heart still racing.

She'd been with other women before, mostly nobles, and it had always been knowing that it was a fling for mutual pleasure and nothing more. She could never have more.

But this was something more, surely. She was still floating. She wasn't sure she'd stop floating at all that day.

Lesander gave a self-satisfied snort, then stretched like a cat and rolled out of bed. "We'd better get to the palace, do you think? You'll need to be seen coming home today."

Dressa blinked at her, her mind and body still unattached, not computing the things of the ordinary world.

Lesander looked back down at her from tugging on her shirt, fastening the buttons. She smirked and stalked toward the door.

"Where are you—"

"Just the bathroom. I'll be back."

Dressa sighed in a relief that held her chagrined.

Adeius, *what* was happening? How had they gone so far, so fast? She'd been expecting weeks of probing Lesander's wishes —she hadn't at all expected Lesander would like her right back. Would things be awkward now? They hardly knew each other.

They knew a lot more about each other now than they had an hour ago. And she couldn't think about that again if she wanted to get anything done today.

Dressa rubbed her face, got out of bed, and dressed herself.

She had to be careful. She had to be so careful, because Lesander made her crazy, all of which was currently heightened to the state where when Lesander came back in, the hair around her face curled from splashing water on her face, she wanted to seize Lesander's collar and drag her right back to bed.

Had she been the one in control? Had Lesander? She didn't know. Both. They'd been so entangled. She'd never felt that synchronous with anyone in bed before. She'd never been with someone who hadn't, on some level at least, been afraid of her and her power.

Dressa stood near the bed, breathing more heavily than she could smooth away.

Lesander was a Javieri.

Lesander was her wife. Her consort.

Lesander watched her, and some of the bravado left her posture. She approached slowly, more tentative this time, and held out her hands.

Dressa took them and pulled Lesander against her, she couldn't help that, just to feel her warmth again.

"I'm not your enemy," Lesander said, as if she'd read Dressa's mind. Or more likely, her body language.

Dressa closed her eyes as Lesander pressed her lips to her neck. She shivered, and she'd have to stop this soon or they'd be back in bed again, wouldn't they? Not that she didn't want that with everything in her. She curled her toes into the floor against the need.

She gently pushed Lesander back. No, Lesander wasn't her immediate enemy. But she wasn't sure why Lesander had decided to kiss her before, she wasn't sure why Lesander had wanted to sleep with her. Had it been innocent, had it been mutual attraction, mutual comfort? Or had it been a deliberate seduction? Lesander absolutely had evaku training. This was the Rhialden court, where such seductions were common maneuvers. Had Lesander seen Dressa's crush on her and leaned into it? Had she truly felt attraction in return?

Ceorre's warnings about the Javieris were running through Dressa's mind like blaring sirens. The Javieris wanted to overthrow the Rhialdens. They wanted to be close to power. It didn't get much closer than this.

"You're upset with me," Lesander said, her posture growing more closed.

Dressa saw the tactic for what it was, saw Lesander trying to put her on the defensive. Was it a deflection of true hurt, or did Lesander want to push on her emotions?

Dressa sidestepped the statement, taking a gamble of her own. “I'm the Truthspoken Heir. You understand that I can't, absolutely can't, trust you on word alone.”

“Because I'm Javieri?” Lesander spat.

Dressa refused to be moved by that ire, either. “Yes. I'm not a fool, and you're not a fool. Can we agree to that?”

Lesander swallowed, and Dressa watched her throat constrict with growing heat again. She wanted to press her lips to Lesander's silky neck. Again.

Lesander inhaled sharply, half turned, let it out again. “I was prepared for Arianna. I was not prepared for you.”

That hit Dressa with a thrill to her stomach, but she still held it apart. “In what way?”

Lesander made a frustrated sound. “Do you want me to outright admit I'm trained to manipulate?”

Dressa shrugged. “So am I. I only care what you're trying to do with it. With me.” She had to ask. She just had to straight out ask—she had a sense Lesander would appreciate that far more than subtlety. “Why did you want—” Her throat closed. She waved at the rumpled bed. “Why did you want to be with me, why right now?”

“Because you've been driving me crazy since I saw you, two —no, is it three days ago now? Three days ago. Arianna is not my type, and I felt zero attraction from her. I knew that would be a loveless marriage. My parents knew that—your parents knew that. I think they wanted that. I knew I'd definitely not get to have—” She waved at the bed. “And I didn't want that with Arianna. But you are—” She took in Dressa, as if the statement was self-explanatory.

Dressa bit her lip, and she did work to calm her body's heat then. In this conversation, she couldn't just be Dressa. This conversation was about politics.

But she was reading sincerity from Lesander. Not fully sincere in all angles, no. But there in most of them, and strong where they were. Of course Lesander would have her secrets. As Truthspoken, so would she.

Dressa stepped closer again, and closer, cupping Lesander's cheek. As Arianna, Lesander had towered over her, but as herself, Lesander was only a centimeter or two taller. She could look her straight in the eyes. Lesander leaned into the touch. Dressa was watching closely. That was not a response Lesander could easily fake.

And neither was the hunger when their lips brushed again.

Lesander pulled back first, resting her forehead against Dressa's. "We need to get to know each other. I get that. But Dressa, please don't tell me I can't share your bed. That was incredible."

She couldn't say no. The words would not come. She didn't want to say no.

Who did she have in her arms? Her enemy? Her lover? Her wife? Only time and observation would tell that.

Dressa stretched up to kiss Lesander's forehead. "Let's go. You're right that I need to make a show of coming back. And you need to be there to greet me."

Was it crazy that she was looking forward to that moment, where she could embrace Lesander as herself in public? Or should she be more sedate? She didn't publicly know Lesander —she as Ondressarie would not have spent the last day and night and this morning with her.

She ran her hand down Lesander's arm, tugged her fingers, and then let go. "Come. The day's show awaits."

2

THE SHOW

> *Sometimes I think the entire point of being Truthspoken is to put on a show.*
>
> — HOMAJ RHIALDEN, SERITARCHUS IX IN A PRIVATE LETTER, NEVER SENT; PUBLISHED IN *THE CHANGE DIALOGUES*

It was certainly a show. Truthspoken Ondressarie stepped out of a car that arrived in a procession from the city's spaceport—which she'd actually gotten into at the palace and had the driver, one of her father's guards and under the strictest security, drive to the port in the city and come right back again.

She smiled and waved for the nobles lined up at the palace receiving entry, and the reporters and vloggers with all their attendant camera drones. But she didn't smile too widely, because of course this was a solemn occasion. Her sister had stepped down, and now she was it. This was her first appearance where the worlds knew she was the future ruler of the kingdom.

Appearance was everything—but then, appearance was Dressa's specialty. She wore a gold dress with little frill that flattered all of her curves. Gold was absolutely her color. Her long black hair hung loose, makeup subtle. Her presence, though. She dialed that up to ten.

Dressa greeted Lesander as if they had not, in fact, been together that morning, and her touch did not, in fact, make Dressa burn.

Lesander's performance in return was worthy of an award, clasping Dressa's hands and exchanging a polite kiss on each cheek. Lesander was her usual charismatic self, elegant in a dark green suit, but she made no attempt to outshine the future Heir.

Their party made it through the palace entry hall, voices echoing. And then to the right, down the long corridor that led toward administrative offices and the guest wing. They stopped at the bank of doors leading to the courtyard where the Adeium sat. That was where Arianna had made her abdication; that was where Dressa would be confirmed as the Heir.

Truthspeaker Ceorre was waiting on a dais outside the Adeium, resplendent in full formal vestments of violet, black, and red. The Seritarchus stood beside her, as calmly neutral as he'd been the day before. He only smiled briefly and nodded at Dressa as she approached, trailing her guards.

The courtyard itself was not as crowded as Dressa would have thought, but then, security would be vetting everyone here today so nothing like the attack on Arianna could happen again.

And the First Magicker was there as well, Dressa saw with a start, standing a little ways off from Ceorre. Mariyit Broden turned, his lined face crinkling in a smile. He stepped forward with hands out, which drew some gasps from the crowd, but they didn't know what Dressa knew—that the attack at the engagement ball hadn't been an attack at all. And that the First

Magicker could hardly do violence to her here, even if he had wanted to.

She clasped the First Magicker's calloused hands, inclined her head as he bowed his own. Beside her, Lesander stood stiffly—but then, she didn't know the whole of it, either.

"Truthspoken," Mariyit said, his bass voice rumbling over her. "I am pleased to see you well. My apologies, my most sincere apologies, for the circumstances that have led up to this day."

She met his dark blue eyes. The sunlight glinted off the edges of the holographic seal on his cheek, the fractal patterns it showed intensely intricate.

"Thank you, First Magicker," she said, loudly enough that those watching her would hear. "I'm honored to have you at this confirmation."

Still holding her hands, he could feel her sincerity, she knew. And he'd feel that she knew he was in no way responsible for any of this. She, in turn, saw some of the strain around his mouth that he was doing a good—but not expert—job of hiding.

Since he'd taken his post three years before, Dressa had always seen him as sharply observant, and Arianna had said before he had a keen eye for politics. He'd been kind to Dressa in the few times they'd met before, in a way that made his kindness sincere when it didn't have to be. Not in this court.

"May the gods keep you well and whole," he said, voice low, then asked, "May I give you some peace in this moment?"

Dressa nodded, and warmth flowed into her, a calm that steadied jittering nerves, though it didn't make them go away. She needed that sharpness to navigate the day.

He let go of her hands and stepped back, accompanied by another murmur from the crowd. What, had they been waiting for her to fall over like Arianna had?

Lesander touched her arm, and Dressa tensed again. She met Lesander's eyes, saw the slightest flick toward the crowds.

They were on display. Right. She hadn't lapsed far, but she smoothed her body language back into the shape it should be: gracious, open, and now attentive as she stepped up between Ceorre and her father.

Her father. He'd always been a closed book to her, but today he was more opaque than usual. His makeup impeccable, long hair pulled up in a looping braid and held with pins sparkling with pale teal Zeoman glass. His ornate shirt flowed in layers of teal and white. But his expression—his expression was so closed beyond the surface projection of emotion that she had no idea what he was thinking about any of this. Was he angry with her, and how much? But she couldn't stare and try to dissect his body language just then.

Ceorre opened the Book of Ceremonies, licked her finger to turn the ancient pages. She began reading a long litany about the place of the Truthspoken in the Kingdom of Valoris, their direct connection to Adeius and the Truthspeaker, and their holy mandate to keep the kingdom whole and holy.

Dressa tried to listen, she truly did. But she'd had to let go of Lesander to step onto the dais, and she kept feeling that lack. Lesander steadied her. How had Lesander gained so much space in her life so quickly? Lesander stood on the far right of the dais, on the other side of the First Magicker, which Dressa doubted she was happy about.

And she kept being distracted by her father as well. There was something unsettling about his demeanor—and it wasn't just her dread of what he'd say about all of this later in private, that fear was a given. She sensed something more, something just slightly off. His lack of visible emotion, maybe, but then, no, that wasn't unusual for him.

He slanted a look at her, face still impassive. Their eyes met briefly and—

Dressa broke into a cold sweat.

This person was not her father.

3

THE IMPOSTER

> *If a Truthspoken can be anyone, then they can be you. They can be me. They can be your parent or your spouse or your closest friend. They can be your help in your time of need, and you'd never know it. They can be cold, and you'd never know why the relationship broke down.*
>
> — DR. NDARI HADI ESYN IN "A SOCIETAL MORPHOLOGY: TRUTHSPOKEN IN THE MODERN AGE"

The Seritarchus, the person standing beside her, looking very much like her father in every way that mattered, wasn't her father. Dressa didn't know how she knew—was it in the posture, was it in the tilt of his head? But no, those were all perfect. Every detail, perfect.

"Truthspoken Ondressarie," Ceorre said, her voice in ceremonial cadence, "do you, under the eyes of Adeius, in the will of Adeius, agree to uphold the will of Adeius in the rule of this Kingdom of Valoris, for the benefit of all in this kingdom—"

Dressa's heart pounded in her throat. *Stay calm.* She had to listen to the oath. This was *her* oath.

"—to give of your heart fully, your mind fully, your body fully to the prosperity of this kingdom—"

Did Ceorre know this person wasn't her father? Ceorre could always see through everything. Could she see through him now?

"—to be the will of Adeius where the Truthspeaker is the word; to govern now as the Truthspoken Heir, and in the future as the Truthspoken Ruler; with equanimity and benevolence, with your people first at heart and Adeius above all?"

Adeius, and if he wasn't her father, who was he? Could he be her father's bloodservant, Iata? But she'd never known Iata to Change beyond the basic things he'd taught her and Arianna, helping the Seritarchus with their training when they were children. He'd always claimed an extremely minimal amount of Change talent, far less than Bettea and Pria had. He was acerbic and strict and had a tendency to telegraph his tells —this person couldn't be Iata. His portrayal was very nearly perfect. And if he wasn't Iata, he would have to be a plant from the nobility. An agent, or an assassin, and where was her father—

He looked at her again, raised a brow. Exactly her father's gesture.

She caught her breath. Had she been mistaken? She saw little of what had disturbed her moments ago. Was she simply that stressed?

She became aware of the hush. And remembered Ceorre's last words—the oath. She had to take the oath.

Dressa cleared her throat through Change. She didn't trust herself otherwise.

"Yes," she said, her voice ringing out, amplified into the courtyard and its dozens of vid cams. She repeated the oath from Ceorre, an oath she'd memorized as a child, inserting herself into it. Feeling the words and their weight even as she frantically tried to parse the puzzle that was the person beside her.

Ceorre pronounced her the Truthspoken Heir, and the ceremony continued.

Her father brought out the engagement contract—a fresh version, unlike the official document she'd signed the day before, which was now a marriage document. But this document was identical.

Lesander came close again, and Ceorre led them all through the terms of the contract and exactly where they were amended—namely, only from Arianna's name to Dressa's. Some of the crowd stirred at that, likely Javieri sympathizers who wanted to make a fuss at the change, but Lesander skewered several of them with her gaze and they subsided.

Lesander signed first, and then Dressa. Ceorre signed, and so did her father—the exact same signature he always used. But then, all Truthspoken were trained in the art of forgery.

He stepped back and gave Lesander a tight-lipped smile. "Welcome to the family, Prince Javieri."

He didn't use her first name, as was typical, but her family name. Emphasizing her family connections. Which was a very like-her-father thing to do.

"Thank you, Seritarchus." Lesander dipped into a shallower bow than would have been proper moments ago—outwardly gracious, but Dressa read the wariness. Had Lesander picked up on the oddness with the Seritarchus, too? No, Lesander would be uneasy with any version of the Seritarchus right now after what they'd done yesterday.

Dressa's neck and arms itched with her unease. She could feel tension crackling around her and didn't know if it was hers, or her father's, or Lesander's.

Did she dare challenge her father's identity? Not in public, surely. But if he wasn't her father, if there was even the slightest chance that he wasn't, she couldn't let him just walk away.

She looped her arm in Lesander's. They were supposed to march back through the center aisle of their audience, but Dressa instead turned to her father. She made sure her throat amplifier was off.

"Father. I would like a word, in the Adeium." There were few places in the palace complex she knew were not bugged, fewer still that she knew her father couldn't absolutely control, and Ceorre's office was one of them. Whatever happened, there could not be a scandal.

She glanced at the First Magicker, who was watching her with a slight smile that raised the hairs on her body further. What did he know? Green Magickers at his rank could sense if a person was Truthspoken or not, but could he tell if her father was Truthspoken-trained but not actually her father?

"I'd like you to come as well, First Magicker."

"Oh, no, you don't need me," Mariyit waved. His aura flared, emerald green rippling in the trail of his hand. "Go work it out. You'll both be fine."

And how was she supposed to interpret that? Did his words mean he already knew about whatever was going on with her father and wasn't concerned? Had he planned it, was he a threat after all? Or was he simply begging out of her family's internal politics? But he'd be able to fully confirm her father to her if he was holding her father's hand and she asked her father directly. And she'd be able to tell the truth from Mariyit if he held her hand in turn and spoke it to her directly. That her father was, in fact, her father. Or that he was not.

She couldn't push. Lesander, aware of the growing tension but not knowing what it meant, stood solidly beside her, waiting.

Her father gestured toward the palace instead. "I'll walk back with you, Daughter. Prince Lesander."

She glanced at Ceorre, who raised her brows, and Dressa could interpret that signal. It meant, "I'm in full knowledge of this situation, why aren't you?"

So Ceorre did know something was off. Something—and Dressa still wasn't sure what, or what signals she should be believing. Her father now read to her—mostly—as her father. She could spot some of his tells, and tells were an intensely private thing among Truthspoken. No one knew them outside the Rhialden family, their bloodservants, and the Truthspeaker and Truthspeaker in Training if there was one, which at the moment there wasn't.

Reluctantly, Dressa followed her father—the person who may or may not be her father—through the crowd of well-wishers and into the palace.

4

LEAD ON

> *My father the Seritarchus taught me how to wield control like a knife. Or maybe that was my father the Consort.*
>
> — HOMAJ RHIALDEN, SERITARCHUS IX IN A PRIVATE LETTER, NEVER SENT; PUBLISHED IN *THE CHANGE DIALOGUES*

Dressa mostly listened as they walked through the palace toward the residence wing, which wasn't her habit—and her father would know that.

He made small talk with Lesander, who gamely rose to the challenge: how are your parents faring? Do you find the palace to your liking? Here's an elaborate description of a crêpe I sampled from the kitchen this morning, and wouldn't that be a nice thing to have at the wedding?

Dressa tried to read jabs at her into the dry conversation, but she had nothing to hold on to. And she rarely saw this family side of her father these days, when he was actually himself and not playing another role or being the Seritarchus with his power wrapped around him like a cloak. She wasn't sure she knew enough to judge if this was how he would act, and that disturbed her.

In the residence wing, her father stopped at the door to Dressa's apartment.

"Prince Lesander—will you wait here, please, while I speak with Dressa?" Though the tone hardly gave room for Lesander to say no.

Dressa reached for the handle, waited through the pause as it scanned her hand and the locks clicked open. She opened the door but didn't go in, and Lesander hesitated.

They'd unofficially been to her apartment that morning after stealing away from the Adeium, but only in her bedroom, through the back corridors. She'd introduced Lesander to Pria —who was still Bettea, and Dressa insisted her bloodservant rest a few days before she tried to Change back, though Pria wasn't happy about it. Or happy about missing everything that had gone on while she was in her long Change trance.

But Lesander had never been alone in Dressa's apartment before. And not when she was publicly engaged to this apartment's occupant and had a social right to be here. Maybe that shouldn't have made a difference, knowing they were married, but Dressa sensed it did.

Or maybe her hesitation was because of the Seritarchus, waiting semi-patiently for Lesander to go in so he could get on with talking to Dressa. Dressa could fully understand being intimidated by the Seritarchus.

Lesander smiled at Dressa, no obvious signs of strain. Dressa caught the slight widening of Lesander's eyes, though, as they met hers. She caught the question: will you be okay? Do you want me to force the issue to come with you?

Dressa's throat tightened. People so seldom asked her that kind of question.

But she had to be Lesander's shield now, whatever lay

ahead. She was the one with the authority to protect them both, even more so now that she was officially the Heir. Dressa couldn't protect herself from her father's wrath if he was her father, though. And if he wasn't?

She was increasingly sure that he wasn't. But she couldn't let Lesander know that. Not yet, not before she knew what was going on.

Lesander must have read some of her decision, because she said, with just the right notes, "I'll be fine."

But she was speaking to two Truthspoken who'd know better.

Dressa reached for Lesander's hand, squeezed it. "There's enough for a light meal in the night kitchen, ask Pria to show you. Or send for a meal to be brought up." Her thoughts raced ahead—the prep room and bedroom would be locked, she'd have to key them to Lesander's genetic signature later. She could have done so that morning, but . . . but.

"I won't be overlong." Adeius, she hoped she wouldn't be. "Ask Pria for anything."

Lesander nodded, dipped the slightest bow to Dressa, and a deeper bow to the Seritarchus.

"Truthspoken. Seritarchus." She glided inside, and Dressa shut the door again with a soft click.

Then it was her, the person who may or may not be her father, and two of his personal guards. Her own guards, picked up again after the ceremony, would be following at a discreet distance; it was understood that when a Truthspoken was near the Seritarchus, his guards and his safety took precedence.

She met her father's eyes, his dark eyes staring back at her. He didn't look away, but there it was again, that very small difference she still couldn't pinpoint that made her skin crawl.

If it came to it, would her own guards protect her, or him?

And if it came down to it in his study, where there were no guards, could she disable him in a fight? It would depend on this person's martial arts training. With her father, absolutely not. She only practiced her own martial arts . . . well, occasionally. She would have to start practicing more, but that wouldn't help her now.

But Ceorre's response to her at the ceremony meant she knew what was going on. If Dressa was in danger, wouldn't the Truthspeaker have warned her? Found some way to signal that danger?

Unless this was a coup. Unless the entire royal family was meant to be replaced.

No. No, she'd been with Ceorre a significant portion of the day before. Ceorre couldn't have hidden that kind of intent from her. And why would Ceorre have helped her become the Heir if she'd meant to replace her shortly thereafter? And why would the First Magicker have been there to witness? Her father was known to be sympathetic to the magickers' cause.

This had better not all be a test of her skills, with her father projecting just enough strangeness to throw her off. If he was playing the role of someone else playing himself—

Adeius, no. She had to think he wasn't so petty, not when the kingdom was as unsteady as it was.

This wasn't a coup, this wasn't a test. This was something else.

She waved down the corridor. "Lead on. Father."

She knew he'd caught the edge of sarcasm in her voice—anyone who could mimic him so closely would be able to catch that—but he didn't show it.

"My study," he said and turned, leading the way.

They walked past the cross corridor that led to her mother's apartment and Rhys's old apartment. Past four more of her father's personal guards that signaled the start of the Seritarchus's private territory.

He nodded to the guards by his door and pressed the doubled security measures of his door handle and a much more sensitive biometric palm lock panel. He leaned forward to murmur the pass phrase of the day, which she couldn't hear.

The door opened.

Dressa drew in a long breath, shoulders tight, following him as he repeated the procedure to the door to his study.

An agent of another house couldn't possibly have penetrated this far into her father's domain, could they? But there were no other Truthspoken unaccounted for. There were only officially three, and their bloodservants, who had lesser training and abilities. Unless her father had trained someone else in secret—which, no, she wouldn't put that past him.

She watched him wave her to the couch, then sit on a wingback chair across from it, all of his movements exactly and perfectly her father's.

Iata. He had to be Iata, no matter that Iata had always claimed to have little ability to Change. And that would be just like her father, wouldn't it, to perpetuate a very, very long game like that.

She sat on the couch, her posture and tone casual.

"Where's my father, Iata?"

5

THE SERITARCHUS

> *There are some secrets even Truthspoken don't share with each other.*
>
> — ARIANNA RHIALDEN, MELESORIE X IN *THE CHANGE DIALOGUES*

At Dressa's challenge, the person who may or may not be her father, and was most likely from everything she'd been able to tell his bloodservant, Iata, smiled and sat back. She watched his expression and posture subtly change. She was watching so closely for any clue she was right —any clue that he might not be Iata, either.

And yes, she did read Iata in the way his lips compressed into a smile, his eyes narrowed, head tipped back to study her.

"Good. Thank you. I've told Maja I don't like to be Homaj around you or Arianna. I can only bury myself so deeply, and it's not a particularly comfortable part of the process—but you'd know that."

Not her father. Definitely not her father.

Okay. Okay.

So Iata was—Adeius, Iata would have to be fully trained as a Truthspoken to pull this off. He'd been out in public as the Seritarchus, at a ceremony as important as her confirmation as Heir. He hadn't seemed nervous at all. So this wasn't the first time.

And Ceorre knew. Ceorre, the Truthspeaker, had to have known it was Iata, not Homaj, who'd formally and legally witnessed the ceremony that day and signed the engagement contract—even if it was a copy. That signature still meant something. If a Truthspoken was being someone else in truth, it could convey the same legalities as if that person was actually there. Ceorre would witness that Homaj, in fact, had been there, if Iata had been Homaj in truth. Just as she'd witness Arianna had abdicated the day before, when Dressa was Arianna in truth.

Except—had Iata been fully Homaj in truth? She'd noticed that extremely subtle difference that had given her pause. And she'd been right.

She studied him back. He'd wanted her to notice the difference, hadn't he? If he played the role of her father so well, at such a fraught time, he must have done this before and she wouldn't have noticed—had even Arianna noticed? He had her father's tells down perfectly. He'd been so identical she still hadn't been sure, even after all the close scrutiny. She'd only seen those tells, and the differences she'd sensed more than seen, because he'd wanted her to.

"But—" She had too many questions. And she wasn't sure if she'd be able to tell if his answers were truthful. Was this on his own initiative, or her father's?

Ceorre knew. It had to be something official, or at least, not something devious.

"You're doing this for my father?"

He shifted again and some of the femme bled out of his

mannerisms. Adeius, Iata wasn't genderfluid like her father as far as she knew, but he had those mannerisms down, too.

"Yes. And no, he's not in the palace right now. He needed—a break. Yes, Ceorre knows about this. So does the First Magicker—your instincts at the ceremony were correct on that. And now you know."

She spread her hands, fighting bafflement. "But . . . but does Arianna know?"

"No," he said, voice hardening. "Maja—your father—didn't want to tell either of you until you were older, but you are already adults. And I think it puts all of us at a disadvantage for you not to know. You handled this whole situation with Arianna and becoming the Heir extremely well, in my opinion. When I'm the Seritarchus, this is my call, and I'm making it."

When he was the Seritarchus?

"Then, when you're my father, you're not just playing my father. You're not a body double."

"Hardly. Yes, when I'm the Seritarchus, I *am* the Seritarchus. I'm not your father, I'm not even your father in truth right now, but right now, I am the Seritarchus."

Her father, her control-loving father, trusted Iata so much he'd let him have his persona, and use his power? And the way Iata was phrasing it, it was as if he had power of his own.

But Iata was a bloodservant. Bloodservants weren't meant to have that kind of power. Dressa loved Pria, she trusted Pria, but she wouldn't want Pria to *be* her and make decisions for her. That wasn't a bloodservant's place.

Iata's lips thinned further. "There's something else you should know."

"Something more that my father didn't want to tell me?" she snapped, then bit her lip. She didn't know what ground she stood on here. She knew Iata mostly as a background presence, a steadily acerbic force who hovered behind her father. She knew him from the basic training sessions he'd given when she and Arianna were children—the only training he'd claimed he was capable of giving, and even then he'd seemed grossly inadequate at Change.

She didn't know Iata at all.

He inclined his head, opened a hand.

"The bloodservant line is seen publicly, and by most in our household, as a service branch of the Rhialden line, making bloodservants distant cousins to the Rhialdens."

Yes, and that was why they could be trained with light Truthspoken training, and why they were known to be loyal, and why they were called bloodservants. They were blood.

But they weren't meant to rule. They were definitely not supposed to be a ruler in any kind of truth. Iata said he *was* the Seritarchus.

"Okay, so are you saying that's not true? We're not actually cousins? Or—what?"

His lips twisted. "It hasn't been true for some time." His shoulders twitched, and she marked the movement as the first time in this conversation he'd shown any kind of nerves. She quick-scanned his body language and found other little signs of anxiety, and that in itself was alarming.

"So then, what is true?"

Iata watched her closely as he said, "I don't know how long it's been this way, or when the bloodservant line switched over from a service branch, if there ever was a service branch. But your father and I realized when we were both younger that he and I were blood siblings. Actual, full siblings. I'm actually the elder—our parents must have started my incubator a year before Homaj. He was their second *acknowledged* Truthspoken child. But if you're counting purely by Truthspoken siblings, I was the third, and he the fourth, counting the first Heir and their bloodservant."

"What?" Dressa felt her stomach falling out. "You're saying you're my uncle? You're—"

She sat forward, fingers digging into the edge of the couch. "Pria and Bettea. Are they my full siblings?"

But he was shaking his head. "No. Homaj and I agreed—it's too dangerous to raise blood siblings as servants. Not to mention all kinds of unethical, especially not telling them." He grimaced. "Pria and Bettea are my children, with a donor parent. They know this. I made sure they knew, though they are under orders from Homaj not to tell anyone until he has given the order. They're also fully aware that they have a choice to live their lives separately from the palace, with a promise of an estate and title if they choose they do not wish to be a bloodservant. We agreed, Homaj and I—bloodservants are far too important to be forced into their loyalties."

Still cousins, then, but close cousins. And—and they both had an out and chose to stay. Pria had just put herself through a difficult Change, and she hadn't had to. She could have just left.

But Iata.

Dressa's gaze sharpened back on Iata. Who was currently wearing her father's face. Who was currently, by his own words, the Seritarchus. He'd said he wasn't Homaj in truth just now, and that was plainly clear. Beyond his appearance, she didn't see as much of her father in him just now. Being someone in truth was an excellent imitation, a legally upholdable imitation, but still an imitation. Iata had meant he held the title fully.

If he was the elder sibling, he *should* be the Seritarchus, shouldn't he?

"What about your loyalties?" she asked.

He waved a hand glittering with her father's rings.

"No, I know what you're thinking, and my loyalties were never in question, not even by myself. I've been the Seritarchus often enough that any ambition to rule is satisfied, I assure you, and I don't envy Homaj having the greater share of that burden."

Often enough? How long had her father and Iata been

doing this? She was still having a hard time seeing her father sharing his power at all, but she could also see the draw of being able to have both the Seritarchus in play and the most skilled Truthspoken in the kingdom off gathering whatever information he felt was important at the time.

Adeius, yes, she could see the draw for her father—he wasn't content to live just one life, he wanted to live two.

"Is my father on a mission now? When will he be back?"

"No. Well, he will likely turn it into a mission, he always does. But as I said before, he needed time away. He left last night. I suspect he'll be back within the week, he can never stay away for long." But he looked troubled, and Dressa knew he wasn't saying everything.

"Okay," she said, trying to collect her thoughts with all this new information. And none of this was small and neatly manageable information, was it? "So—you're telling me now because I'm the Heir now? And Arianna really doesn't know any of this?"

"No. Arianna is—well, she is very much like your father, or at least she tries to be. The trouble is, your father is also very much like your father, or at least he tries to be, too. He's not well suited to be a Seritarchus, did you know that? He chose that style of rule when he became the ruler, because he assessed the state of the kingdom and saw what it needed. He thought the kingdom needed a strong hand, a rule by dominance after his parents had been assassinated, and he wasn't wrong at the time. But he should have been an Ialorius, ruling with assessment and fluidity—which is exactly what he did to determine he should be a Seritarchus and rule with strength and control."

Iata rubbed at his eyes. "The truth of it is that he can't always uphold it, projecting a personality that is so counter to his own. It's become a large part of his own over the last twenty-three years, but it's not fully natural to him. And when he's pushed, when there is too much going on or the stakes are too high, he needs to pull away for a time, recenter in himself, and then come back. That's when he goes on his missions."

Dressa's neck was so tight it started to ache. She forced herself to breathe, but she could in no way reach a Change trance to smooth the pain away just now.

"What about you?" she asked. "Are you more a Seritarchus style, then?"

"Yes, but as I said, I have no designs on your father's power. I want what's best for the kingdom, and for Homaj. I only ever want that."

"And yourself?" she pressed. "What about what's best for you? Did my father push you into this? What do you get out of it, what do you plan to get out of it, if you say you have no designs on my father's power? If you say that right now, you're actually the Seritarchus?"

His smile broke over his face like a sunrise, relaxing planes that never relaxed on her father's. It was disturbing, and so was the look he gave her—not because it was actually disturbing, but because it showed something her father never, ever showed her. Adeius, was that actually approval? Was that possibly pride?

She had to smooth back a sudden sting in her eyes. That sort of look he only gave Arianna, on this face just now—she couldn't handle it. She didn't know how to handle it. This still wasn't her father.

Iata sat forward, smile dropping, projecting sincerity in every nuance of his posture. Another thing her father never did.

"Dressa. Your father thinks Arianna is his perfect Heir because she's bent on crushing herself into a person resembling him, and I don't think he gets the irony of that. But you just outmaneuvered him. You've made your bid to rule in a way he can't ignore. I can't promise you he'll take this easily, but I can promise he won't continue to ignore you. You're going to be an excellent Heir—you already are. And one day, you'll be an excellent ruler."

There was something in the way he said it that made Dressa chill. It was the same feeling she'd had when he'd said her father had needed rest. He was troubled by what he said, and what did that mean? Was her father needing a break more than a temporary burnout?

Try as she might, she couldn't read any malice into Iata's words or gestures this entire conversation. But he wasn't telling her the whole truth—she knew that. Of course he wasn't telling her the whole truth, not if he and her father had been playing out this elaborate act for long enough that Iata could fully be the Seritarchus in his turn. And he'd demonstrated today that maybe . . . maybe her father wasn't the most skilled Truth-spoken in the Kingdom of Valoris. Not if someone else slipped in and out of his life with ease.

6

THE BOOK

> *The most damning secret of all? We're Human. We have needs and wants like anyone else, though we work hard to make you think otherwise.*
>
> — ARIANNA RHIALDEN, MELESORIE X IN *THE CHANGE DIALOGUES*

Dressa swallowed hard. There were too many thoughts in her head.

She stood, moved around the couch, continued in a circuit around her father's study. She'd never pace the room if this had actually been her father, oh Adeius, no, but Iata didn't seem displeased. And she was still wrapping her head around the fact that his opinion did matter—had absolute weight at the moment, if he was the Seritarchus. Her whole world had shifted on its axis and she was frantically trying to find north again.

"You say I'm going to make a good Heir, but I'm not fully trained," she said finally.

Iata opened his mouth, his expression projecting protest, and she waved a hand.

"No, I know I'm fully Truthspoken. But I haven't been trained like Arianna—"

"We always have room for improvement." Iata tracked her around the room, brows quirked. "But I don't believe you're not ready."

"I'm not a good Truthspoken, Iata." She stopped behind the couch, leaning into the soft synth leather. "I don't like Change. I don't like being other people. The social stuff I'm good at, but—I know that Change is a part of all this. I need to get better at that, and at the politics of it all—I need to be more aware."

"Not all Truthspoken rulers rule with as much emphasis on Change as your father has. You can Change yourself, or delegate others who can, or not place the emphasis on Change at all but run extensive intelligence networks. You are Truthspoken—you have the ability to shift your body and your personality presentation, but it's a tool, Dressa. It's not the end result, at least it shouldn't be."

Which was ironic, perhaps, coming from the man who looked and sounded identical to her father.

She pushed down on the couch and let go. "Will you train me? Not my father. You."

His brows went up, absolutely one of her father's gestures. Or maybe it was a gesture they'd both picked up from Ceorre.

"I'm not sure that's a wise idea. When I am myself as Iata, I shouldn't be training anyone."

"You do have as much training as my father, though?"

"Yes, he and Ceorre fully trained me. But I am a Seritarchus personality, Dressa. My style won't be yours. You, I think, will be a Melesorie. Maybe an Ialorius, but I think Melesorie. You have momentum, and you use it."

That warmed her heart, and she knew it shouldn't mean so much, but she held it close all the same.

"That's why," she said. "You can see I'm not Seritarchus, so you won't try to make me into one." Like her father had done with Arianna. Like her father tried to do with her and everyone around him.

So had Iata trained her father how to rule as a Seritarchus, if that was more his own style? She still had so many questions, but she didn't want to push. She was getting a better feel for Iata's personality in this conversation, and she thought he'd only give out information on his own timetable. Throughout this whole conversation, he hadn't used dominance tactics like her father. He hadn't had to—this sort of charisma was natural to him, wasn't it?

And the Iata she'd known all her life, the brooding bloodservant who'd said he couldn't Change well, who'd only trained them in the most basic of basics when they were younger—she, Arianna, Bettea, and Pria all, and later sometimes enlisting Rhys to help in their practice, too—she could see that person in him now, yes. Before, she'd only seen what he'd allowed her to see, and no more. That was likely still true now. He had secrets as deep as being, in part, the Seritarchus.

All of that was true control. That was being a Seritarchus. The difference, demonstrated so clearly, made her father seem like a petty tyrant.

Iata hadn't been the kindest teacher, no. But he'd been fair. And those early lessons had stuck with her in a way many of her father's hadn't—mostly because she'd spent much of her time with her father trying not to listen when he implied that she should just be able to get these things; Arianna did, after all.

She dreaded the thought of having to go back into training with her father. If there was any other alternative, even this new angle she wasn't sure about, she'd take it.

"Please," she said, turning her palms up.

He grimaced and stood, coming around the couch to take

her hands, turn them down again, as if even that slightest gesture of subservience disturbed him.

"I'll ask your father, when he comes back." But he added, "We can start tomorrow, if you wish."

She didn't doubt he had high sway with her father, if her father trusted him this much. He would train her if he wanted to.

"Today," he went on, and his voice and bearing flowed back into that of her father, "we have many, many meetings and people to greet in the Reception Hall. People will want and need to meet you as the new Truthspoken Heir. Go and dress the part—we'll want Lesander there, too. The Javieris must be seen close to the seat of power to sate their appetite for it, for the moment."

He paused, halfway to the large desk at the back of the room. "I saw the marriage contract."

Dressa froze. "And—my father? Did he see it?"

Iata hesitated, and her insides grew cold.

"He's angry," she said. "He's—"

"He has a week, or however long he's away, to process it, and realize why it was a good decision, regardless of whether or not it was his own. And to realize that the goal of raising Truthspoken is to raise rulers, who make their own decisions."

She bit her lip. Would her father see that? She had absolutely no confidence he would.

"In any case," Iata said, shuffling papers on the desk and waving away a holo standby signal, "the point will be irrelevant soon anyway—you'll have a public wedding in two months, that's as soon as I could shift the schedule to accommodate travel time, public functions, planning for a large event, all of it."

He looked up, met her gaze. "He will likely be more accommodating when he comes back. That's how it usually goes." Though she could tell he was still troubled about her father being away. Something more than usual—if anything could be called usual in all of this—was going on.

"Is my father . . ." Adeius, for all she was dreading seeing him, she didn't like how cagey Iata was about her father being away. She especially didn't like the weight he'd put on her becoming the ruler someday.

"Is he okay?" She had to ask. Her father was still her father. And he was still the Seritarchus by holy mandate.

She couldn't imagine a situation where he'd willingly take a break. And she truly couldn't comprehend anything that could rattle him, even after all Iata had said. Had Arianna getting sick finally broken his composure, and what would that mean for the kingdom?

She'd thought Iata would come back with reassurances, but he looked down, nudging a stack of papers on the desk into some unseen alignment.

"Captain Zhang is with him," he finally said. "She'll set him straight. And if he needs more time, if he needs to be out of the palace, I have no objections to remaining Homaj for however long I need to. I'm comfortable enough in this role, though I would not want to stay in it indefinitely."

Dressa inhaled—he understood. He absolutely understood what it was like to have to become a sibling for the sake of the kingdom, though it didn't seem to bother him as much as it had bothered her.

He must have read the consternation in her face, because he held up both hands. "I'm also fine, Dressa, truly. I've never had an issue remaining long in a role, and while I'm usually Homaj for only a few hours or a few days as needed, I've been him for weeks at a time before."

She was absolutely not going to ask when, but she knew she'd lay awake that night, examining past interactions with her father.

The thought was horrible, but she was starting to wonder if

the few good times had actually been Iata. Or had it been Iata when her father was distant, cancelling training while he single-mindedly pursued some mission or political problem?

Iata opened a drawer in the desk and reached down to press a palm lock inside. Dressa heard a soft click as the lock released, and he pulled out a paper notebook. He held it out to her.

Cautiously, she crossed the room and took it.

It was a calendar. A year per page spread, and while the first few years held no markings—those would have been before her father had been the Seritarchus—most of the other years had black circles around some of the dates. Sometimes single circles only. Sometimes several circles in a row. A very few times nearly an entire month.

He'd marked the days, or maybe her father had—dangerous to have such a thing recorded in this way, but then, few others would ever have the context. And maybe, more dangerous not to have it recorded. They would have to remember who made what decision when, who had said what so they could reference things if they came up later.

Dressa had no direct internal reference for the dates, but the whole picture showed that Iata had been the Seritarchus around a fifth of his entire rule. Including, she saw as she neared the end, both this day and the day before. Though not the night of the ball, when her father had commanded her to be Arianna.

Iata had said he was the Seritarchus just now, but she hadn't understood just how true that was.

Carefully, she closed the book and handed it back. She knew what he'd just entrusted her with and how dangerous that information was. Even more than the revelation, and the explanation, the actual evidence going back over twenty years was a piece of information so hot it could set the kingdom on fire.

He returned the notebook to its drawer and locked it in again. Shut the drawer. Looked up at her, waiting.

She hesitated the barest moment before nodding. "Seritarchus. Thank you. I—thank you for all of this."

He nodded. "Go. Get dressed. I'll meet you in the antechamber to the Reception Hall in an hour."

7

TREATMENT

> *While Truthspoken have a highly trained ability to heal themselves of sickness and injury, not all injuries can be dealt with on their own. Because of this, the Rhialden line employs the best physicians in the kingdom for their private use at the palace.*
>
> — DR. IGNI CHANG IN "DISCOURSE ON THE HUMANITY OF OUR RULERS"

The morning after she'd arrived on Hestia, Ari woke to sunlight streaming through the windows of her bedroom, and the soft sounds of voices in another room.

She froze and strained to listen.

"No, no, please come back another time," she heard Bettea say. "She's still resting. Yes, I know you have other patients, but—"

A physician?

Ari pushed back the covers and tumbled out of bed, her feet hitting the floor with a definite *thunk*.

The voices paused.

Ari looked herself over in the mirror. If she was Arianna, she would need an hour at least to dress and make herself the perfect statement for whatever message she wished her visitors to receive.

But she wasn't Arianna. Imorie Rhialden méron Quevedo didn't care nearly so much about how people saw her, or what they thought.

She touched the rings on her right brow, still a little sore from the recent piercings.

Right. And the sooner she saw the resident physician, the sooner she could start treatment, the sooner she could get back to Valon. That, now, was her only goal.

She pushed open her door just enough to poke her face out. "Jis? Tell the doctor I will be ready in five minutes, if they can wait."

Bettea looked back at her, scowling, but faer face softened when fae saw her. Unlike Ari, Bettea had been able to solidly Change on the way to Hestia, and now the planes of faer face were sharper, hair short and golden, eyes a dark burgundy.

Ari didn't wait for the answer but pulled the door shut and unzipped the duffel neither of them had touched the night before.

Everything, of course, was a bit rumpled. But she was seeing a physician, not going to a ball.

Ari pulled out a flowing black shirt and forest green leggings, stepping into them as quickly as her pounding heart allowed. She had to pause for breath once, hanging onto the bed post.

She glanced in the mirror again—her makeup from the day before was still mostly intact. She hadn't washed it off last night, and she had no time to fix it now, but it still did its job of reshaping the contours of her face. What Change she'd been able to manage on the way here had pushed her eyes a little farther apart than Arianna's, skin tone a lighter brown, her brows thicker, fine dark hairs above her upper lip.

As Truthspoken, Ari should have been able to accomplish the far greater Change than Bettea as her bloodservant. Her lips tightened. The cosmetics would have to carry the rest. It would all have to do for now.

Ari entered the sitting room to find Bettea standing with arms crossed, talking to a wiry person with flushed, pale skin, and brown hair tied back in a tight bun. They were perched on the couch, a black instrument case resting on their lap.

The person stood and gave a slight bow. "Ser Quevedo, I presume? I'm Dr. Lin, he and him, here to give your first examination. I promise you, I am discreet, and my contract is bound to Windvale's resident privacy policy. You needn't have any concerns that anything we say will go beyond these walls."

Ari saw sincerity in his mannerisms, if also a tired boredom. And how many guests to this estate had he said those same exact words to?

She nodded. "Can we do the exam here?"

"Of course. If you can sit here, please." He waved at the chair across from him, then opened his instrument case.

Ari sat, eyeing Bettea, still standing with faer arms crossed. Bettea's brows rose in a "let's see how this goes" gesture, and Ari nodded. This was the place her father had sent her to. She couldn't imagine him sending her anywhere that wasn't discreet or that had incompetent staff.

But then, she couldn't imagine him letting Dressa take her place as the Heir, either—Dressa, as herself, not holding the place for Arianna. And that had just happened.

She pressed her lips tight.

She must endure this, and get better, before she could go home.

Dr. Lin asked a series of questions about her energy levels, if she was experiencing any pain, and what she was eating and how much. He felt around her neck and gave her a silver bracelet that had medical monitors inside. He checked her heart with one instrument held in front of her, and her lungs with another. He held a gene and blood scanner to her arm then pulled it back, the diagnostic holo popping up overtop of it.

Adeius, had she Changed her DNA enough? She knew she'd scan as close kin to the royal Rhialden line, closer than her claim as a lesser contract member had a right to be. She'd done her best to shift the Delor markers to sister lines during her Change, but she'd been exhausted. She was exhausted still, and knew some markers were still there for anyone to read if they knew what to look for.

The actual Truthspoken markers, at least, were safe from view. They hid themselves among the junk DNA—or else everyone would have a Truthspoken-detecting scanner, wouldn't they?

In Imorie's official records, Bettea had listed ancestors with Delor ties, just in case those markers in conjunction with Rhialden markers were ever called into question. Because there was only one recent, official pairing of Rhialden and Delor bloodlines, and that would mark her instantly as Truthspoken.

She'd thought she'd be safe here. She hadn't had to go through the customs scans that most worlds required—Hestia wasn't controlled in that manner and trusted its people to screen anyone coming in if they felt they needed to.

Her heart pounded in her ears as she watched the physician read his instrument.

It was a medical instrument, she told herself, not an intelligence scanner.

People used medical scanners every day. Medical scanners didn't do full sequence referencing, only partial sequencing. Full sequencing was for government use alone, or special permit cases like determining parentage or preparing a child.

Not even most security scanners used more than partial sequencing.

That didn't, of course, stop most nobility or criminals from using it.

But Lin was a physician. He wasn't going to be comparing her genetics to high-security Rhialden files. And from everything she'd seen so far, Windvale Estate was the farthest thing from a criminal enterprise. Her father wouldn't have sent her into a criminal enterprise for treatment. Would he?

Ari let out her breath slowly.

She still resolved to find a way to push her genetics . . . elsewhere.

"Hm. It's definitely the Bruising Sleep," Dr. Lin said, "all the symptoms point to that. We can't, of course, get a hundred percent certain diagnosis, as the disease has no known association with any pathogen, but the lack of any pathogens is telling in its own way."

He began packing his instruments away. There was no indication of alarm anywhere in his body language. Not even over the Bruising Sleep—but then, he'd dealt with that often here, hadn't he?

He was just a physician.

And her thinking was veering dangerously into paranoia.

Ari, her heart an unsteady rhythm in her chest, struggled to get enough breath to ask what she needed to ask.

"Is there a cure?"

Her father had said no—but then, her father wasn't a physician who treated the illness every day.

"I'm sorry, no." He snapped his case shut. "But we've been successfully treating the Bruising Sleep here at Windvale for over a decade. Those who come here often go back to their lives with only slight adjustments in schedule to accommodate their energy levels."

"And—how long?" She flipped her hair out of her eyes. "How long until I can go back to—my home and my family?"

He gave her a sympathetic smile. "That will depend on how you respond to the treatment. Some people are able to handle higher doses of the medications and recover more quickly. Some need a lower dose over time."

He opened another compartment in his case and pulled out two sealed medical patches, one with a green striped border, one with black. "I'm going to start you in the middle, both with a nutrient boost and a medication we've found to lessen the effects of the Bruising Sleep, and then I'll be back in three days to check on your progress and any side effects." He recited a list of possible side effects, but Ari's ears were ringing. She took the patches, reading the labels.

She had never taken medication before a few days ago. She'd never needed it.

Ari glanced up at Bettea, who actually seemed to be listening to the physician, thank Adeius. She clutched the patches to her stomach like they were treasures. Her hand trembled like they were grenades.

If she could get well enough, just well enough to fully enter a Change trance again so she could heal herself, she could get back to Valon and sort out this mess of her life. Set everything right, get her title back from Dressa. Yes, of course she'd be able to do that. She wasn't just any minor noble here for discreet treatment, she was Truthspoken.

Bettea's gaze shifted to meet hers, and Bettea's focus sharpened with alarm.

What? What was she showing, what was she projecting? She didn't know, but she slipped her thoughts firmly back into Imorie's patterns. She was pissed at having the illness and pissed at having been sent by her family for treatment. That was all.

Dr. Lin finished his instructions, then smiled politely and

gave another bow. "I'll see you again in another three days. In the meantime, be sure to use both patches. Rest, and avail yourself of the house and its extensive gardens. Many of the plants in the gardens are medicinal in nature and soothing to walk among. Or glide, as we have ample hover chairs if needed."

Ari flinched at the thought.

He leaned forward. "You're here for healing—there's no need to push yourself for anything. If you need dinner brought up, your comm should have the interface to request it. Have you met our host, Count Badem, yet?"

"Uh—no, not yet."

"She's not one to push herself on any of the guests," the physician said, moving toward the door. "Indicate on your comm if you are up for seeing her, or if you'd like to schedule an appointment. You will, of course, see her at the common dinner if you go downstairs. But again, there is no pressure. You're here for healing."

Ari blinked slowly. There was something in his voice, something a little off. Too cheerful, maybe a little pushy. She was growing too fatigued again to parse it just now, but she filed away her impressions to examine later.

"Thank you, Doctor," she said, and didn't make an attempt to stand up—and he didn't seem to expect it.

"Of course! Thank you for coming to Windvale—I hope you have a pleasant stay."

He shut the door behind him, and Ari glanced up at Bettea. Had fae picked up on the odd undertones, too?

Bettea held out faer hand. "Can I see the patches?"

Ari reluctantly handed them up, waiting as Bettea read the labels.

"Mm." Faer shoulders were tight, brows pinched. Wary.

Bettea met her eyes again, and Ari saw the mistrust there as fae cut a glance to the door.

Ari took the patches back. Were they safe to use? But then,

why wouldn't they be? No one here knew she was Truthspoken. She presented as a Rhialden, yes, but a minor contract member of the house. She was only at mild risk for assassination here. She didn't even need to have guards.

Even if she had testing equipment, she had no baseline to test the patches against. She'd have to trust, somehow. She was here for treatment, and she needed that treatment so she could go back to Valon. That, of everything else, was foremost.

Ari tore the seal on the first package, shook the bright green and white-striped patch out into her hand, and stuck it high on her left arm. She did the same for the other, placing it just below the first.

They both waited in silence for a full five minutes. Nothing happened.

Ari sat back, heart racing again. She was jumping at ghosts. Everything since that night at the ball had made her jumpy—even knowing her father had been the magicker, even knowing that, she couldn't stop seeing shadows.

The physician's reactions had been . . . odd at points, for reasons she couldn't describe. But that could have been from anything. This wasn't Valon court. Hestia might turn on more ordinary rules, like people being worried about the comfort of their jobs or the contentment of their families. Not the life and death of a capital city court and its Truthspoken rulers.

She raked her hands back through her hair, prompting a soft protest from Bettea.

Adeius, how could she relax with all of her training? How could she rest at all?

"Help me back to bed," she said, and Bettea came around to help her up. "I'll rest for a bit, then I want to see Count Badem and give my respects to the house."

It was, she decided, something Imorie would do. And if Ari herself wanted a better feel for the people at play in this household, well, that would serve its purpose, too.

8

DINNER ESCORT

What we know about the Bruising Sleep is so little and inconclusive that the majority of papers on the illness are about what we don't know.

— DR. A. MADRIC, FROM *THE COLLECTED SPEECHES OF THE GENERAL ASSEMBLY, FOURTH EDITION*

Ari didn't, after all, wake up in time to see Count Badem before dinner. She slept most of the day, only waking again when sunset colors shown through her bedroom windows.

"Fuck," she said, scrambling out of bed for the second time that day.

It wasn't a thing Arianna would say. Which was good.

Bettea stepped in. "You're awake."

"You should've woken me!"

Ari stumbled past faer into the small bathroom. "What time is it? When is dinner?"

"We have time yet."

Ari held onto the sink with one hand as she tried to make something of the mess of her dark blue undercut hair. It was sticking up at all the wrong angles.

"Help me," she demanded.

Bettea huffed a sigh but produced a comb and a tube of product. "I'll have to redo your makeup. It's smudged."

"Am I even in good enough shape to go to dinner? Is the treatment working?"

"I doubt it's instantaneous. Tilt your chin up."

Ari closed her eyes, still unsteady from her jump out of bed. She gripped the sink tightly as Bettea wiped her old makeup off.

Bettea had said she had time. But how much time? She had to make a good impression here. This was her life now—she couldn't start it off with antagonizing her host. She'd been here a whole day without presenting herself yet. She'd met the physician before she'd met the host, and that was entirely bad form on any world.

"I'm not making a good impression on the house."

"Does that matter here? Really?"

She made a frustrated noise. Yes, it mattered. Appearances always mattered, and why couldn't Bettea, who had enough truthspoken training faerself, see that?

Or was Bettea saying that Imorie Quevedo wouldn't be so concerned about appearances?

Well, maybe. Maybe, but this was her life. She didn't know how long she'd be living as Imorie, and she had to have control over *something*.

She shuddered out a tight breath, managed to catch it again and inhale. Slowly, slowly, she brought her heart rate down through sheer force of will.

Imorie or Arianna, she was still a Rhialden. There was always the Rhialden name to uphold.

Yes, she'd seen the physician before the host, but the host

knew the kind of guests who'd come here. They were the kind that needed the treatment before the introduction, weren't they?

But was the treatment working? Did she *feel* any better? Ari tried to dip into a light trance, just to scan her body. She felt all the usual aches now, but she couldn't trance deep enough to tell anything more. She didn't feel any different. As Truthspoken, she was supposed to heal quickly. She was supposed to be able to heal herself and get better faster than anyone else so she could get back to her life at the palace.

Ari squeezed the edge of the sink until her finger joints creaked.

And then she remembered, like she should have remembered all along, that she shouldn't have this much emotion here. If anyone was watching, anyone at all, she had to be Imorie. Only and ever Imorie. This was an enforced vacation for her—yes, she wanted to be better. But she didn't have anything urgent to get back to. Not as Imorie. She was annoyed, yes, and frustrated. But she didn't have a kingdom on the line.

Ari tensed her shoulders, then forced herself to relax. She leaned against the sink rather than death gripping it.

Bettea worked quickly, and the too-recognizable contours of her face, far too close to Arianna's, smoothed away into Imorie's.

Ari let her own concerns go. It was the only way to inhabit a role, especially when the lines between this role and her palace life were dangerously thin.

She rechecked her posture and body language. Very different from Arianna's. In a few more days, it would be second nature, and she'd be able to relax a bit more.

She jumped at a knock on the apartment door. What the hell was this, a receiving hall?

Bettea gave her an intense lookover, nodded. "You'd better get dressed. Everything else is good—I'll handle the door."

Ari slipped back into her room and found the duffel's contents had been emptied into the closet sometime while she'd slept. She grabbed a long, split-paneled coat and deep blue shirt with swallow pins on the lapels to match the holo tattoo beside her eye. She glanced in the closet's wall mirror just long enough to cement her mental image of Imorie.

When she came out again, she stopped just inside the main room.

Etienne Tanaka, their chauffeur and professed gardener from the day before, stood gawking at her.

Oh, Adeius, what now? He was so intensely awkward, and she didn't want to deal with that.

He coughed and straightened. "Imorie? Ser Quevedo?"

"Imorie's fine," she said, eyeing him back. He was a good deal cleaner than he'd been the day before, dressed in a black shirt and cream trousers. His dark brown hair was combed down, and she'd swear he'd trimmed around the edges of his scraggly beard.

"Aren't you supposed to be in the gardens? You said you were a gardener."

Ari saw Bettea shift and winced inwardly. Okay, no, that hadn't been nice. She had to switch her mind out of the language of palace politics. Had to.

She wasn't used to playing roles of any kind that required . . . niceness. Not that she had to be nice as Imorie, but Imorie wouldn't treat Etienne like just staff, would she? Imorie was a good deal more rungs down the ladder than Arianna.

And she had to stop comparing herself—her *selves*—too. A long-term role was meant to be fully inhabited. She wasn't yet ready to be Imorie in truth, but she had to get close.

Etienne flushed, actually flushed, red from neck to forehead. Adeius, he had a crush on her. And how was she supposed to handle that?

But the look he gave her as he held his arm out wasn't the

sort of fawning adoration she expected. It was . . . decidedly sharp. Which gave her pause. Why had Etienne, who wasn't a chauffeur, picked them up at the port field, and why was he here now, apparently on escort duty?

"One of the porters is sick," he explained, and offered a small shrug, looked away. "I was done with my chores for the day, so."

She took his arm just to stop the awkwardness. It wasn't endearing. He—flinched when her hand brushed his.

Ari exchanged a look with Bettea. Painfully shy or something else?

Bettea shrugged.

"So, we're off to dinner?"

Etienne straightened. "Yes. Uh—" he turned back to Bettea. "Staff meals are served in the hall beside the kitchens. I can take you there after I take Imorie to the dining hall, if you'd like."

Bettea waved a hand and opened the door for them. "I know my way around staff. I'll manage." Bettea marched off, not even looking back, leaving Ari alone with Etienne in the upstairs corridor.

Which wasn't bad, exactly, but still awkward. Did Etienne think he should hold her arm the whole way down, the whole way to the dining hall? He was staff. Staff didn't escort guests in the same way other guests escorted guests. And he was hardly holding his arm at the right angle. From his rapid breaths, she was pretty sure he was as uncomfortable as she was.

She didn't pull away, wanting to see what he'd do next.

He shot her a glance, then they started walking.

Near the top of the stairs, he said, "Are you—are you well? Do you like it here?"

Ari sighed. Arianna knew how to manage painful small talk, but Imorie wasn't as adept. Imorie had a touch of the awkward herself.

"I haven't been here long enough, but the sunset's nice. And I'm well enough. Thank you for asking, Etienne."

"Eti," he corrected, as if the response was automatic.

Ah. Yes, he had said that before.

But it was too like a private name, too familiar for a person she didn't know and had no particular wish to know. He was a *gardener*. Not even Imorie Rhialden méron Quevedo would seek to make friends with the staff.

But he had stated a preference. She had no solid reason other than her own preferences not to follow it.

"Eti," she repeated, dampening her cringe. And maybe it wouldn't be a bad thing to have an ally in the house. Her father made allies among the palace staff in his various personas, though she hadn't managed as well at that feat, to her chagrin. Maybe it was time to practice that.

As they neared the end of the corridor, she glanced over at him, at his rigid discomfort. Had he meant anything more than polite conversation by asking how she felt?

If he worked here, he had to know that people came to Windvale when they were sick. At least, some of the guests did. Were all of them sick with the Bruising Sleep? And what about the party the night before? How had anyone else tolerated all that noise?

They walked with halting steps down the stairs to a crowd of guests gathering below. So far, she'd been Imorie with Eti, one of the porters, and Dr. Lin. Her true test of the role, though, was about to begin.

9

SHARKS

> *Most people can identify the two most common types of courtiers: the sharks, and their prey. But many forget the water itself holds danger for those not suited to it.*
>
> — ARIANNA RHIALDEN, MELESORIE X IN *THE CHANGE DIALOGUES*

People were gathering in the entry hall to Windvale House, and a few looked up as Eti and Ari descended. It was a weird déjà vu to the last time Ari had been at any kind of social gathering—had that only been a week ago? Then, there had been hundreds of faces watching her as she descended, all the sharks just waiting for her to show weakness. Then, she'd barely made it down without Dressa's help.

She wasn't having as much difficulty now. Did that mean the treatment was already working?

She knew palace court sharks, but how would these people be? Of the dozen or so milling in the entry, on some faces, she saw that particular variety of closed politeness that court players learned to wield as weapons. But not all. Many were dressed well, even fashionably, but again, not all. She recognized a few minor nobles, but there were more that she didn't recognize, and she didn't have the energy to parse body language and try to see if anyone had used cosmetics or surgery to hide their identities while they were here for treatment.

Or maybe there was just a variety of people. Hestia was a resort world, after all, and not just frequented by Valorans. She spotted a couple hovering near the back of the group who wore the gauzy dresses popular right now in the Onabrii-Kast Dynasty—that style hadn't taken off yet in Valoris.

Among the faces she recognized, though, were a few she'd known to have left the court recently. She could see the bruising under some of their eyes. Could they see hers?

Of course they could.

She watched recognition in some faces as they looked at her, but it was recognition of a family line, not a person. She was being seen as a Rhialden, which would give people pause, but there would have been a different reaction entirely if they'd seen her as Truthspoken.

One person who'd been talking to another in the corner turned around, and Ari almost stumbled. Eti seemed to anticipate the fall, though, and steadied her just in time.

Oh, hell. Duke Kyran Koldari, scion of the lowest ranked of the high houses, and someone she had gone out of her way to avoid in the Rhialden Court. He'd met her before when she was Arianna, but only in passing. The Koldaris, like the Javieris, preferred to keep to their own worlds, and that was fine by her. The man was boorish, and she was certain it was deliberate.

He smiled at her now, and the smile seemed genuine. His black hair was oiled and twisted into knots, tan face holding a rugged beauty, but not the perfection Ari identified with those who had illicit beauty training in Change.

His dark eyes met hers.

He had to see her own recognition after she'd stared a beat too long. Oh, hell. Could she turn it into attraction? Imorie wouldn't flow in the same circles as the duke. But the very last thing she wanted to do was have to play out an attraction to this man.

She wasn't sure she was up to sparring with him, either, on any level. Dinner was a bad idea. She should go right up those stairs and call for dinner to be sent up. She still clung to Eti—she didn't think he'd protest turning around. He seemed to have stiffened up as eyes turned to them, too.

Duke Kyran was already cutting toward them, though. While she'd be justified in claiming illness—Adeius, the thought of doing that, among these courtiers and various nobles, with having that as their first impression of her, shot iron up her spine.

There was only one thing to do. She didn't have the energy to track both her thoughts and Imorie's, so she'd have to fully be Imorie.

Ari took a breath and submerged.

Imorie stepped down from the last step and tilted her head in bemusement as the duke was there to greet her, giving a shallow bow.

"Rhialden," the duke said, and some of the conversation around them quieted.

Imorie felt her face heat. Adeius, but she didn't want to have that conversation here.

"Contract Rhialden," she corrected. "And very much a minor line. You don't need to bow, Ser Duke."

"Contract Rhialden, then," he said, straightening with a smile. And it was a devastating smile. "May I have a name, Contract Rhialden? I don't recognize you, or at least, I don't think I do. One can never be sure if one's met these days, especially in this house."

A quiet, nervous twitter from those watching.

"I'm me," Imorie said with an ungraceful bow. "And absolutely sheltered. Imorie Rhialden méron Quevedo. She and her."

"Quevedo," he said. "Ah, an excellent family. Out from Fial?"

"Gray Moss, actually."

"Ah. Excellent wineries on Gray Moss." He held out his arm. "May I escort you in to dinner?"

He glanced at Eti, who was still glued to Imorie's side. "You may go."

But Eti didn't, at first, let go. Which was endearing in its way, if unwise here. Imorie saw annoyance flash in the duke's dark eyes and unwound her own arm from Eti's.

Eti gave her a wary look before turning his gaze back to the floor.

"Thank you, Eti," she said, and he nodded without looking up. He hesitated, made a clumsy bow, then headed off down one of the branching corridors.

"Awkward kid," the duke said dismissively. "I'm Kyran, by the way. He and him."

He looped his own arm in Imorie's and pulled her just close enough to him to be slightly uncomfortable for her, though he seemed to be fine.

The people around them acted like it was natural for Kyran to claim a guest for himself. They moved back as he led Imorie toward the doors at the back of the entry leading into a wide corridor.

Should she try to create more space between them? He vastly outranked her, and the others here seemed aware of that for themselves, too.

She didn't create more space. She didn't know if he was just unaware of his physical boundaries, but she wasn't about to make an enemy on her first full day here or an enemy as powerful as the duke. He seemed like the sort of person who'd be disproportionately offended if things didn't go his way.

ETI, standing in an alcove off the main corridor that ran through the center of the house, watched Duke Koldari and Imorie pass. They didn't see him—of course they didn't see him, because he didn't want them to.

He hated making himself disappear with his magics, and it always took him hours to recover afterward, but he didn't like at all how the duke had attached himself to Imorie. Imorie hadn't liked it, either. The shine of her soul had dulled and gotten jagged with distaste when the duke had taken her arm possessively.

Imorie, who had a many-layered soul. He was determined not to think too hard about what that would mean, because his handlers demanded he report everything to them.

He told himself, as Imorie and the duke moved on, that Imorie was just a noble. She acted like a noble. She'd let the duke take her into dinner—someone who was more than a noble would never let the duke push her around like that. That's all she was. A noble.

But earlier, when the duke had dismissed him, he hadn't gone back to his own duties but hurried down the service corridor, through a parlor, and hesitated at the pocket door back to the main corridor, deciding whether leaving it open would be suspicious or not. All the doors were usually kept closed, as guests would gather in different rooms. He'd run out of time to decide and ducked back out to the main corridor and into the alcove. Behind a large vase that absolutely wouldn't hide him if he didn't turn himself invisible.

He had to make sure she wasn't in any danger. He'd learned long ago not to ignore when his gut was showing him danger.

Eti craned a little out of the alcove to watch them walk on. Was she safe? Did she think she was safe?

He studied the density of her soul energy. Even from here, he could tell she was uncomfortable, yes, and annoyed, but he didn't think she felt she was in immediate danger. And Koldari's soul was all blocky chords of self-satisfaction. Some darker notes, yes, but then that was the same with many of the nobles. So why had Eti felt such a need to watch out for her just now?

Eti waited for all the guests to pass, then quietly withdrew back through the parlor to the service corridor. This led to the side of the house and the gardens beyond—his domain.

He'd promised himself he wouldn't get involved with the guests of this house. That's what his handlers wanted—they wanted him to tease out the guests' secrets and report to them. How convenient to have an unsealed Green Magicker under their control. Eti could pick up anyone's surface emotions with proximity and a look. Or more deeply, and sometimes with accompanying thoughts, with a touch.

But he'd seen Imorie on the landing pad the day before, Imorie and her servant both with heavily layered souls, and weighted beyond that with a distress that ran to their cores. Most of the people at Windvale had some kind of distress—few were here by any kind of choice but the necessity to treat their illnesses.

But then Imorie had looked at him. He'd seen more than the usual distress, an unmooring of her soul. He'd looked away, but—he hadn't been able to look away.

Eti strode out into the fading sunlight over the gardens. He trailed his hand over a hedge row, never touching, not disturbing the souls of the bushes. But he asked softly for their help as he walked and the bushes gave him the extra sunlight they'd stored that day, warming his soul. He needed that warmth after the soul-injury it took to make himself invisible.

He asked of the planet's earth beneath his feet and felt warmth from there as well. He wove through the more cultivated areas of the gardens to the wilder places, the streams and their soft whispers, the taller, older trees. Finally, he came to the tree he wanted, one that was hundreds of years old and always had more to give him.

Eti settled against its gnarled trunk, his heart aching from all he'd done that day and all he carried, and sighed as he felt the tree's soul touch his. A soft chime of joy and recognition.

"You can have some more of my memories of music today," Eti said softly. It didn't cost him anything, and the tree truly enjoyed them, every song Eti could think of.

In return, the tree extended its soul aura around Eti, drew him back to rest, held him in that place where all was well and as it should be. And in that place, some of the ashes of his soul drifted away again, the injured patterns restored.

Arianna. Her name was Arianna.

Tree, can you help me forget? I have to forget.

His handlers would clasp his hand when he debriefed them, and they'd know if he was lying or withholding anything.

The tree rumbled its distaste of this request but understood his need. The earth beneath him joined in the tree's desire to help ease his distress.

Eti drifted toward sleep knowing, for now at least, that he could keep her safe from his handlers.

10

THE RECEPTION HALL

> *There are fewer times nobles are more petty than when in arbitration.*
>
> — KIR MTALOR, SOCIAL COMMENTATOR, IN A POST ON THEIR PERSONAL FEED

"I know we said all our formal greetings here yesterday, but this is your first time holding legal court in the Reception Hall," the Seritarchus said.

He turned toward Dressa, brow raised, smile on the sour side of mocking. He didn't ask if she was nervous. He damn well knew, and that look was a challenge.

They were sitting at a table set up on a dais in the palace's Reception Hall, the hall still empty except for them, their staff, and their guards. Dressa sat at the table's center, a legal clerk to her left, the Seritarchus to her right. At the Seritarchus's end of the table, Commander of the Palace Guard Jalava themself stood watch, unwilling to take any chances at this first Reception after Arianna's attack at the ball.

She smiled back at the Seritarchus, all sweetness. "You have, of course, trained me well."

His grin showed teeth. "Then you have nothing to be nervous about."

Strangely, whatever he'd hoped to accomplish with that bout of sparring eased some of the tension in her shoulders. She was trained for this, even if she didn't actually have the practice. But she was absolutely determined to not let her lack of experience show.

By rights, the Seritarchus should sit at the center, hearing the cases brought before them and making his judgements. But she was the Heir—Arianna had done this and done it well enough that she'd taken over the duty almost entirely in the last few months. He was only here now because it was her first time. Well, and to continue to show his public support for her as his Heir.

"The public doesn't see me like they see Arianna," she'd said in his study an hour earlier. "They're not going to trust the judgements I make like they trusted hers."

She'd spent most of the last few years setting herself up as the perfect foil to Arianna's air of authority and control—she was the fun sister, she was the one you could approach. But that reputation wasn't helping her now. She'd seen the feeds. People were highly skeptical of someone who'd spent most of her days until now in vapid social gatherings and parties.

"Don't try to be Arianna. They'll mistrust that most of all. You're approachable, Dressa, and that's an asset. Use it."

Now, in the Reception Hall, Dressa eyed the Seritarchus as the double doors at the far end opened, and a group of waiting petitioners were escorted in. When Iata was the Seritarchus in public, he was almost perfectly her father. It was unsettling, knowing it was a different person behind that familiar edged smile. She'd decided to think of him as the Seritarchus in those times, because he was. He wasn't her father, but he certainly wasn't Iata then, either.

Dressa took a breath and tried to set the Seritarchus out of her immediate thoughts. He was here to support, but she was running this Reception today. And she did know the formula, she knew how this Reception should go. She'd sat beside her father many times growing up as part of her training. She'd watched Arianna's Receptions a few times from the audience, anonymous and observant.

Her gaze edged back to the Seritarchus. Had some of those times she'd sat with her father been with him instead?

He inclined his head toward the steward, who was waiting to announce the first petitioner of the group.

Dressa refocused and gave the steward a nod.

The steward in maroon velvet livery turned to the dozen or so petitioners who'd been allowed entrance. Often, there were as many as fifty at a time in the Reception Hall. They'd sit in the rows of chairs and wait to be called, watching the show all the while. With the heightened security in the palace, though, Commander Jalava had insisted that the groups be smaller and more manageable if there was a problem.

Jalava watched the petitioners now with iron suspicion, but Dressa saw no signs of their alarm. Not that she thought there would be—Jalava was one of the few people who knew that the magicker attack hadn't really been an attack at all.

The steward held up her comm, which flashed blue and chimed loudly in the large space. Any remaining chatter or rustling from the petitioners died down.

"The Truthspoken Heir, Ondressarie Rhialden, is now accepting petitions to her judgement. Will Lord Madrol, their opposing party Lord Ramirez, and all support please approach the dais and stand on the gold-marked section of the floor."

Dressa internally checked her expression—pleasantly neutral—and settled in to listen.

The first petitioner, Lord Madrol, spoke of a contract they'd signed with Lord Ramirez to have a child; the child, now two years old, was shown to have some of Lord Madrol's DNA, but not as much as they should. Lord Madrol, tears streaming down their face and running their eyeliner in a way Dressa was sure had been calculated, explained that the child had been given the genetic material from three parents—one being Lord Ramirez's longtime partner.

"And that," Lord Madrol said, their voice rising to a hysterical pitch, "is a breach of contract! I want compensation for this breach, and another child who is half mine! I want proof of parentage this time, not falsified lab documents!"

Dressa sighed to herself. It was only fitting, she supposed, that her first petitioner was one of the dramatic sorts. She could read their body language easily enough—they didn't care about the child at all for the child's sake, they'd only wanted the prestige and business assets of having a blood relative who had a tie to the Ramirez shipping lines.

Dressa held up a hand, and Lord Madrol stopped talking, though they continued to sniff loudly as they dabbed at their eyes.

"Lord Ramirez, care to share your perspective?"

Lord Ramirez, a short, stocky man with thinning red-black hair, smiled tightly. "Lord Madrol stipulated that they didn't want part in any raising of this child. I told them that if I was going to fully raise this child, I wanted my child to not be just mine, but my partner's as well."

"Ah," Dressa said. "Lord Madrol, that seems fair. Did you agree to this?"

Lord Madrol waved a hand. "Well, it was only talk. It wasn't in the contract."

Lord Ramirez turned to Lord Madrol. "We wrote it into Section Three." He produced a tablet, touched the screen a few times, and handed it to Madrol. "Here."

Madrol bent over the tablet. "That wasn't there before. You added that clause after the contract was signed."

Dressa admired Ramirez's restraint as he took the tablet back and handed it to the steward.

"For the Truthspoken Heir to inspect," he said.

Dressa took the tablet from the steward, but she already knew what she'd see. The tablet was one of the official varieties used specifically for the signing of formal contracts. While it wasn't quite the contract paper of her marriage contract, it functioned in a similar way. The firmware of the tablet was hard coded to fundamentally change when the contract was signed, and it was tamper-proof afterward. The contract couldn't be changed after it was signed by all parties without logging that change in bold in the contract header itself, stating that the changes weren't signed. There was none of that here.

"Lord Madrol," Dressa said, handing the tablet back to the steward, "do you wish to raise this second child you demand?"

"No! Of course I don't. I don't have the proper lifestyle to raise a child, they would only get in the way of my business—"

"Lord Ramirez, do you wish to contract another child to Lord Madrol?"

"No, Ser Truthspoken."

"And are you happy with the agreement as it stands now?"

Ramirez cut a glance at Madrol, who was dabbing at their eyes again. He was regretting the contract at all, Dressa knew. But he said, "Yes, I am content with the agreement as it stands."

"Then I want custody!" Madrol shrieked. "If the child isn't as much mine as it should be, I want custody! It's only fair!"

"No," Dressa said. "The contract will stand, as it's valid and legal. No clauses will be added or taken away. That is my judgement."

Madrol let out a moan, but Ramirez bowed deeply before they were both escorted out.

Dressa smoothed her fingers against her own tablet in front

of her, her stylus beside it if she wished to take notes. But a court secretary was on her other side, taking all the notes she'd ever need.

Those two nobles should have handled their dispute in a court of civil arbitration, but Dressa was sure Lord Madrol had thought they could sway the Truthspoken into coming down in their favor. How they'd deluded themself to that plan, she didn't know, but it wasn't uncommon among the nobility to think they'd be able to use hysterics where facts wouldn't do.

Dressa glanced at the Seritarchus. But he only looked back, impassive. He was only there to observe and help if absolutely necessary, right. He wouldn't tell her how she'd done until the end. She tried hard to read into his body language, but he was as maddeningly opaque as her father right now.

"Next petitioner is Count Tegan Griel of Sangor Brec, under the rule of Duke Kyran Koldari, and her daughter and heir, Lord Iva Griel."

Dressa settled in for another tedious account, but sat up straight when Count Griel opened with, "Ser Truthspoken. My land has suffered an attack from the Kidaa."

11

DINNER AND CONVERSATION

> *Dinner among courtiers is not for those with weak digestion.*
>
> — LORD ESARA TEOH MÉRON BRINT IN *A GUIDE TO ETIQUETTE AT THE PALACE RHIALDEN COURT*

Count Badem fully inhabited the space she occupied—tall and animated, with an infectious laugh and razor wit that set her dinner guests rolling and caused not a few incidents with napkins not getting to mouths and noses in time.

Imorie could see why she ran an estate that specialized in treating the Bruising Sleep—the count herself was medicine.

Imorie had been tense with the duke on her arm, but now, seated beside him, with others chatting around her and the count carrying on a raucous overview of the party the night before, her tension began to ease.

It was all a bit much. The spread of food, too many spices, too many bright colors in the clothing of the guests, too much laughter, when she didn't truly have the energy to laugh. But the laughter was good, at least.

She found herself thinking of Eti—was he in the staff dining area with her own servant, Jis? Had he gone back to the gardens, which was where he was supposed to work anyway? He was odd, and shy, but she liked him. He'd gone out of his way to be kind to her, and that wasn't something she was used to. He'd been ready to take her all the way into dinner in the entry, to protect her from the duke, or anyone else who she didn't want to be with, she suspected.

She was pretty sure he had a crush on her, but she didn't think that was at the core of his help. He seemed the kind of person that would help because he thought it was right. In the circles she moved in, in her family, the ambitious Quevedos who'd reached high enough to get a contract child from a Rhialden, that was so rare.

Her head stabbed with a sudden pain, and Imorie winced, touching her forehead.

"Are you all right?" Duke Kyran asked, leaning close so others wouldn't overhear. A bit too close.

"Fine, yes, thank you. Just—"

"We don't talk about why we're here in public," he said, still close. His breath smelled like the white wine he was slowly swirling in his glass. "We can talk in the gardens, we can talk in the various rooms about the house. But not here at dinner. This is where we forget."

She glanced over. "You just asked me if I'm all right."

"We don't let each other fall into our dinners, either." He smiled, drew back. "Have you tried the candied beets? They're one of the milder dishes, I promise."

Imorie breathed out slowly as he scooped a mound onto her plate. She'd only been picking at everything else, her stomach churning too much to handle the flavors. But slowly, she poked her fork at the beets, and they had some flavor without being overwhelming. Honeyed and sweet, with a light, tangy sauce.

"This is good."

"The dishes are color-coded," he said, waving around the table. "Blue is mild. Violet is medium-adventurous, and red isn't for the faint at heart."

She did a quick glance around the table. Yep, she'd been picking from mostly violet and red dishes so far. Why hadn't he told her that earlier? Was he having fun trying to rescue her now?

Her shoulders tightened back up. She found herself wishing for the buffer of Eti, not that he would be a lot of help in this sort of company. Adeius, she despised formal dinners.

This wasn't, truly, a bad dinner. And it wasn't supposed to be formal, anyway, though the caliber of the guests forced it to be more than casual. Count Badem helped defuse it all with her running commentary, but that didn't stop the career courtiers from being . . . well, themselves.

Had she thought she could relax here? Was she truly that tired?

"Imorie," Count Badem boomed, and Imorie jumped. "It is Imorie, isn't it? How are you finding our estates so far?"

"Uh, yes, Imorie. She and her. I—"

Her hands were shaking. Was it the illness, was it nerves? Was it being startled or the eyes of everyone around her, which were all turned on her?

She'd never been good around a lot of people, especially nobility. Yes, she was a contract Rhialden, but she wasn't a courtier by birth or inclination. She did have some social training, though. Her Quevedo mother hadn't let her enter the world at large without as much training as she deemed necessary to honor her Rhialden mother's name.

"I think the estates are lovely," she managed. "And, um, good company, too."

"Oh, excellent! Well, welcome, Imorie—everyone, make her feel right at home, will you? We're all family, here." Count Badem turned to another guest and began a lively discussion about their grandchildren.

Imorie felt like a searchlight had just passed by her and now she could breathe again.

Kyran grinned. "She does have that affect. But she makes this place interesting. Would you like to see the gardens? I could take you on a tour after dinner."

Imorie almost choked on the bite she'd shoved into her mouth.

"I—sorry, I'm still travel-lagged. Maybe another day?"

She wasn't sure why his suggestion had made her skin crawl. Maybe it was that he'd left her to navigate an unknown food system, knowing she'd be uncomfortable. Or was this system widely used on Hestia, and he'd just assumed she'd known? Otherwise, he'd been pleasant, mostly civil. He had personal space issues, but she'd met other people like that, it wasn't always a red flag.

"Of course," he said. Then twirled his chopsticks in the air. "You came down the stairs with that gardener boy? You probably want to keep your distance. He's a little strange. He caused a bit of a stir with the Dynasty couple last week. Bumped into them on the path, wasn't looking, just plowed straight into them, didn't look back, didn't apologize. It was odd." He shrugged. "You don't know with some of these service types."

Imorie looked at him askance. Eti seemed awkward, sure, but not oblivious. Well, okay, not totally oblivious, but that was hardly a warn-able offense to her—she'd grown up with siblings.

She gave a non-committal shrug and was saved from having to say more by Count Badem ringing her glass and calling for dessert.

Imorie looked out through the bank of windows lining the

dining hall to the gardens, the sun fully set now, the sky still fading pinks and blues. Why had the duke singled out Eti, of all the people here? Was he jealous that Eti had escorted her down and seemed protective of her? Really—was he, a duke, jealous of the gardener?

She'd see the gardens when she could, but not with Duke Kyran. She'd have to find out what Eti's schedule was.

12

THE CLAIM

> *We have, so far, found only the runic system as evidence of Kidaa written language past or present. Runes serve as broad conceptual signifiers, such as 'planet' or 'water,' clan designations, and navigational signals. We have yet to find evidence of complex grammar in their written language, though it is certainly complex in their spoken language, to the point where our translation algorithms struggle to understand.*
>
> — ADMIRAL BRYNC QUACH IN HER REPORT "THE STATE OF AFFAIRS WITH THE KIDAA"

The air in the Reception Hall hung tense and charged as what Count Griel had just said sank in. She was claiming her land had been attacked by the Kidaa?

Count Griel's daughter, Lord Griel, stepped forward. "Ser Truthspoken. There are *signs* this attack might have been the Kidaa." She gave her mother a reproachful look. "We don't know it was the Kidaa."

"The Kidaa have never shown themselves to be aggressive, let alone attack anyone," Dressa said. "What signs have you seen, what made you think it might have been them? What kind of attack did your land suffer?"

She studied Count Griel and her daughter—both were dressed well, but not as extravagantly as most courtiers in the Rhialden Court. Tegan Griel's collar was a little rumpled, her knee-length coat a few shades less than the black it might have once been. Her daughter's hair was mussed on one side, like a hasty fix had come undone again. They both looked as if they'd come to the Reception Hall after hours of attending to other business. Or, maybe, straight from the spaceport.

Beside her, the Seritarchus said quietly, "Dismiss the rest of the petitioners. I want to hear this one privately."

Dressa nodded and looked up to do that when one of the back doors opened and a familiar figure with blazing red hair stepped in.

Adeius. Lesander. Dressa didn't need distractions right now, and what was Lesander doing here? Did she have an actual purpose in coming? Was she bored? Dressa didn't know her well enough yet to tell, and she didn't have the mental bandwidth just now to try and figure that out. She had a count who'd just said she suspected an attack from the Kidaa.

Dressa glanced at the Seritarchus, who wasn't quite frowning. Could she send the rest of the petitioners out if Lesander had now placed herself among that audience? Lesander shouldn't have been let in, but with her status now as betrothed to the Truthspoken Heir, she could have talked her way through the guards easily enough.

Or maybe not so easily, Dressa thought, by Commander Jalava's tight glare. The door guards would likely get a stern rebuke from their commander later, and she didn't envy their positions.

Dressa read the tension in the room, growing, shading into

an ugly sort of restlessness. If she dismissed the petitioners now, what was said here next would not be on public record, but that would bring its own attention and fire up gossip. The initial damage had been done—someone had publicly claimed a Kidaa attack, and the court would be buzzing with the anxiety of that within an hour.

But she knew if the Griels' claim was a ploy, or a mistake—or, worse, if it was in any way true—it had to be handled delicately.

Adeius, why did something like this have to come up on her first day?

"Count Griel, Lord Griel, please stay. The rest of the petitioners—this Reception is adjourned for the next hour. Please wait in the waiting room, and you'll be notified if I'm seeing any further petitioners this day."

There was no protest. There was a tightening in the air that Dressa didn't like. Not quite fear, and not quite malice, but something of the kind.

She narrowed her eyes and held up her hands. "Wait. Everyone in this room, you are sworn to not repeat anything you have heard in this room until I publicly release this information. Please state your acknowledgement of this command."

The petitioners looked at each other, then looked past her to the Seritarchus.

Dressa gritted her teeth. She was in charge of this Reception, not him.

"I will hear your acknowledgement of this command," she said with quiet weight. It brought their eyes back to her, but she realized with a grimace that she'd used one of Arianna's signature moves—tone of voice and everything. She'd have to come up with some of her own, but, well. It had worked, for the moment.

The petitioners, including the Griels, all gave their acknowledgements, and the remaining petitioners filed out.

Lesander, of course, still sat in the back, an island of her own.

Dressa's lips parted as she met Lesander's gaze, too far away to read her closely.

Then she looked past Lesander, set her firmly out of her thoughts, and focused back on the Griels. She'd bet on Lesander's discretion before. This, at least, wasn't nearly as dire as their secret marriage.

Maybe.

"Now," Dressa said, folding her hands in front of her. That move was one of her father's, and she decided to let it be. She definitely didn't look to the Seritarchus to see what he'd thought of that. "Count Griel. Please explain what happened and why you think it was done by the Kidaa."

13

EVIDENCE

We have such little commonality with the Kidaa that how can we even say for certain that they have a moral code? Do they have concepts of violence being wrong, or non-violence being good? Or do they simply have no concept of violence at all, and therefore don't do it?

— HIGH GENERAL BANAMAR ABRET IN A LETTER TO TRUTHSPEAKER ADUWEL SHIN MERNA

Count Griel straightened, smoothed down the front of her coat, and nodded, bobbing her short salt-and-pepper hair.

"It happened nine days ago. I sent a report to the Seritarchus—" the Seritarchus nodded, and that was the first Dressa had heard of it "—but I wanted to come myself. Truth-spoken can read the truth of a situation, same as the Green Magickers."

Dressa stirred. Hardly the same, but she wasn't going to argue that point now.

"The attack happened in one of our fields. I had a large herd of cattle moving from the lowlands, and all the handlers with them. The cattle were spared except for a few minor injuries, but one of the handlers behind them was killed, and another severely injured in the stampede after." Her mouth pulled tight. "She died shortly after."

Dressa swallowed. Adeius. But why would the count think the Kidaa were interested in her handlers? Kidaa hadn't shown any interest in Human affairs at all as far as she knew, beyond a minor curiosity for Human ships near the border. Rhys had warned her, though, that the Kidaa might not be as docile as they seemed. But . . . cattle handlers?

Wasn't it infinitely more probable that this was an attack from another of the lords on Sangor Brec?

"Did you take this matter to Duke Kyran Koldari?" she asked.

Count Griel shifted. "Duke Koldari is away from Sangor Brec. His staff has no word on when he will return, only saying, 'soon.' I tried the onworld agents for the other two worlds in Koldari's holding, and all said the same thing—he isn't on those worlds, either, not at least that they know. I took it to his estate steward, who promised to look into it, but xe seemed to think I was crazy to suggest it was a Kidaa attack. Xe just wanted to dismiss the whole thing as a petty vengeance crime or bizarre accident. But it was a *rune*."

Griel stopped for breath, looking flushed. "Truthspoken—I respectfully request you launch a full company of reserves to support my holdings, as well as reinforce orbital security over Sangor Brec."

Dressa sat back, trying to fit the nature of this attack with the proportionate response Count Griel was asking for.

"You're saying this was an orbital attack?" She glanced at

the Seritarchus. “Was there word of an attack on the world? Or Kidaa in-system? Surely the Navy would be aware of that?”

“No,” he said. “I did read your account, Griel. A rune was burned into the site.”

“Yes.” Griel leaned forward. “One Kidaa rune, though I don’t know what it means. But it fits the look of other Kidaa runes, we looked it up. The rune *was* the attack. There were deep, scorched gouges in the ground, and—and everything in the path of whatever burned it. Including my handler. About fifty meters to a side, just missing the herd. It looked like an attack from orbit, or else, I don’t know how else to explain it.

“When my surviving handlers commed me, I sent up drones to better assess what had happened, and that was when I saw what had really happened. It wasn’t accidental, not lightning or anything else that might have made an attack like that —and I can’t think what else naturally would. The Kidaa have runes carved into their skin, do they not? They have runes on their ship hulls and use them in their tools.”

“The image file you sent was denied at the planetary origin,” the Seritarchus said. “Not enough to cover the cost of sending interstellar. I requested it be sent again under my seal but didn’t receive a response.”

Griel grimaced. “We were already en route. Apologies, Seritarchus. As I said, I thought it best to address this in person.” She pulled a thin tablet from her jacket pocket and started forward.

Commander Jalava stiffened, hand on their holstered pistol, but the Seritarchus reached for the tablet as Griel stretched up to give it to him.

Dressa didn’t have to ask to see it—he angled it toward her while he examined the image.

It was an overhead view of a field, green grass scorched into a complex shape.

Dressa’s stomach churned as she took in the details—this

would have been taken right after the attack happened and spared nothing—but she forced herself to keep looking, to flick through more of the images. Was that truly a Kidaa rune? Could there be another explanation? She hadn't thought the Kidaa placed a lot of weight on written language beyond clan and ship markings, preferring oral traditions. They didn't, as far as she knew, have anything like Human books or databases or comm feeds.

But then, that was speculation. Like every other thing about the Kidaa.

She wanted to talk to Rhys. She wanted to know what they knew, all of it.

"Do you have enemies, Count Griel?" the Seritarchus asked.

Griel stiffened. "A few, but none so malicious as to kill my handler. Or even kill the livestock, if that's what they were aiming for and missed. I have thought maybe this was supposed to be a warning, too, and my handler got caught in the attack by accident, but that still doesn't explain the rune, and I honestly don't know who'd want to warn me like that. Losing a handler—losing two—it's a tragedy and they will be sorely missed, but it doesn't take me out by any means."

"Mm." The Seritarchus studied the image again. He zoomed in, panned around.

Somewhere in there, he'd taken over this petition, and while some part of Dressa chafed that he'd needed to, she didn't want to have to deal with this on her own. And she hadn't known all she'd needed to know. Had he kept that from her, or had there just not been time, among all the myriad other things she urgently needed to know? She had to get up to date on . . . everything.

"It's possible it's an attack from a rival house to Duke Koldari, not yourself," the Seritarchus said.

"But still, why attack in the shape of a rune?" Griel's daughter asked, stepping closer to her mother. "The rune doesn't make sense. I've studied the Kidaa. We're closer to the border than Valon, though not right on it. They've never done anything like this—why would they? And why would someone think this would look like the Kidaa, and why would someone want it to? Everyone knows the Kidaa are docile. They don't fight. They just don't do violence."

She looked over at her mother. "I don't have my mother's conviction that this was the Kidaa—there's no evidence of a Kidaa ship. There were Navy ships and trade ships and local system ships in orbit, but none of them saw the Kidaa. But . . . if this *was* the Kidaa . . ."

She trailed off, looking at a loss.

And Dressa felt it, too. On the surface, this was nothing to rush to the capital over. There were squabbles, even violent squabbles, among the nobility all the time. There were accidents. Weird things sometimes happened.

And yet. All of Dressa's training in reading patterns was telling her that this pattern didn't add up. Or rather, that it was adding up in a shape she didn't like. Whether it had been the Kidaa or not, this meant trouble. The Seritarchus had been right earlier to dismiss the other petitioners. Whatever this was, rumors could be even more dangerous than the attack itself.

The Seritarchus set the tablet down. "Please stay in one of the guest rooms of the palace—my steward will get you accommodated. I want you on hand if I have more questions."

"Of course," Count Griel said, bowing. "Thank you, Seritarchus, Truthspoken, for hearing our petition. Will you be sending troops to my land?"

"I'll send an investigation team. I won't commit to more than that, as I don't want any potential conflict escalating."

Count Griel looked like she wanted to protest, but nodded. "Yes, Seritarchus." She bowed again and looked to the steward, who with her own bow to the dais saw the Griels out.

14

SOMETHING TO DO

> *Why would I ever want to be in this room, when you are in that room?*
>
> — COUNT JIN HEART IN THE VID DRAMA *NOVA HEARTS*, SEASON 6, EPISODE 2, "ISN'T IT A LOVELY DAY?"

The Reception Hall was empty now of all petitioners. There was only Dressa and the Seritarchus, her clerk to her left, the door guards, and Commander Jalava, whose shoulders had gone stiffer throughout the conversation.

And Lesander.

Dressa caught Lesander's eye, and Lesander stood, approaching the dais.

Dressa sifted through and discarded several openings that all amounted to, "Why are you here?" and instead stood, holding out her hands as Lesander climbed the side stairs up to Dressa's level. Lesander caught her hands, and Dressa placed a quick, chaste kiss on Lesander's cheek.

"That was interesting," Lesander murmured.

"You will, of course, not repeat this anywhere."

Lesander arched a brow. "I already gave my oath. Forgive me, Dressa, but the walls were closing in and—" Her eyes darted to Dressa's lips.

Dressa suppressed a groan. She and Lesander hadn't worked out yet how they were going to handle themselves with the court. After the initial introduction to the court the day before, in this same Reception Hall, they'd both been tired. It had been a big day, after all. An absolutely cosmos-shattering twenty-four hours. An abdication, a secret wedding, a confirmation, a real betrothal.

A wedding night, or rather, morning.

Last night, they'd fallen into Dressa's bed with intent to rest. But, well. Maybe not intending to rest after all. Rest was not nearly so good as . . . mm. Other things.

Adeius. How the hell were they supposed to keep this marriage secret for another two months?

Beside her, the Seritarchus also stood.

"Lesander," he said cordially, but with an edged enough smile that Dressa saw Lesander tense.

"Seritarchus. Forgive my interruption."

"Not at all. You'll need to be aware of what goes on in the palace, of course."

He turned away, abruptly dismissive. "Jalava, you should be in your office. You don't have to babysit me—one of your juniors will be fine, I assure you."

Adeius, did he have to be so obvious about his displeasure with Lesander? Dressa moved a little closer to Lesander, their shoulders almost touching.

Jalava, ever the seasoned Commander of the Palace Guard, weathered their own rebuke without a twitch.

"Ser Seritarchus, we don't need panic about an attack from the Kidaa on top of panic about an attack from the Green Magickers. Two groups, I might add, that shouldn't be violent, so tensions will be high. I've already restricted magicker access to the palace except for the already approved magickers—the First Magicker, of course, and any of the overly diplomatic set that always shows up at balls and parties to reassure people that they're harmless. You might want to make a statement, ser, about handling things with the Kidaa. Something nice and reassuring."

Dressa didn't know Jalava well, though the commander had always been a fixture in her life. Jalava had headed the Palace Guard since before she was born. Did Jalava know that this Seritarchus wasn't the same person they usually guarded? She had to assume they did not.

The Seritarchus let out a slow breath. "See to order in this palace, Commander. I'll handle rumors as they come up. They might even be useful rumors. Dressa, if you will join me in my study. Lesander—" He stopped, looking back to regard Lesander. "Do you legitimately want something to do?"

She blinked. "Yes, Seritarchus. I'm not in a position to make inroads in court without Dressa's help, not yet, with things as they stand. And I am absolutely sick of apartment walls."

"Yes, I can see that. Well." He motioned to the clerk beside Dressa. "Your tablet."

The clerk handed over her tablet, and he tapped at it quickly. "This tablet now belongs to Prince Javieri—see requisitions for another one." He handed the tablet to Lesander. "This has send and receive privileges to my personal account, as well as Dressa's. Fill out your information to make your own personal palace account. Then find out where Duke Koldari has gone and send that information directly to me. This tablet has extra security measures, but do you know how to perform an untraced search?"

"Yes, of course."

"Good. Do so. You can have Office A-5, you'll already have access. Where are your guards?"

Lesander clutched the tablet, looking a little flustered. "Uh, outside. The door guards wouldn't let them in with me."

"As they should," Jalava said, crossing their arms.

The Seritarchus waved their comment off. "Your guards do not leave your side, except for when you're alone with Dressa or alone in your office. When you're finished with tracking Duke Koldari, I would like every instance you can find of Kidaa runes showing up within the kingdom—whether from artifacts brought in, copies made by Human artists, or any other circumstance—in the last two hundred years."

"Father," Dressa protested, "she's not a clerk. She's not even staff."

"No," he said, his voice low. "I know exactly who she is, and what trust I can place in her discretion."

Lesander froze, and for the barest moment, Dressa thought she saw her pale. Or was it the lighting? Lesander tilted her head in acknowledgement, and her coloring seemed normal.

"Yes, Seritarchus, and—thank you. I'll have this information for you."

"Good. Dressa?"

The Seritarchus headed toward the back door. Dressa took one last glance at Lesander, whose own gaze was hovering on shell-shocked, then hurried after him.

15

THE CALLBACK

> *Most people think that for Truthspoken, assuming another personality is easy. Usually, though, we don't assume personalities in truth, we only stretch and extrapolate from our own personalities, even the darker aspects. We inhabit a role, we steer its boundaries, we allude. We use a vast repertoire of traits we've learned through observation and training to give the illusion that we are someone else. Once in a while, we'll push past those bounds, but we are trained so carefully not to lose our centers when we do so. Playing a role is far different than being another person in truth. When you truly believe you are another person, then you are.*
>
> — ARIANNA RHIALDEN, MELESORIE X IN *THE CHANGE DIALOGUES*

As Duke Kyran wished to continue the evening with the other guests in one of the sitting rooms, and Imorie was struggling to keep herself present even at the end of dinner, she sent one of the waiting staff for Jis. It was on Jis's arm, not the duke's or Eti's, that she slowly took the stairs up to the second floor, and the tiny lift to the third. She had to pause outside the lift doors for breath, and then, with Jis supporting her, she walked the last stretch to her suite.

Imorie was trembling when Jis helped her sit on the couch. She pressed her hands into her stomach, trying to still herself, hold herself together.

"It's not working," she gasped. "The treatment's not working."

"It's—Adeius, it hasn't been a full day. It's not going to work overnight."

But it should. She knew it should, and why did she know it should?

Jis shifted from one foot to the other, sighed, and sat beside her. Reached out a hand, and she took it.

"Hey," fae asked softly, "did dinner go well?"

"I—"

Imorie sniffed, wiped at her eyes. "Yes. Sort of. There's a duke here, Kyran Koldari—"

She felt Jis stiffen.

"You know him?"

Jis gave her a long, searching look. "I've heard of him."

"And? He's—well, he wasn't exactly uncivil, but he was pushy. And he got in my space. I think he's jealous that Eti brought me down."

"Huh. That—" Jis bit faer lip. Fae was staring at her again.

"What?" Imorie asked.

"Are you planning to see more of him?"

Imorie loosened her grip on her stomach, sighed back into the couch. "I don't see how I can avoid it. He's like his own Seritarchus here, with Badem as the Truthspeaker. I can't figure out if he wants to use whatever Rhialden connections he thinks I have, or if he's genuinely interested in me." She thought a moment. "He didn't offer to escort me back upstairs. Also, why does this place not have a lift on the ground floor? Why only the second floor and up?"

"I suspect it's for the charm, though I agree, it's a weird decision in a house full of sick people." Jis pushed errant bangs out of faer eyes. "Imorie, can you come with me to the bathroom? I want to wash off your face before you go to bed—not good to keep that makeup on all night."

It wasn't an unreasonable request, but it felt . . . off. Jis was acting weird, a little jumpy, and fae was entirely too familiar just now. Sure, Imorie had known faer for years now, they were as close as any person and their staff could be, but Jis was still staff—

Adeius, and why was she even concerned about that, here on Hestia, where all the rules seemed a bit sideways, and Jis was the only familiar face among the crowd?

Jis stood and reached down a solid hand, hauling Imorie up. Imorie found, at least, she could walk without support to the bathroom. There was that small dignity.

Inside the cramped space, Jis shut the door and turned on the shower. Then, the sink.

Imorie leaned against the sink, watching faer. "What are you doing?"

Jis ignored the question—or maybe fae didn't hear—and approached Imorie with a cleansing cloth. Fae cupped Imorie's face in one hand and said, "Ignoble speaker, how deeply your courage offends me."

Imorie pulled back. "What?"

Jis stared at her, mouth tightening. "For you have traversed the stars, and know the call of the void."

A pain hit Imorie between her brows. She grunted, rubbed at her forehead.

"Jis, what the hell?"

Jis swore and leaned forward, grabbing both of her arms.

Fae spread faer fingers out across her forearms, close on one arm, apart on the other. It felt like a pattern—

Ari gasped and clutched Bettea as her knees gave.

Bettea caught her, tripping back hard into the wall. But fae held her upright.

"What the hell?" Ari breathed, and the words, the same words she'd said seconds ago, felt entirely different.

Bettea put faer mouth right by Ari's ear, and Ari still strained to hear. "Imorie. You can't do that. You can't go that deep. Adeius—this is so dangerous. Do you understand what I mean?"

Ari blinked, more of herself coming back to herself. She'd buried herself in the entry earlier—she hadn't had the strength to match wits with Duke Kyran, so she hadn't. She'd let Imorie handle that.

"I—"

This conversation was definitely dangerous. The shower was still running. The sink was starting to fill up. But bugs could filter for such sounds—water was a deterrent, not a shield. And Imorie wouldn't know how to do the more thorough sort of bug search that she and Bettea could do. Imorie shouldn't be looking for bugs at all.

Ari rested her forehead on Bettea's shoulder, trying to think. She'd met Duke Kyran as Imorie—she had to continue as Imorie in truth, at least for the next few days. At least until the treatment started to work. She truly didn't have the strength to be both herself and Imorie.

She'd be better prepared for the next time, though, and more fully construct and center herself in Imorie's personality. She saw the uncertain gaps from being unprepared tonight, and that was no good. She still felt Imorie's heightened anxiety from that.

Ari leaned close to Bettea, and Bettea bent faer ear to hear her better.

"I have to. Have to again."

"I almost—" Bettea bit faer lip. Fae shook faer head, and small water droplets from hastily turning on the shower shimmered in faer light gold hair. "Just, sleep on it? Then, in the morning? If you must."

Fae pulled back, searched her eyes. Ari nodded, looking back with all her conviction. She'd had no other choice, in the sort of crowd she'd been in that night, but to submerge herself. Her mind was too hazy to cover every detail otherwise. She'd slip up, she'd say something she shouldn't, or make one of her own gestures, not Imorie's, and the sharp-eyed courtiers among the bunch would see. The evaku-trained, as Kyran certainly was. Her father had told her not, under any circumstances, to break her cover. Whatever was going on at the capital, she still couldn't do that.

Could she beg off from socializing here? Surely there was precedent, with so many people getting treatment. She'd seen another of the courtiers at dinner who'd left court a few weeks before. Duke Kyran—was he sick? She couldn't tell. He'd insinuated that he was a part of that particular group of guests with his comment about not talking about how they were feeling, but that didn't mean it was so.

Her head throbbed, and she took back every time she'd ever told Rhys to tough it out when they said they had a headache and couldn't help with training practice that day. Every single time.

Etienne. She'd go form a friendship with Eti as Imorie. Eti, at least, seemed safe enough. Unpretentious. Absolutely not skilled in court etiquette. Eti seemed the closest thing to safe there was here.

Ari's head snapped up. Bettea had used two phrases of the callback stanza from *Alter Gaian,* a prose poem that was popular four hundred years ago and which Ari had no particular love for. Her callback couldn't be anything that could easily be traced to her. She wondered now, though, if they should try to establish another callback that had more emotional attachment—but they couldn't, now. Not with the sort of repetition and conditioning she'd need to make it work.

Adeius, it was dangerous to submerge herself again when her verbal callback hadn't worked. The tactile callback had, though—they'd just have to use that, and pray it would also work again, or that the callback failure this time had been because of her fatigue, or maybe the treatment.

Well, she'd constructed Imorie to be different enough from Arianna, but enough of herself that she could fully inhabit the role without much personality strain. There was that. She'd have no difficulties being Imorie in truth for a few days or a week if she had to.

She had absolutely no intention of losing herself in Imorie, though. "We'll do this every night," she said. "Call me back every night. If it gets worse than this—I'll stay in bed that day."

"Stay in bed tomorrow," Bettea said, sounding strained. "Please. You'll probably need the rest anyway."

"Okay. Tomorrow." And maybe the next day, but she'd have to go out again sometime. She didn't want to isolate herself and rely fully on the hospitality of the house, either. She needed some social leverage here, too, in case anything ever went sour.

If anyone called on her, she'd have to submerge again. Well, or maybe she wouldn't have to if it was only the physician, or even Count Badem. She had a feeling Count Badem was noise enough to drown out whatever inconsistencies she might show here.

Maybe rest would help. Maybe if she submerged again, it wouldn't be hard to bring herself back out. She'd still only been here a day yet and had only just started treatment.

Slowly, she pushed herself back from Bettea and reached to shut off the sink. Bettea hesitated, then turned off the shower.

Fae hadn't touched her makeup—she'd need to keep that

on, only to be washed off in the moments before a new layer was applied.

One of the new piercings on her left ear throbbed. She sighed.

"Bed," she said, and Bettea helped her to it.

16

DISTRESS

> *People ask me sometimes if my aura as a Green Magicker hinders my vision, like I'll only see green, because that's what they see around me. But my aura is an extension of my eyes and my senses. I don't notice the green at all unless I'm looking down at myself, at my own hands.*
>
> — FIRST MAGICKER MARIYIT BRODEN, AS QUOTED IN *THE CHANGE DIALOGUES*

Dressa followed the Seritarchus through the back corridors, taking the narrow stairs behind the Reception Hall up to the second floor, and then down and up again as the layer that sat between the first and second floors of the palace wove in and around the architecture of the rooms and corridors around them.

Why had he assigned Lesander the task of finding Duke Koldari? What did he know, and especially what did he know that he hadn't told her about the Kidaa?

She was finding it hard to focus on the Kidaa, because she

kept getting distracted, now that she had time to think about it, remembering how the light in the Reception Hall had fallen across the curve of Lesander's cheek. Of how Lesander, sitting at the back of an empty hall, had slowly run a hand up and down her wrist. A nervous tic? A stim? A purposeful gesture?

The Seritarchus unlocked and opened the door into his study, and the familiar surroundings brought her back to herself.

"Are you trying to separate us, so I'm not distracted?" she asked as he went to his desk, calling up the holo controls so he could adjust something on the display.

"Are you distracted?"

Adeius, he wasn't dropping the role of her father at all. It made her want to squirm and absolutely change the subject.

She forcefully ejected Lesander from her thoughts, though it took more effort than she'd want to admit.

"Okay, so, the Kidaa. What don't I know about the Kidaa? Do you know if they're behind this attack? Do you know more than what we heard today?"

"Of course I know more," he snapped, and that paused her momentum. That wasn't her father's ire. Her father seldom lost control of his temper—everything her father said was absolutely calculated.

He closed his eyes, leaning on the desk.

There was something in his posture she didn't like. Not fatigue, maybe not quite strain. But he was tensed against something. His mouth was pulled thin in a grimace.

Should she even ask?

Yes, she decided, she should. If something was going on that would affect how he ruled the kingdom until her father came back, and how he interfaced with her in the meantime, she'd better know. The kingdom was still on precarious ground, and maybe even more so if there was something going on with the Kidaa.

"Wait," he said, and made swift strides for the door that led to the rest of his apartment. He opened it with a wide swing and slammed it closed behind him, rattling the pictures on the walls.

She stared after him, blinking. What had just happened? Did he have to use the bathroom? Was he sick? But he would have excused himself in a different way, surely.

But *was* he sick? Were there any signs that he might have the Bruising Sleep, like Ari? She hadn't noticed anything, but then, she hadn't noticed much with Ari, either, until it was too obvious to miss.

She took a step forward. If it wasn't the Bruising Sleep, could he have been poisoned? Truthspoken could heal themselves from poison, but that didn't mean it wasn't a painful or dangerous process.

Dressa started for the door, jaw tight, already reaching for the handle.

But the door swung back open again, and she jumped back.

Iata peered at her, looking absolutely collected. That would have to be a blatant lie.

"What's wrong?" she demanded.

He stepped back inside, shutting the door much more gently this time.

"Forgive me," he said, but didn't offer any more explanation as he crossed back again to his desk.

What the hell? Not long enough for Changing poison, surely. Not long enough to use the bathroom, hardly long enough for a comm call, even, or to check on information. Whatever he'd needed to do so urgently, whatever had caused him that distress, he hadn't had enough time to actually do.

He reached his desk and studied it for a long moment. Dressa came back around to face him, trying to think what she could say to get whatever he was keeping from her out of him. If he'd just been Iata the bloodservant, she could have ordered him to tell her. He wasn't, though. He was still the Seritarchus, and with that title, he didn't have to tell her anything.

Iata sighed and finally let himself ease out of her father's mannerisms and back into his own. He tugged on the tight knot of hair at the back of his head and let it fall loose, combing his fingers across his scalp.

Maybe it was best if she didn't see him as adjacent to her father, or just the Seritarchus, but as her father's twin. That concept, at least, was easier on her nerves.

Iata looked up, half-grimaced a smile, and led her to what was becoming their accustomed place to talk at the sitting area.

"Iata," she started, but he held up a hand as he sat.

"I'm fine, truly. Not getting enough sleep." Which explained exactly nothing. She wasn't going to get it out of him no matter what, was she?

She sighed and settled on the couch across from him. Her father's twin, right. Full of all his own idiosyncrasies, and in his own way, as complex and implacable as her father.

He leaned back into his chair, closed his eyes for a brief moment. "You'll understand that part soon enough. Truthspoken Heirs aren't known for their quality of sleep, either." He made a placating wave. "Don't worry, I'm not throwing you in the deep."

Dressa did a quick catalogue of all of his tells. Some Iata's now, some still her father's, even when it seemed he'd relaxed from the role of her father.

She fidgeted in her seat on the couch. This was the least put together she'd seen him—but, okay, she got that a Truthspoken couldn't function at one hundred percent every moment of the day. Maybe he'd been pushing too hard. And she herself knew the strain of inhabiting a specific role that ran counter to her own self, or a role for any length of time. He'd said he was okay with that, too, but was he really?

But that marked calendar book in the desk gave more

weight to his claim than to her own theory about it. He'd been doing this for years—so what was different now?

"Is this about the Kidaa?" she asked. He hadn't seemed rattled at all before the Griels had made their petitions. She'd seen absolutely no signs of distress until they'd come back here.

He pulled his hair back up off his shoulders but tied it more loosely this time. "The Kidaa, yes." He cleared his throat, and the control he normally had slowly came back.

17

DEBRIEF

> *Yes, the kingdom was founded with the support of the high houses, but I think those houses have mostly forgotten what they were supporting in favor of what they wish they themselves were ruling.*
>
> — HOMAJ RHIALDEN, SERITARCHUS IX IN A PRIVATE LETTER, NEVER SENT; PUBLISHED IN *THE CHANGE DIALOGUES*

"This isn't the first attack like this," Iata said, "though it's the first with any casualties. The other two destroyed some land, one clipping an outbuilding, though it was little used and no one was hurt. I'd thought, whoever was doing this, that they'd wanted to avoid casualties." He grimaced.

"The first was on Neyan, in a forest clearing near a nanotech factory. That rune was carved into the grass, which was fortunately wet enough that it only smoldered before it was put out. The second was on Espiral, also carved into a field like the Griels', though there were no casualties there. The incidents were only notable in that the runes were Kidaa in origin, though there was no evidence the Kidaa themselves carved them. There is no evidence they didn't, either. Your father and I —we saw the Kidaa connection, of course, and there have been other reports from ships along the border that the Kidaa have started behaving . . . oddly, sometimes. Their ships coming too close to ours, or they'll suddenly leave one of their settlements and abandon a world. Or suddenly decide to settle. We don't know if any of this is related—we don't know enough about the Kidaa to know if this is just a natural part of a cycle for their civilization.

"When I got the report from Count Griel, I of course sent back for more information, though I didn't expect her to come herself. And this time . . . lives have been lost. That these attacks have actually been made by the Kidaa is, on the surface, ludicrous. It's far easier to believe this is a grand conspiracy to disrupt the kingdom by the high houses, or any number of other parties."

"But who?" Dressa asked, sitting forward. "Who would even think that's a good idea? Or that the Kidaa themselves might not take offense at being framed for this?"

He spread his hands. "But that's the point. The Kidaa don't take offense to anything, and we've certainly given them cause enough over the years. Are they taking offense now? Or are they still the Kidaa we know—or rather, don't know—and this is someone else trying to work people into a panic, get us to commit our resources to figuring this out while they move forward with their own plans?"

"Yes, but—" She could think of plenty of high houses that would want to destabilize the Seritarcracy, but not necessarily the kingdom itself. They'd want to claim the kingdom for themselves. "Is this a hostile operation? From outside Valoris—the Dynasty, maybe?"

"The Onabrii-Kast Dynasty also shares the border with the

Kidaa, and they've been aiming to expand into Kidaa space for a while now." Iata's lips thinned. "They think the Kidaa won't do anything but pull back. They might be right. But they most certainly might not be, too. Have they sent scouting parties? Are these runes made by the Kidaa in retaliation for that, or warning?"

"What do the runes mean, though?" Dressa asked. She'd seen Kidaa runes before, of course, every child who attended primary school had seen holos of Kidaa runes.

"The first said what we think is 'being,' as in a person. The second, we didn't recognize, though it shared some characteristics with the rune for 'galaxy.' The third . . . I'll have to have analyzed, now that I'm able to see it."

"None of that makes sense," Dressa said. "It's not anything like a warning or threat, like 'danger' or 'stop' or anything like that, if they even have words for those things. Is that why my father sent Rhys to find out more?"

Iata's brows went up. "I'm the one who sent Rhys, if that makes a difference. But they're only one of many assets we've put into play—academics, strategists, analysts, and both Navy and civilian research ships near the border."

He'd sent Rhys? Well. Well, and she didn't know just now if that did make a difference. "You know that wasn't fair to place that on Rhys. They're working hard to separate their Navy life from their palace life."

"Fair, maybe not. But necessary, yes. Of all the assets we've put into play, they're one of the only ones I actually trust."

Dressa looked down, smoothing out the edges of her thigh-length tunic.

Would she, knowing what she knew now about this mess of questions around the Kidaa, and how it may or may not be the Kidaa—well, wouldn't she have done the same? She trusted Rhys. She trusted Rhys with her life, and Iata was, in a way, trusting them with the kingdom.

Was this what her life was becoming? Sifting through all these multi-layered plots and moving the pieces she thought best to block them? She didn't want to see people as pieces on a game board. That was Arianna, not her.

But could she afford for it not to be her?

"What if it is the Kidaa?" she asked quietly. "What if they are finally showing signs of violence?"

Iata studied her. Maybe he sensed she was stretching beyond herself just now, because his voice softened, too, though the words themselves were hardly soft.

"If it's the Kidaa, we'll need to prepare for war, however we can."

Which thought was . . . terrifying. The Kidaa had no weapons on their ships that anyone knew of, but that didn't mean they couldn't cause damage. Any chunk of rock or space debris could become a weapon if aimed properly. Any sufficiently large ship falling on a planet could wipe out all life on its surface, and Kidaa ships weren't generally small.

Dressa remembered Rhys in the terrace garden a few nights before. They'd been trying to fill the silence, talking about the Kidaa, and she hadn't been paying as much attention as she wished she'd had now. But Rhys's uneasiness, their conviction that something was off, that something everyone thought they knew about the Kidaa was vitally wrong, weighed heavily on her. Rhys didn't rattle easily.

And maybe it was best that Rhys was in play now with information gathering, too. Rhys was seeing things she was sure no one else was seeing, or at least, not ignoring what others might be dismissing out of hand. Rhys, with all their second-hand evaku which had, over the years, grown almost as honed as her own training—they would be able to see things in body language and patterns, in social habits and communication, that even the most disciplined researchers might overlook.

Rhys had what amounted to a doctorate in social and behavioral analysis.

And so did she. And so did Iata.

She clamped down on her frustration, refusing to let it show. None of them were acting on impulse here, or even necessity, but on what they'd been trained to do—maneuver everyone around them to enact the most desired outcome.

"In any case," Iata said, straightening, "we'll go back to finish the Reception for the day. Continuity will do much to calm any fears."

18

TRUST

> *You all have made me feel so welcome.*
>
> — HANERI NE DELOR RHIALDEN, SERITARCHUS CONSORT, IN A SPEECH AFTER HER WEDDING

Dressa nodded, rising with Iata, her thoughts still churning over the Kidaa, and Rhys, and the high houses, and what this all meant.

"You did well, by the way," Iata said. "I don't think I'll need to sit second to your Reception tomorrow."

Dressa started. "No, my father sat with Arianna for weeks before he let her sit Reception on her own."

"Your father isn't so great at letting go of control." He gave an ironic smile, standing near the hidden panel door to the back corridors, waiting. Once in, they wouldn't be able to talk until they got to where they needed to go. The back corridors were sound-dampened, but only to the point of masking footsteps. Part of their point was being able to hear what happened in the palace around them.

Dressa drew in a long breath. He thought she was ready to sit Reception on her own? To make these huge and sweeping judgements in the lives of the nobles and merchants and diplomats, for the course of the kingdom?

But she was going to be the ruler someday. She would have to learn, wouldn't she?

"If you wish," he said, "we can go over the Receptions each night and if there was anything you might wish to have done differently. But at the moment, we're a bit understaffed in the Truthspoken department, and I trust your judgement."

That was a statement that would never come out of her father's mouth. And what would her father do when he came back? Would he just take over sitting Reception again? Or would she have to suffer through long days of him sitting by her side, sniping at her efforts or silently—and loudly—disapproving?

Dressa stood up straighter. "If you think I'm ready, then I'll be fine to finish the Reception today."

"You would be, yes, but again, continuity. If we're both there, there's less reason for anyone to think there's something wrong."

Well, okay, yes, that made sense.

"As for Lesander," he said, "I know you like her, Dressa—and that's fair, she is your wife—but she is also still a Javieri. And of the many people who would stand to gain from unrest in the kingdom right now, the Javieri family is high on that list."

Dressa's focus sharpened. If he didn't trust Lesander, why had he set her to finding the whereabouts of Duke Koldari? "And Duke Kyran Koldari? Do you think he's involved? The Koldaris have always played dirty."

"He wasn't connected to the other two attacks, as far as I can tell, but I don't like that no one seems to know where he is. For now, I'm reserving judgement. And as for why I gave Lesander a job—well, better to have her tracking missing dukes than loose in the court while you're busy elsewhere."

"I'm not going to do to her what my father did to my mother." Her father had tried to keep her mother within his tight sphere of control, and whatever had happened, the whole result of it was her mother's long seclusion.

"No," Iata said quietly. "Which is also why I gave Lesander a job. She can work alongside you, to the degree that you feel you can trust her. Maybe, in the end, she will be your co-ruler—that is always the most desired outcome. But be careful, Dressa, until you do know you can trust her."

She hated that she didn't have that trust yet, but . . . yeah. She nodded.

He reached for the door into the back corridors, but Dressa pointed to his hair. It was still the looser, messier style he'd knotted back in place. Her father might wear a style like that in public, but not to a formal Reception. Not unless he was trying to make a specific point, and she didn't think Iata was.

"Do you want me to fix that?"

He frowned, but reached back, pulled out the knot, and quickly braided it tightly down his back. Which, yes, was a favored style of her father's. And it wasn't unusual for her father to change hairstyles throughout the day, either, as his gender shifted, or just simply his preference.

She wondered at the lapse, though. In all other things, she'd only seen him play her father's persona perfectly. Was this related to his weirdness earlier, when he'd had to run out of the room?

But, his hair checked and approved by her, they slipped into the back corridors, and there was no more to be said. They made the winding trek back down to the antechamber of the Reception Hall.

Dressa's thoughts strayed back to Lesander. With her wife's direct ties to one of the most powerful and ambitious of the high houses, when would Dressa ever know she could trust her? She was certain her father had never reached that point with her mother, who'd also been the heir to a high house princedom. But then, she was certain her own parents had never had anything approaching love.

What did Dressa have with Lesander? Not love yet, surely. There hadn't been time. She couldn't get Lesander out of her thoughts, though, and maybe that counted for something. Or signaled danger all around.

She felt an ache, an absence of Lesander just now, that she wasn't sure how to handle. Would Lesander be in the Reception Hall the rest of the afternoon? But the Seritarchus had assigned her a task and given her an office. And maybe that had, in some part, been to separate them for the moment, though Dressa was already planning how she'd integrate Lesander more directly into her days. Well, and maybe she should ask Lesander if she *wanted* to be integrated.

The Seritarchus opened the door to the royal Reception Hall antechamber, then froze.

Dressa heard him take a breath in surprise, just one small breath, then that tiniest lapse of control was gone.

What? What in the worlds had made Iata stutter like that?

She looked around him and had to bite down hard on her own curse.

Lesander stood in the antechamber . . . with Dressa's mother.

19

HANERI

> *There is little I can say about my mother—that I would wish to say—that the court doesn't already know. Despite her very public presence throughout much of my father's rule, my mother is a very private person.*
>
> — ARIANNA RHIALDEN, MELESORIE X IN *THE CHANGE DIALOGUES*

Dressa's mother. What the hell was her mother doing here? Her mother never came out of her apartment these days, and now, of all days—Adeius, did Haneri know about Iata? Did she know the person staring at her was not, in fact, the person she'd married? Did she even know Dressa's father well enough to tell the difference?

The Seritarchus recovered and glided into the room, his mannerisms sliding deeply femme. He gripped her mother's hands, a sardonic smile quirked, and leaned in to kiss her on both cheeks.

Not the lips. But then, that had never been her parents' kind of marriage.

Dressa's heart was trying to pound outside of her chest. Iata had been playing the role of her father on and off since before her parents had married—he had to have been around her mother before as her father. Had to.

"Haneri. What brings you out of your deliberate seclusion?"

Ah. Okay, and there was the edge, and did he have to press on that very sensitive subject? He wasn't sparing any of her father's personality on this one. She wouldn't be surprised if he'd just submerged himself to be Homaj in truth.

"I found I've gained another daughter," Haneri said, waving a hand with a single ring, her ornate, heavy wedding ring. Well, and that couldn't have been without planning.

Adeius. It had been years since Dressa had seen her parents truly interact. She understood so much more now, and all of it, just all of it, was painful to watch.

Then what her mother had just said sunk in. "Gained another daughter"—she knew that Dressa and Lesander had already married. How did she know? The marriage contract would have been sent only to her father, and only he—and, apparently, Iata—had access to that account. The only other people who knew were Ceorre and the speaker who'd witnessed the ceremony. Well, and Lesander.

A quick glance to Lesander told her little, but she didn't think Lesander would have dropped that information on her own.

Dressa took a breath and swept to her mother's side, setting herself between her mother and Lesander. What had her mother been talking about with Lesander? What damage control would Dressa have to do later?

"Mother, how do you know that?" Dressa asked in a low voice. There was no one else in the antechamber—the room would be on security monitors, but Dressa knew the Seritarchus would have that intercepted and erased as soon as possible.

"You don't need to worry about ears," Haneri said, waving at the room around them, the side tables, the four uncomfortable chairs set to one side, the deep eggplant walls with gold vine patterns. "Commander Jalava turned it off while we waited."

Would Jalava have complied with her order, or would they have listened to what was going on here instead? Dressa was going to go with the latter, but at least the Guard Commander was aware of what was happening. And if they were listening, they now knew of Dressa's secret wedding, too, if they hadn't already.

Dressa found herself the subject of her mother's intense scrutiny. Steeling herself, she stared back impassively.

Up close, she could see that Haneri was wearing a faint holographic overlay, like a crown, across her pulled-up braids. Well, and she was the Seritarchus Consort.

Dressa hadn't been to see her mother in a while, but her mother didn't look any different, not even a little, from the last time she had. Her makeup was perfect, her skin, as usual, flawless. Her tightly coiled brown hair box-braided with pale rose extensions, which complemented her pale rose dress. And that holographic crown with its intricate patterning—which, Dressa was just now realizing, Haneri had probably sculpted herself. It had the same feel as her other light sculpture work, intense and vaguely judging.

"How did you know about—us?" Dressa asked again. "Ceorre wouldn't have—"

"You could have told me," Haneri said. "Rhys, at least, came to me. I haven't seen you in months, and you live only a few doors down from me, not at the Kidaa border."

Dressa opened her mouth, closed it. She was not going to get into a fight with her mother. Not here, not now.

She turned to Lesander, gripped her hand hard—and Lesander gripped it back.

She leaned in and kissed Lesander, not quite chastely, on the lips. And that was the kind of marriage she was determined to have. Let her mother see that, whatever else she'd learned already from Lesander. Hers would not be a loveless marriage like her parents'.

"Haneri," the Seritarchus said mildly, "there will be a small gathering in the Lilac Hall later tonight. I hadn't planned to attend, but if you'd wish an escort, a re-introduction to court, I'd be happy to."

"I'd like that, Homaj," Haneri said, as if his suggestion had been her due.

"Mother, you're planning to rejoin the court?"

Dressa didn't know if that was something to be happy about, or an unmitigated disaster.

"You've just become the Heir," Haneri said, sweeping out her hands. "I will, of course, support you in any way I can and prepare you for what's to come."

Dressa couldn't help the exasperated look she shared with the Seritarchus. And she was sure Haneri would see that, too, likely on both of them. But Haneri didn't act like she'd noticed.

Her mother hadn't shown any interest at all in helping Arianna be the Heir. But she'd shown little interest in Dressa's life before now, either. Was Lesander the tipping point? Arianna's illness? Her own marriage?

Something else?

Could it even be all this mess that may or may not be the Kidaa? Iata had said the Javieri family was high on the list of those who'd want to destabilize the Seritarcracy, but if that was the case, so was her mother's family, the Delors.

"And—what's to come, Mother?" she asked, picking up on her mother's last statement.

Haneri gave her an arch look. "Your public wedding. I won't

let my daughter be married without having a hand in the wedding."

20

MOTIVATIONS

> *Never underestimate the power of a noble wedding, or better yet, royal. Alliances can be brokered, rivalries sparred and won, all while glasses are raised and smiles abound.*
>
> — LORD ESARA TEOH MÉRON BRINT IN *A GUIDE TO ETIQUETTE AT THE PALACE RHIALDEN COURT*

Her mother wanted to help with her wedding?

Beside Dressa, Lesander shifted. "The Seritarchus Consort offered to turn the Reception Hall into a living light sculpture."

Dressa blinked. Well—well that wouldn't be so horrible, would it? Her mother's work was well-admired. Dressa had always thought it was a little off-putting, a little too intense, the lines of her geometric designs trending toward harsh. Did she want that at her wedding? Maybe not exactly, but she'd also already had her real wedding.

And she didn't want to say anything that would make her

mother go back into her seclusion again, no matter the difficulties her coming out might bring.

"Yes, that would be nice!" Dressa said. "Oh, excellent."

Haneri's smile was knowing, and not entirely kind.

Yes, Dressa decided, she *was* glad to see her mother step outside her apartment, let alone attend a gathering with courtiers. As much as it gnawed at her gut that Iata would have to be flawless in his performance tonight, at least he'd be there to help temper Haneri if she was giving offense, whether deliberate or not.

But seriously, why now? And if the deciding factor was Lesander, her mother hadn't shown any interest, as far as she knew, in Lesander's engagement to Arianna. Was it because Dressa was now already married? Already tied to the Javieri line?

Lesander had mentioned the light sculptures, but that would be the means to whatever her mother's end was, not the end goal itself. What did "prepare you" mean in Haneri's definition? And why had her mother sought out Lesander first and not Dressa? Or had she? Had Lesander being nearby been a coincidence?

Dressa's eyes narrowed.

Yes, like Lesander, Haneri had been a high house prince before she'd become the Seritarchus Consort. The Delors had never been allies to the Rhialdens beyond her parents' formal marriage contract, and of course they'd continue their plots in the background, that's what high houses did. But the Delors were known to ally themselves with the Javieris. So was her mother's sudden reemergence about Lesander and not actually Dressa at all? And what would that mean in the political landscape of the court?

The Javieris and Delors couldn't be allowed to gain more power than they already had—she was sure her father would have factored in her mother's former political influences when choosing Lesander as the next consort. He would have decided Haneri wasn't active enough to pull her Delor background into play with Lesander's Javieri ties. Haneri shouldn't be a threat—she was almost a non-entity at the court.

Yet here she was.

Dressa remembered keenly her mother going on tirades about how the Rhialden Court was run when she was younger. Her mother raging against the necessity of the Truthspoken, or the necessity that she'd had to marry one.

"I'm sure your father's done the best he can with starting the wedding preparations," Haneri said, not even looking at the Seritarchus. "But he is busy. I will help you from here. If that's acceptable, Homaj."

"Perfectly acceptable," the Seritarchus said, and Dressa could feel the slow boil of his irritation from across the room, a dozen little signs playing out, noticeable to everyone in the room who had some sort of evaku training, which was all of them.

Dressa had the urge to turn to Lesander and ask her what she thought about her mother helping, but no, what reason would Lesander have to refuse? Haneri had faded in the court's eyes the last few years—she just wasn't talked about. Everyone knew the Truthspoken could be anyone, and no one wanted to be the one to spread gossip about the Seritarchus Consort to the Seritarchus himself.

Lesander's shoulder brushed against hers, as if she knew Dressa needed that extra bit of reassurance here.

Dressa wanted to be reassured by that touch, and it did warm her, but the ground she'd thought she'd stood on had slipped sideways again. Now, with her mother in play again, Dressa would have to keep a close watch on the court, adapting her own presentation and narrative on the fly. She didn't need this. Not on top of everything else. Her head was still spinning with everything she'd just learned about the situation with the

Kidaa, or rather, the dozen new questions that had sprung into place of what she'd previously thought was solid fact.

And still. Her mother, here, standing in light other than the purposefully dim confines of her apartment, made her chest ache. Had Rhys said something to her, even? Was that why she'd come out now?

Haneri turned back to the Seritarchus, reaching up like there was something on his face. But then she pulled him down in one swift move and stretched up to kiss him on the lips.

His hand spasmed in surprise, but then eased as he gripped the back of her waist.

Dressa watched in horror as he kissed her mother back.

They broke apart, eyes locked on each other, faces unreadable.

Had her father ever kissed her mother? Would her mother be able to tell now that this wasn't him?

Adeius, why had she kissed him like that?

And why had he kissed *her?*

Haneri tilted her head, still studying the Seritarchus. "Tonight, then. Pick me up at my apartment. When?"

"Nine," he said, voice a tiny bit hoarse.

"Nine, then." She nodded to Dressa. "Dressa, Lesander. I'll be in contact about the planning shortly."

She moved to the door and gave it a sharp rap. The door opened and the bulky form of her bodyguard, Ina Vogret, stepped in. Vogret smiled at Dressa, gave a perfunctory bow to the Seritarchus, then offered her arm as Haneri stepped out again.

The door closed.

The silence made Dressa's ears pop, and then begin to ring. She didn't even attempt to smooth the ringing away—she couldn't pull her thoughts together.

She glanced at Iata. He was still showing to her, flawlessly, as her father. Not a single tell out of place. How far had he just buried himself, and would he need a callback? Did she even know his callbacks? Adeius, no. She knew some of her father's, but not Iata's.

Then he blinked, and his posture briefly, ever so briefly, shifted, before it shifted back.

"Let's finish Reception, shall we?" He headed for the door. "Lesander, I'll assume you're here because you found something?"

"Not yet, Seritarchus. I thought you'd need a clerk who knows the details of the matter with the Kidaa earlier."

He raised his brows but didn't comment on that as they stepped back into the Hall. And he didn't point out that Dressa's legal clerk had also been there in the Reception Hall, and Dressa wasn't about to point that out, either. She wanted Lesander nearby. She needed someone to steady her against these crosswinds.

Maybe it was dangerous to make that someone Lesander, or at very least, not wise.

Well, she could be wise tomorrow. They sat again, and this time, Lesander took her place beside Dressa on the dais.

21

PHOSPHORESCENT GREEN

I'm just saying, the safest way to travel from world to world is on the cruise liners. They've got everything—comfort, security, a nice compliment of weapons, though they're hardly warships. But the liners are slow, so sometimes you need to bunk on a freighter.

— XINANDER, VID COMMENTATOR, IN THEIR VID "CRUISE LINERS VS FREIGHTERS: COMFORT OR ADVENTURE?"

Rhys was fine with tight spaces—it was almost impossible to serve on an active starship and be claustrophobic, because every starship was filled with tight spaces—but the fast freighter they'd booked as the first ship off of Valon headed remotely in the direction they needed to go was getting to them. It wasn't designed to be a passenger ship, and yet the crew had converted one of the holds into passenger space with thin prefab walls sectioning out ten tiny cubicles with barely adequate cots and a slightly larger cubicle as a mess/rec space.

Rhys had lain awake for hours the night before listening to the person in the cubicle next to them talking in their sleep. And the night before that—*and* the night before that. In Farani, which Rhys knew only a few words of, and all of them dirty. They'd had a bunkmate at the Academy who'd come from a predominantly Farani-speaking planet near the border to the Farani Protectorate, and they knew exactly what kind of dreams their neighbor was having.

That passenger, thankfully, had left when the freighter docked at the orbital above Kilaire V. Rhys had an hour to stretch their legs on a circumference of the small ringed station and check the station's news kiosks.

They'd had updated news on their comm as soon as the ship had connected again to the inter-system network coming out of Below Space, but their comm projection area was small, and they wanted to read what they could from Dressa's posture and body language on a bigger display.

She'd done it. Adeius, Dressa had done it—abdicated as Arianna, and been confirmed as the Truthspoken Heir as herself. At the kiosk, Rhys had looked over vids and images of her and Lesander, her and Ceorre, and her beside—her father. The Seritarchus's body language showed nothing, absolutely nothing.

Rhys's gut churned, and Adeius, they hoped she was weathering that particular storm with her father well.

Then their comm pinged with an alert from the freighter recalling all passengers.

On ship, the freighter's comm ordered them to strap into their cots for orbital maneuvers—the cots weren't even bolted down.

That had been an hour ago. An hour in which Rhys, still strapped into their cot, had opened their comm, reading as best they could in the awkward position, trying to understand all the reactions to the sudden shift in Truthspoken leadership.

Rhys finally set down their comm and glared up at the red alert light jury-rigged to the bulkhead above the cubicle walls. Turn green, dammit. Turn *green*.

If this freighter was even remotely up to code, they shouldn't need to require strapping in—they hadn't lifted from a planet. They'd never even left space. But then, Rhys had only had to take one look at the bathrooms installed next to the passenger cubicles to know this ship was definitely riding fast with ship codes, and if the gravity cut out when maneuvering —well.

There was a clunk from the cubicle next to theirs. The one whose former occupant had talked in their sleep.

Rhys grimaced. What fresh hell would this neighbor bring? Well, or maybe it wouldn't be so bad. The person on the other side of them hummed to themself sometimes, but at least they were decent songs.

"Fuck," they heard through the cubicle wall. Then, "Well fuck if I forgot my—ahhh!"

Rhys glanced at the straps still holding them to the cot, then shrugged and released them. No sirens went off, and they wondered if anyone else was even strapped in?

They grimaced. Dammit, had they even really had to strap in? Their military training was showing. You always followed the safety rules on ship, no questions asked, but this was hardly a Navy ship.

"Oh all the blazing hells!" was followed by another clunk.

Rhys pulled their curtain door aside and padded in socked feet to their new neighbor's curtain door. They hesitated only a moment before they knocked on the cubicle wall. "You okay in there? You need help?"

The rustling sounds from inside the cubicle stopped. The curtain pushed open and—and a femme person stepped out, who was a magicker? No, who had phosphorescent *green* hair. Their hands were on their cheeks, mouth open, staring up in appreciation at Rhys's own phosphorescent white hair. Which was dulling a bit now, but it still glowed.

Rhys grinned.

"Nice," the person said, nodding. Then, "I'm Misha. She/her. Uh . . ." She faltered as her eyes went down to Rhys's rumpled off-duty uniform, pale blue shirt and dark blue slacks. Their junior lieutenant's pins. A Navy officer always wore a uniform in space, no matter if they were on a Navy ship or not. It was their duty to protect anyone in space, wherever they were.

"Uh—sir!" She straightened and saluted.

Rhys saluted back out of habit and then blinked. She'd let go of her face to salute, and they had to use every bit of the evaku they'd been working hard to shove down the last few days not to react. They'd thought she wasn't a magicker.

But on her cheek was a holographic seal, and that covering of her face, the glow of her hair—which actually was phosphorescent green—was a clever cover. Rhys didn't know magicker rankings well, but they didn't think the fractal rank swirl shown on her seal was low. Maybe not high, though, either? And the pale green glow around her, which they'd at first thought was from her hair, was just as evenly spread around her saluting hand. It was the palest aura they'd ever seen on a magicker. It made her look ethereal.

Their heart started to pound, and they thought of the magicker in the crowd at the palace ball, flickering in and out of sight, heading toward Arianna. Rhys hadn't been able to stop them. Dressa hadn't been able to stop them. They knew that attack wasn't what it had seemed—they knew that. But what were they supposed to do with this person now? With this magicker, who'd been trying not to show she was a magicker?

They kept their face and body from reacting, but they watched Misha's open expression close.

Adeius, what had she seen in them? Magickers could read

emotions and sometimes even whole thoughts just by looking into a person's eyes. At least she hadn't touched them.

Misha shifted, one phosphorescent green brow tilting up. "You're thinking about what secrets I now have of yours, right? Am I right?"

Rhys looked away. Evaku or not, it was useless to try and lie to a magicker. And also, shitty. "Yeah. Sorry. I—I just wasn't expecting—"

They were making a fool of themself. A totally ridiculous fool.

What happened at the palace was at the palace, and everything at the palace had its own skewed meaning.

They were not in the palace anymore. They had to set that, and everything happening there, aside. Rhys the officer, and Rhys the regular person who was just minding their business, had nothing against magickers.

"Sorry. Really. Start over? I'm Lt. Rhys Petrava. They/them. Headed for *Occam's Storm*."

"What a coincidence," she said blandly. "I'm Ensign Misha Moratu, also headed for *Occam's Storm*."

Rhys only now noticed she was also in off-duty blues. They wanted to smack their forehead. For being highly observant, for knowing *evaku*, by all the stars—Adeius, they were thick today, weren't they?—they hadn't done a good job of actually being observant. But they'd been trying to let go of their evaku away from the palace. Well, and they'd been too focused on her hair, too, which was very cute, and what she'd thought about their hair, and then that seal.

They felt their face heat and defaulted to a bow, to court manners—no, that wasn't right, either. They didn't use their court manners in space. They weren't Delor out here, just Petrava. Just . . . Rhys.

They straightened to Misha's bemused expression.

Rhys stepped back, holding up their hands. “Sorry. Truly, for disturbing you.”

Misha glanced up at their hair again, then nodded inside her cubicle. “Want to come in? I’m having a crisis. You’re welcome to join me.” She ducked back inside without waiting for an answer.

After a moment, Rhys shrugged and followed.

22

THE CRISIS

> *Can you imagine? Adeius, seriously, they just had the most gorgeous eyes you could ever think of. Or maybe it was their lips. Or maybe it was their everything.*
>
> — TIFFAR DOTRAL MÉRON WU IN THE VID COMEDY *I SAW YOU AT THE HOLOCLUB*, SEASON 1, EPISODE 6, "WHEN LIGHTNING STRIKES"

Misha's cubicle, for her only having arrived on the ship an hour before, was a disaster. Clothes were strewn about the deck—mostly slinky, stretchy things in various shades of red and black.

"Those," Misha said, watching where Rhys's eyes fell, "belonged to my girlfriend. *Ex*-girlfriend. I definitely can't fit into those." She stuffed them into an open duffel.

Why she had them and why they were strewn about the deck if they belonged to her ex was not a question Rhys was about to ask.

On the wall over her cot, she'd already tacked a small holo portrait of First Magicker Mariyit Broden, with blonde hair and bushy brows, considerably younger than he was now. He definitely hadn't been the First Magicker when that was taken. And next to it was a list of what looked like the steps of a meditation exercise? And another thin holo sheet with what looked like a stylus-drawn, abstract, geometric design.

Rhys stared at the design, feeling a weird sense of familiarity.

They pointed. "What's that from?"

"Not for non-magickers," Misha said. But she didn't take the holo down.

They started to feel . . . woozy.

Rhys shook themself and focused back on Misha. "Uh, you said you had a crisis? You forgot to bring something? Sorry, the walls are thin."

"Okay, well, that's good to know," she huffed. Then ran a hand through her hair. It fell back again at all the right angles. She caught them looking and smiled.

"I doubt *Occam's Storm* has a better view of inter-ship relationships than any other Valoran Navy outfit, so I'm just going to stop whatever that is right now."

Rhys's face got so hot it hurt. They held up their hands. "Sorry. I—yeah. I know."

She rolled her eyes. "Fine. Lieutenant. And yeah, I know sometimes you can still fall in love with someone in under a minute despite it all. I did." She sighed at her pile of slinky things, now in the duffel. "So, yeah, my crisis. I grabbed my girlfriend's duffel, not mine. Mine had all my uniforms, my underwear, my toothbrush and stuff. Hers has—well, there's a toothbrush, but I don't know if I want her spit in my mouth anymore."

"The *Storm* has a decent ship's store," Rhys said. "There's a good clothing fabricator, and all the toiletries and things."

Misha finished putting the rest of the clothes back in the duffel and scowled down at it. "Yes, that's fine, but it's another ten days to the Storm, isn't it? And I can't fit into a single thing in this duffel."

She looked askance at them, sizing them up. "You're tall and fit enough—broad, okay, and maybe I'm bigger around the waist but it's better than what I have. Do you have a spare anything, and then I can wash this one in the sink?"

They didn't really have spares. They'd packed light and had planned to take advantage of the palace's laundry service, which hadn't happened. Rhys had just enough uniforms if they cycled through off-duty, duty, dress, and formal to get to the *Storm* in reasonably good smelling order.

But her eyes were intent on them, and they read the tension in her posture. They read her expecting them to say, "no."

They had one pair of civvies, a stretchy, tighter-fitting athletic set they wore when they hit the gym on ship or on station.

Rhys opened their hands. "Do you mind being out of uniform?"

Misha shrugged. "You outrank me here, Lieutenant. I won't tell if you won't tell. It'll be better than wearing this for ten days, I can tell you that. If you can hear through these walls, you can probably smell through them, too."

"Okay. Okay, wait here."

Rhys ducked into their own cubicle and rummaged through their duffel, coming back with the athletic set in one hand.

Misha took it dubiously. "Clean?"

"I washed it on the way to Valon, didn't get a chance to wear it when I was there."

She stretched it out, and then shrugged when she found it stretched well. "Okay, I'll try it. It'll probably fit better than a uniform. Turn around."

Rhys turned, biting their lip as she cursed the buttons on her uniform shirt.

"Coming from Valon, huh?" she asked. "What's on the capital? Family? Duty?"

"Family," Rhys said.

"That was a pretty bow. Are you nobility?"

Rhys parsed her tone carefully.

It was wary, with an edge of challenge. How much had she seen when she looked into their eyes? Or, was she wary of nobility in general? Which, honestly, they couldn't blame her for that. Nobles weren't generally kind to magickers.

Which made them doubly annoyed at themself for how they'd reacted when they'd seen her seal.

"Partially," they said. "My father is military." Which wasn't really an answer.

Rhys shifted. "So, you're coming to be the *Storm's* magicker?"

"Yup." There was a pause. "Okay, you can turn around now. Does this look okay?"

She was clad neck to ankle in burgundy stretch wear, and it didn't hide a single curve.

More than okay. She looked more than okay. She'd rolled up the ends of the pant legs, and the shirt was a little long, but that didn't matter. And her freaking phosphorescent green hair.

"Hey," she said softly. "No starting anything, okay? We can't finish it. We know we can't finish it."

23

HOW MAGICKERS DO THINGS

"In the first heart of the universe."
"In the heart of She Who Wakes."

— UNKNOWN, A TRADITIONAL CALL AND RESPONSE GREETING AMONG GREEN MAGICKERS

Rhys shuddered out a sigh. What the hell was wrong with them? Misha was right. She was absolutely right that they couldn't start anything, and while Rhys occasionally appreciated their crewmates aesthetically, they'd never even thought to take it beyond that. They couldn't. They had to work hard to not show the privilege of their birth. They were absolutely not going to be seen as "that noble officer" who dallied about with their crewmates, thinking it would have no consequences.

But Adeius, she made their fingers want to curl into their palms, their toes into the deck. That didn't usually happen to them this fast.

Misha smiled. She tugged out the collar of the athletic shirt, letting it snap back. "Thanks for this. I guess I'll have to figure a way to wash my uniform. Or does this ship have laundry?"

"Crew only, I'm guessing." Rhys shrugged. "We're not even let out of this makeshift passenger area. They bring meals to us here. Not very good ones, I might add."

Misha looked up darkly at the metal walls of the hold encompassing the cubicles and everything else in here. "I'd report them if I thought it was worth it. But, I've got a reputation to uphold. Can't go telling anyone's secrets." She waved at her magicker cheek seal, her lips twisting in painful irony.

"I—I'm really sorry. I had a bad run-in with a magicker a few days ago, it was a fluke, I was just startled. Really. I'm sorry."

She pushed her hair out of her eyes. "A run-in? We're not violent—"

"No, I mean, I know that—" They frowned. She hadn't reacted at all to what they'd said. "You haven't seen the news?"

She tilted her head. ". . . no? I was kind of in this whirlwind thing with my girlfriend—my ex—who followed me to the station so she could say goodbye, because you know, we were ending a three-year thing, and we were already over, but we just wanted the sex one more time because it was really good—"

Her eyes were narrowing, her smile growing more smug. She saw them squirming, knew exactly what her words were doing to them.

"So, no." Her face grew more serious. "Was a magicker in the news?"

Rhys took a breath, then held up a finger and went back to their cubicle again, coming back with their tablet. They opened their news feed and the articles they'd saved, tapping one from three days ago into a holo.

Green Magicker Attacks the Truthspoken Heir at Her Engagement Ball.

Misha stared, her mouth tight. She held out her hand, and

Rhys gave her the tablet. She flicked quickly through the text, her lips growing thinner.

"You were there?" she asked.

"I—yes. Do you know this magicker, Sodan Iseban?"

Misha clicked off the tablet, handed it back. The playfulness was gone from her now, leaving sharper edges. "Contrary to what the nobility might think, there are over four hundred thousand magickers in the Kingdom of Valoris alone, another two or three hundred thousand at least in the Dynasty and other nations. I know that's not a lot in a kingdom of trillions, but we don't all know each other."

Rhys drew back. "I didn't mean—they were high-ranking. I saw them flicker—"

Her gaze sharpened. "You saw that? You were there when this happened? Do you have that thing that the nobility has where you can read people?"

Rhys hesitated. That wasn't quite how it worked, and she was oversimplifying things, but, "Yes. A little bit."

They regretted the lie as her lips twitched, and not in a good way.

Rhys held up their hands. "I know evaku." They met her eyes. "And that doesn't go beyond here, okay?"

Could they trust her? Adeius, they hadn't meant to say that much. They hadn't meant to talk about evaku at all, or their parentage, or what they knew about the magicker and Arianna. But she'd already learned that they were high enough ranking that they were at the palace engagement ball, and close enough to see this attack happen.

"I don't share people's secrets," she said, her voice chilled. "Especially ones they didn't give willingly." She sighed. "Sorry. I shouldn't have called you on that—but I think you read on me that I called it on you, right?"

Rhys clasped their hands and front of them, playing with

the skin between their thumb and index fingers. "Okay. Okay—what do you want to know, then?"

"If you saw this attack—and you saw the magicker flickering—what did you read from them? I mean, could you read anything? What was their body language like?"

Rhys hesitated. They thought back to that night, their gut tightening. They'd seen the magicker approach Arianna, bearing self-assured, but shoulders tight with—what? Distress? Fear? Rhys had been moving through the crowd yet, they hadn't been close enough. They'd seen Dressa slash the magicker's face, but then that's when Arianna fell, and Rhys had of course run to her.

But looking back, right before Dressa had slashed at the magicker—the fury in Dressa's whole being, the fear underneath it, had seared itself into Rhys's mind. They looked past it now, trying to see that point just before Dressa had reached the magicker, so they could better read the magicker. Rhys moved around the memory, making it holographic like Arianna and Dressa had taught them.

"They were . . . when the Truthspoken Ondressarie attacked them, in Arianna's defense, the magicker didn't react in pain so much as in . . . anguish?"

Oh, no. A horrible thought was wending its way up from the depths of their gut. They wanted to hold up the tablet again and reread the news article they'd picked up while on the station. They wanted to hunt down ten more and go over that whole encounter from every angle.

Because why would a random stranger who'd wanted to attack react with anguish? Even if they were a magicker? That sort of anguish was reserved for family.

"And when they flickered, what was their body language then?" Misha pressed.

"I only saw it briefly, once before they attacked, and then

right after. They seemed determined. Self-assured. Why? What does that tell you?"

"Mm," she said, but didn't elaborate.

Well, okay. Okay, she had her secrets, Rhys had theirs. Or rather, others' secrets they would protect at all costs. No one, absolutely no one could know what they suspected right now.

They avoided meeting Misha's eyes.

Misha sighed. "Rhys. Oh, we're technically on duty, so, sir—"

"Rhys is fine, here. And the *Storm* has a pretty loose culture among junior officers. Not a lot of 'sirs' unless a senior is around."

Misha waved it off. "Good to know. Rhys, I can't read your thoughts when you look at me. I don't actively read people's thoughts, okay? I can't even read them clearly unless I'm touching you, and I wouldn't without consent. I do know when you're lying, that's something I can feel in my bones, and I can't turn that off. And I can feel your emotions sometimes, but that's it. I'm not going to take your secrets—you know that's a myth, don't you? That's not how Green Magickers do things. We have laws and morals, too."

Rhys hesitantly met her eyes. And forced themself to keep their gaze there.

"And that," Misha said, pointing at the tablet in their hands, "is not how Green Magickers do things. Whatever that Sodan Iseban did, it wasn't with the blessing of the Green Magickers, or for the good of the magickers. We don't attack people, for gods' sakes. I'm not even sure he was a real magicker, or just using parlor tricks. You might know that high-ranking magickers can turn themselves invisible, but you don't know what it takes to do that, do you? No? Then don't assume every magicker you meet is going to attack you. We are the least likely of anyone to attack people. You do know it makes us sick, right? We'll literally throw up or pass out if we try. Sometimes even if we just think about it." She passed a hand over her eyes. "Though I swear sometimes it would be worth it to try. Gods, *people*."

Rhys relaxed a bit. Well, and they could understand that sentiment, couldn't they? Maybe not in the same way, but they knew what it was like to be on the outside, having to prove your way to the center. That was their entire life in the military. That had been their entire life at the palace too, hadn't it?

"So," Misha said, "you don't assume I'm the worst of the magicker stereotypes, and I won't assume you're the worst of the nobility's. Deal?"

Rhys snorted. Well, and that was fair. "Deal."

"Right. Now, can you show me where I might wash my old uniform? And is there soap that doesn't smell like chemical vomit?"

"I have lavender soap in my kit. If you don't use too much—"

"I won't, I promise."

Well, and they'd still let her use it if she did use too much, wouldn't they? They followed her to the bathroom section and helped wring out the thick uniform cloth. While she chatted all the while about an art exhibit she and her ex had seen on the station, and how it reminded her of the writings of Lin Pham, a philosopher Rhys had liked in their teenage studies who wrote about conflicts between classes, and how that reminded her of the weird non-conflict with the Kidaa.

Which, after that, they both didn't stop talking until far into the ship's night, perched on Rhys's cot with comm windows open around them for hastily scrawled notes. And Rhys absolutely didn't have to think about the two chips in an inner pocket of their duffel, which Iata had given them. In fact, they hadn't thought of them since meeting Misha.

They only stopped talking when their neighbors, who were trying to sleep, complained.

24

GARDEN TOUR

> *Gardens are strength to me. Gardens are a place where there's no pretense or judgement, at least among the plants and trees.*
>
> — ETIENNE TANAKA, AS QUOTED IN *THE CHANGE DIALOGUES*

The light of Hestia's golden sun shone warm on Imorie's face, and she tilted her head up to meet it, swiping her short dark blue hair out of her eyes.

Adeius. Three days cooped up in her suite, too tired to drag herself to the tiny lift, let alone down the stairs, and anything —*anything* else would be excellent. But the sunlight was bliss. And around her, the mixed perfume of garden flowers, and the light hum of bees, the bird songs, the crunch of gravel beneath her feet. She was so done with being inside.

And the open air of the estate was nothing at all like the city air she was used to, the sounds of the birds and the rustle of leaves a different sort of background noise. Why had she waited so long to take any kind of vacation? Her work managing her family's antiquities trade business wasn't that strenuous, and she did go offworld occasionally to look at this or that piece that had just come on the market. It wasn't as if she couldn't take time off, take a day or two when she was on another station or world, she just hadn't felt the need. Or maybe, hadn't really known who to take time off with. People who might call themselves her friends usually wanted something from the Rhialden half of her name, or else were scared off by it.

Not that this was a vacation, but she was absolutely intent on enjoying this day.

As she walked the garden paths, Jis trailed a meter or so behind her. Imorie had insisted she could walk on her own, and wonder of wonders, she could. Maybe it was the rest, or maybe the treatment was working—the physician had said he was pleased with her progress and had given her another dose of medication. She had no idea what the medicine was actually doing, but her legs were the most stable they'd been in, what, a week? More?

Her thoughts strayed from that path as nothing she wanted to think about right now, and she hummed softly to herself as she made her slow way around a hedgerow and out of sight of the main house.

She'd checked before coming out to make sure Duke Kyran wouldn't be in the gardens that day, and no, he was holed up with three other guests in one of the sitting rooms playing a holo game tournament. She'd heard their loud whoops before coming out.

He hadn't visited her in her rooms while she was sick, and she was absolutely fine with that. Count Badem had, but then, she was the host, and it hadn't been anything but hospitality.

Imorie was turning down another path, fully intent on getting lost—Jis had the water and snacks, at least—when the bushes rustled beside her. And then disgorged a person in a puff of leaves.

Imorie yelped and jumped back, arms up in a warding motion, heart in her throat.

The person skidded to a stop. It was Eti, the gardener. He gaped at her, leaves stuck in his clothes and messy hair.

"What the hell?" Imorie breathed. She swayed, the adrenaline leaving her shaky.

Jis was beside her in an instant, supporting her, glaring at Eti.

"Step back," Jis snapped.

Eti held up his hands and stepped back, gaze falling to the ground. "Sorry. Sorry, I—I need to check some of the new grafts on the trees south of the stream . . ."

He trailed off, dropping his hands to his sides.

"No, it's fine," Imorie said. Duke Kyran's warning about Eti stuck in her thoughts, and she shoved it away again. She wouldn't form her opinions based on the duke's.

"Uh—Eti, would you have time to take me on a tour of the garden? Now, maybe?"

And then she felt like crap for asking, he'd obviously been in a hurry if he'd been cutting through the bushes on his way to wherever he was going. But she didn't know how long she'd feel good enough to walk around. Even that small upset had weakened her legs a little.

Eti was staring at her from under his wide-brimmed hat, cheeks flushed. His eyes darted down again to the ground and back up, as if he couldn't decide if he should look at her directly.

She held out her arm, and he smiled and tentatively took it, like he had the night he'd escorted her to dinner. She braced a little for it to be awkward, and she felt him stiffen when he touched her arm, but then he seemed to relax again. Or at least, not be as entirely stiff.

"Sure," he said. "Yes. The tree grafts, I can get them later, that's fine."

"Imorie?" Jis asked, disapproval in faer voice.

"It's fine. I'm fine. Walk as we were before."

Jis hesitated a moment, then reluctantly nodded.

Imorie took a breath and set off again, this time with a—what, friend?—a person who might become a friend beside her. Could she even think that? He was staff. She was certainly not a high born Rhialden, but her mother had snapped it into her young that they did not make friends with staff.

But Eti was someone who wasn't herself, and wasn't Jis, and wasn't like almost everyone else in the house, with something to hide or something to prove. Eti was refreshing.

25

DAYTWIRLERS

> *Hestian daytwirlers, particularly of the orange and magenta varieties, are widely cultivated for their soft, delicate petals and scent that's often said to smell like summer. Swipe here for holos of celebrities with daytwirlers in their home décor.*
>
> — LURIN OMA IN THE LISTICLE, "*TEN HESTIAN FLOWERS YOU MUST HAVE IN YOUR HOME, RANKED BY POPULARITY*"

"If you need to walk more slowly," Eti said, "that's okay." And then he promptly stiffened again, as if he'd said something wrong.

"No, I'm fine." She was mostly fine. "So, tell me about the gardens. How long have you been the gardener here?"

He didn't look past twenty, surely, around her own age.

"A—a year," he stammered, and she hadn't thought that was a loaded question.

Imorie glanced over, but he shrugged, scuffing at the stone path as they walked. "Just a year. I'm not the main gardener. I take care of the paths, and clear the leaves, trim the branches, that sort of stuff. Ryam's the main gardener." After a moment, he added, "I do get to plant the flowers," as if that made up for the shortcomings of everything else.

"Well, that's nice."

Oh Adeius, it was getting awkward again, wasn't it? She liked Eti, truly liked him, but she wasn't sure at all how to actually talk to him.

"Oh, hey, look," he said, pointing to a small gathering of orange flowers. Their long leaves spiraled up around the blossoms. "These. I planted these a week ago. Orange Hestian daytwirlers. They're native to Hestia—a pretty big export business in some of the larger farms. People like to use them for all sorts of occasions, but I just like the look of them."

He smiled at the flowers as they passed them, and Imorie smiled, too. Who smiled at random flowers anymore?

She stopped and bent to pick one, but Eti pulled her back.

"Sorry," he said. "They just—we don't pick them."

She blinked down at the flowers. Well, okay, she thought she'd seen fresh-cut flowers around the house, but maybe they'd come from another source.

They walked on. Eti showed her first one fountain, then another with iridescent blue and green fish swimming around the base, which led out to a small, artificial stream. They crossed a meter-long foot bridge that was hardly necessary, but Imorie enjoyed the touch all the same.

And Eti relaxed as they walked, his stiffness melting into a chatter about the various kinds of trees and bushes, pointing out differences in the leaves between the high forest cherry and Valon caseca trees, showing her where the bees had cross-pollinated a grove of peonies with native Hestian field roses.

Imorie didn't care much about flowers either way, but she relaxed as well, just listening, just taking it all in. She had a modest garden at her family home in the capital of Gray Moss, and she walked at the nearby municipal park, sometimes. But that wasn't like this at all. Those trees didn't do much to block out the steady drone of aircar engines, the sounds of a large city. And then, she walked alone, as she was usually alone. Her family wasn't high nobility, but her recognizably Rhialden looks tended to give people pause. She'd often walked the parks alone, trailed only by Jis, who could double as a bodyguard in a pinch.

When her legs were growing heavy again, and her breath shorter than she'd like, she didn't have to ask—Eti just steered them off to one side, where a stone bench sat under a caseca tree, with its smooth, indigo-gray bark.

"Thanks. And thanks—" she waved at the gardens "—for the tour. I needed that."

Eti shrugged, growing awkward again for the first time since they'd started out. "Sure."

She hadn't gotten lost after all, though she wasn't sure she could trace her steps back from there. But Eti didn't seem in a hurry to leave her, and Jis was settling across the small clearing, spreading a small blanket under a tree. Jis was better at tracking things like that.

"Do they follow you everywhere?" Eti asked, looking past her to Jis.

"Jis uses fae and faer pronouns. And yes, pretty much. I don't mind, if that's what you're asking. Fae's been with me for a long time. Practically family."

Eti twitched at this, brows drawing together. Had she hit another sore point? Did she dare even ask about his own family?

"I don't have family on this world," he said. "They're on Kalistré. I'm just here to work." He shrugged, and then hunched into himself. She hadn't asked him to offer that bit of personal information, but he seemed to want her to change the subject anyway.

"So, beyond working with the trees and flowers, which you obviously love, what else do you do for fun? Got any hobbies? Anything interesting to do here that doesn't involve loud parties or holo games?"

He snorted. "No, I don't like the parties, either. I, uh—" He brushed hair out of his eyes, squinted up toward the sun overhead. "I used to play the mandolin, sometimes."

She shifted to get a better look at him, grinning. "Oh? Like, in a band?"

His cheeks flushed red. "Uh, no. Mostly classical. I—I never got good enough to be in a band or orchestra—"

He was looking down again and seemed like he wanted her to change the subject again. He was so cagey about anything personal. Should she leave it alone? Was he not supposed to tell her anything about his personal life? Was that against some sort of unwritten staff fraternization rule?

But they'd had easy enough conversation earlier. It hadn't felt like walking with someone on staff, it had felt like walking with a friend. If she actually knew what that felt like.

"I've attempted to play the piano," she confided. "Attempted being the key word there. My family finally asked me to stop."

"Ha. Well—mine liked my playing . . ." His voice trailed off again, and he shrugged.

They sat for a moment in silence until Jis tromped over, apparently giving up on keeping faer distance, and unslung the food cooler from faer shoulder. "You hungry? I am."

Imorie was, actually. Eti started to get up, but she waved him back down. Sandwiches were doled out. The conversation went back to the plants around them, the weather, the overall mood of the estate without naming any of the particulars. All of which were safe topics.

Imorie eyed Eti as she ate, watching him wave his sandwich about as he described a migratory pattern of birds that would be coming in the next week. Some sort of tropical species that made its way north once a year when the weather at the equator became too hot.

Etienne Tanaka was a puzzle. Gardener, yes, and obviously suited to it, but hesitant to give himself any real authority there. Here on Hestia for a year, away from family. Imorie had heard of service workers going from city to city for jobs, but it would be expensive to go world to world for what looked to be a more minor position in the household. Even the porter had talked down to Eti. He didn't act as if he had any particular friends here. He used to play music, but the past tense implied he didn't anymore, and family itself was a sore spot. What sort of situation had he left behind on Kalistré?

Well, it wasn't her business. She didn't need to know, and he certainly didn't owe it to her to tell her. Maybe he wasn't even that big of a mystery—people ran from problems for whatever reason all the time. Or were forced to move away, or whatever. Eti's life hardly sounded unusual in that context. Yet she couldn't shake the feeling that there was something more, something deeper going on with Eti that went beyond the surface of things.

Footsteps on the gravel made her look up, and the conversation lulled. A person who looked to be on the younger side of middle-age, pale and firmly masc, was striding down the path, wide-brimmed hat in hand.

"There you are," they said. "I've been looking for you, Etienne. You were supposed to clear the south side paths today, and did you check on the grafts?" They hesitated as they glanced between Imorie and Jis, then made a curt bow. "Sers. Forgive me for interrupting your meal. Please forgive Etienne for interrupting yours—"

"I asked Eti to give me a tour of the gardens," Imorie said, brushing off her hands as she pushed herself to her feet. "And you are?"

"Ryam. Head gardener here at Windvale. Etienne works for me—or at least, he's supposed to be working for me."

He glared at Eti, and there was no fondness in the head gardener's annoyance.

"I'd like him to stay with me, for the day," Imorie said. "I'm a guest here at Windvale. Surely you offer guests hospitality."

Ryam grimaced, looking away, but they nodded. "Sure. Etienne, stay with the guests, then. But report to me tomorrow, six sharp."

The gardener turned and tromped off again, muttering to himself.

Imorie glanced back at Eti, who'd drawn in on himself, eyes down, shoulders hunched. Adeius, was that the issue? Was he working for a tyrant here?

Could she hire Eti for her own staff? Her family had sent her with funds, but, well, not a salary's worth of funds.

Eti stood. "Thanks, um. I should get back to work. Thanks."

He hesitated, looking between her and Jis. "You know the way back?"

"I do," Jis said. "Go on. But you're welcome to stay." Jis's mouth was pulled tight, looking after where the head gardener had gone. "Plenty more sandwiches."

"I'm fine, thanks." Eti was already backing away, already not looking up at them anymore. He turned and hurried off in the opposite direction from the head gardener, further into the gardens.

When the sounds of footsteps faded, Imorie looked to Jis. "Did that seem weird? The head gardener shouldn't have reprimanded him in front of us. We're guests."

Jis tilted faer head back and forth, not quite nodding. "Some people like their own power. I've seen it often enough among staff."

Fae turned back, smiled. "Maybe it's best we just stick

together, not get embroiled in any petty estate politics. You don't need to be in the middle of any of that."

Imorie nodded but looked after Eti. His reactions had been off, maybe too extreme for the circumstances, maybe calibrated wrong, she didn't quite know. She felt no sense of danger from Eti, but wasn't sure he didn't feel the same from . . . somewhere.

Maybe Jis was right. Maybe it was a mistake to get friendly with one of the estate staff when she was a guest here.

But he looked like he could use a friend, about as much as she could. And if he was in trouble for whatever reason, and there was anything she could do to help, she had to try, didn't she? He'd faced down a duke for her.

She narrowed her eyes. She'd find a way to find out what was going on.

26

CYCLES AND INEVITABILITY

> *There are certainly criminal elements among the nobility—I'd say much of the nobility has at least some ties to organized crime and same for the other way around, whether they actively participate in crimes themselves or not. The determining factor in whether these enterprises are actually considered criminal is who is smart enough to be subtle and even smarter not to get caught.*
>
> — THUR ELSTRAT IN HER CONTROVERSIAL BOOK *THE CRIMES OF THE NOBILITY*

When Eti made his way back to the house, the red was mostly gone from the sky, soft golden solar lanterns lighting up in the trees. He'd checked the tree grafts. He'd done all his work that day, and even stayed longer to trim some of the bushes near one of the fountains. His stomach clenched with hunger, but he'd pulled strength from the ground beneath his feet, from the steady rocks, and in much smaller amounts from the trees around him. He was hungry, but he wasn't shaky from not eating all day. Not shaky from that, anyway.

The soft attention of the grass and the roaming insects followed him as he walked. He felt the fleeting, rioting sense of two bushes that would need to be pulled apart soon, and the churning sense of finality from fallen leaves underfoot. Of cycles and inevitability.

Eti clenched his fists as he approached the two-story garden shed behind the main house. He pushed the door open, flicked on the lights, and dumped the shoulder sack of tools he'd picked up earlier from one of the small auxiliary sheds within the garden itself. Wiping at his sweat-sticky face, he surveyed the mostly orderly array of garden tools and supplies inside, not really seeing any of them.

Then he heaved a sigh and started up the stairs in the corner that led to his tiny room in the attic loft.

"Etienne!"

Eti froze, shoulders tightening as he sensed a too-familiar presence jogging toward the shed door.

He winced. He'd forgotten to close the shed door, again.

"Hey," Ryam said, pushing into the shed, "I told you to keep this door shut, we can't have animals getting in here overnight, we can't have anyone trying to steal the tools, or use them—"

"Sorry," Eti said, eyes on the floor.

Ryam stopped, ran a hand through his short hair, and sighed. "All right. Well. What did you find out?"

Eti's breath was a soft hiss through his teeth. This—this was his real job, not as a gardener. He could be the best gardener on any world, and it still wouldn't matter. He hadn't been brought to Hestia to tend the gardens, that was only the most useful and convenient place his handlers had found for him.

Ryam came closer, hand out.

Eti stared at the hand, dirty from Ryam's own day's work in the gardens, and thought about refusing to take it. He always thought about refusing—and today, oh gods, today. Today he was pretty sure he'd re-discovered something he'd tried to forget.

When he looked at Imorie, he saw Imorie, and he also saw a density around the edges, a layering of souls. It was subtle, not as glaring as it would have been if she'd merely been herself.

When he'd touched her arm—he hadn't tried to listen to her thoughts. And he'd done his best to firmly shut out her emotions. He didn't know who she was, but he'd felt the coiled terror lurking just beneath the veneer of Imorie. And he'd felt that sense of queasy déjà vu he got on the rare occasions that he tried to erase some of his own memories. If he thought too hard, if anyone asked too much or the wrong questions, if he thought about Imorie much at all, he knew what he'd tried to suppress would come out.

Eti stared at Ryam's hand a beat too long.

Ryam reached forward and slapped him, and Eti stumbled back, hand flying to his cheek. It hadn't been hard, mostly startling. But he couldn't fight back, and Ryam knew it.

Ryam thrust out his hand again. "Now, Eti. I'm tired, you're tired, we're going to get this done. The Count doesn't like excuses."

Eti swallowed. He thought of his mother, put her squarely in his thoughts. And his younger sibling. He was doing this for them. He was doing this to protect them, and he had to help them over any stranger. Imorie, though he'd liked walking with her in the garden, wasn't his friend. None of the guests were. He couldn't have friends here.

Eti gripped Ryam's hand and felt Ryam relax even while he himself tensed up.

"Now. Tell me, what did you learn today?"

So Eti launched into a recitation of every snippet of conversation he'd overheard while working among the trees, which hadn't been much, as the guests seldom wandered too deeply into the garden. He reported on the Dynasty couple, who'd found a make out spot near a bench he'd wanted to work at. He'd settled himself near a fountain a distance away instead.

Ryam squeezed his hand hard enough to hurt. "The Rhialden. Contract Rhialden. What did she say to you? You gave her a tour? She was with you all day! You have to have something good."

"We just talked about the garden. I didn't get anything more than that. Oh, well she plays the piano, or tried to. That's it. And she liked the Daytwirlers." Which was all true, but just that shade of trying to obscure anything more, and Ryam sensed it through his touch.

Eti gasped as Ryam crushed his hand in his grip. "Okay, sorry, I—I like her—"

Ryam laughed. An ugly sound, and accompanied by ugly emotions. Eti felt, and didn't want to feel, Ryam's disgust with him.

"Oh, magicker, you can't have any of the guests. They wouldn't want you anyway." Then Ryam let go and gave Eti a friendly slap on the shoulder.

Gods. Ryam had believed it. He thought that's what Eti was hiding. Eti doubted that would work twice—as much as he didn't want to, as much as it twisted his soul, he'd have to find a way to forget again, wouldn't he? If he wanted to protect Imorie from the people he worked for.

Eti clenched his teeth. "You shouldn't have interrupted us. I could have gotten more from her, if you'd let us keep talking."

Ryam raised his brows. "Oh, is that how it is? You just want to spend time with the Rhialden. You have work to do, Eti. I want you to find out her secrets, all of her secrets. It's been a while since we had as big a fish as a Rhialden to deal with."

"Contract Rhialden," Eti corrected, rubbing his shoulder where Ryam had hit it. "She's not anyone important. She doesn't act at all like the high nobility, like the duke."

Ryam shrugged. "A Rhialden's a Rhialden. The Rhialdens won't want their name sullied, and we can use that. Find out her story, why she's here, beyond the usual reasons." He waved and headed for the door. "Six tomorrow, Eti."

The door slammed shut behind him. Then locked.

Eti held his breath for one long, heart-pounding moment.

He couldn't do violence. Even the thought of violence made his ears ring, his head start to spin. He could feel the sense of Ryam's life energy too closely not to have near total empathy with it.

He turned and climbed the stairs to his room, which held a bed, a chair, a cooler and instant oven to one side, and a curtain hiding a toilet, sink and narrow shower stall.

Eti flopped onto the bed, staring up at the open rafters overhead. The air was tight and stuffy, despite the cooling unit in the window.

Why did he feel so strongly that he had to protect Imorie? He owed her nothing. He'd always given the information asked of him. If he couldn't overhear it, he bumped into people. He picked up their startled, unguarded thoughts.

He closed his eyes and rolled over, facing the wall. Carefully, with a shudder, he let his suppressed aura flow back around him, his senses becoming painful before they normalized again.

Imorie was different than the other nobles. He knew that, though maybe not all of it.

Would he risk his family to protect whatever information she had that his handlers wanted? That should be a ridiculous question. Of course he wouldn't risk his family. He was only here because his handlers had his family, and the Javieris didn't take kindly to anyone telling them no.

He should do his absolute best to avoid Imorie—and he was pretty sure he had been doing that, until he'd been rushing too much and hadn't paid attention to where she was, or if she was out of her rooms.

His face heated as he thought of her shock in seeing him, a wide-eyed, skeptical look that looked so out of place in her usually restrained demeanor.

And that thought led, he knew, to information he shouldn't have. That he'd made himself forget.

His head throbbed at that small violence to himself, excising memories from his own mind. He should do it again, but the greater part of himself rebelled against the thought. He was fairly certain he'd already done it more than once.

So Eti would wait. He'd just have to be careful. He could probably be careful. And how long would she be staying? Some guests stayed months. The duke had been here for three so far, and Eti wasn't sure if he'd been sick at all to begin with.

Eti laid awake too long for his tired body, trying to find some way to warn Imorie off from going outside, but he couldn't think of anything convincing enough that wouldn't also get him into trouble.

27

SUNSHINE

> *Was I myself, or was I the role I played?*
>
> — HOMAJ RHIALDEN, SERITARCHUS IX IN A PRIVATE LETTER, NEVER SENT; PUBLISHED IN *THE CHANGE DIALOGUES*

Homaj woke slowly. He felt the texture of the pillowcase beneath his cheek—not satin, surely, but not rough. The warmth of someone beside him. The light, earthy musk of the captain of his guard, Zhang, her breathing steady, just tickling his shoulder. The soft ticking of a mechanical clock on the wall. The drip of a sink—either in the kitchen or the single bathroom.

Sun slanted through the shutters of the safe house, one known only to himself, Iata, and Zhang. The coastal town where they were staying was quiet, only the occasional chirp of birds disturbing his silence.

Homaj sat up, doing his best not to disturb Zhang. He ran a hand through his long brown hair, shoving it out of his eyes. He caught his reflection in the glass of a framed picture across the bedroom. A picture that had deliberately been set in that place for that purpose, so he could re-orient himself.

He'd Changed before he and Zhang left the palace, and then Changed again when they got here the morning before. Waking up after the first night in a completely new body had stopped being disorienting to him years ago. He stared at his reflection—long, loose hair, medium-brown skin, wider eyes, wider nose. When he looked at himself the first morning after a Change, he didn't feel less himself. He looked at himself and always saw himself.

And he looked at himself and never saw himself, too.

Zhang stirred, propping up on one elbow. "What's wrong?"

"Nothing. You can sleep—"

She laid back down. "It's too early in the morning for this conversation."

He scowled. "What conversation? I said I'm fine—"

"You said nothing's wrong." She ran a hand over her face, yawning. "Maja, you're not hiding that 'nothing' very well."

He scowled and levered himself up, grabbing a robe off the bedside chair and padding barefoot into the house's small kitchen. He grabbed two mugs off the counter, filled them from the tap, and opened a drawer to find the instant cartridges—a tea for him, a coffee for her. He dropped the cartridges into the mugs and let them do their thing.

Zhang was sitting up again when he brought two steaming mugs back to bed. She took one, peering at it blearily. He sat back beside her, crossing his legs and pulling the covers back over his lap. He hunched over his own mug, letting the steam heat his face.

"You're not fine," Zhang finally said. "You wouldn't let us talk about it yesterday. But you're obviously not fine."

Zhang had been the captain of his personal guard for over twenty years, there from the beginning. She'd been his friend for as long, too. Deeper than friends, not quite lovers. They sometimes shared beds, for comfort more than anything, and every so often, shared their bodies as well. She was asexual, though she did have sex on occasion, usually, he'd found, when she was stressed. He usually was more attracted to men and masc-presenting people, but on the few times in the last few years she'd asked to sleep with him, he'd never said no.

As they'd done the night before.

He met her eyes briefly, looked away again into his mug. Took a long, slow sip of the rich tea.

She could read him as well as anyone. Better than anyone. He'd taught her how, over the years. Taught her how to find him amongst any crowd, in any role. She hadn't batted an eye waking up just now and finding him with the different body he'd Changed to the day before. Most people would need a few days at least to get used to something like that.

"We can talk about it later," he said.

And she didn't push. They both knew there would have to be a later.

He spent an hour working Zhang's bobbed hair into a spikier, gelled style, and contouring her features into different angles. They'd dyed her hair silver before they'd left the palace, but they had time now for the more thorough transformation. Zhang knew enough by now to change her walk and habitual gestures, to change her accent as needed. She'd never been particularly expert at any of it, but she was solidly adequate, and security here wasn't anything near what they'd encounter in Valon City.

He spent another hour on himself. Not that he needed to Change his appearance any more than he had, but because he wanted to.

They ate breakfast with small talk about Qoriale, the small town where they were staying. They'd been there once before, years ago, on one of his rare, non-working breaks from palace life. Ceorre had insisted at the time that he needed a break that wasn't also a mission. He'd tried to find something in the town that was useful to bring back to the palace, and of course he'd read the usual petty schemes among the tourist trap merchants, the deceptions in the relationships of the passersby. Nothing worthy of the palace, though. Zhang had been annoyed with him that whole trip because he'd stayed in a mood until they'd gone back to his more important work. He'd insisted he hadn't had time for fun.

This day, though, they put on warm jackets and walked the half kilometer toward the waterfront, rented two powered bicycles that looked like they'd seen better days, and set off along the wide, sandy beach. And every time his shoulders started to hunch up, when he thought about all that he should be doing at the palace, when he thought about the mess with Arianna, and oh Adeius, whatever would happen now with Dressa, he looked out toward the ocean and the tension ebbed away again, in the salt air, in the sunshine.

28

OVERLOOK

> *My position as Seritarchus lets me have only occasional contact with the planet itself. When I'm in a role on a mission, I'm almost always in the palace or in the city. There's very little political intrigue to track down in a quiet forest or a seaside town.*
>
> — HOMAJ RHIALDEN, SERITARCHUS IX IN A PRIVATE LETTER, NEVER SENT; PUBLISHED IN *THE CHANGE DIALOGUES*

Qoriale was near the end of a peninsula on the southern coast of Gavri, the second and largest of Valon's two main continents. Lethrin, the continent that held Valon City and all its politics, was eight hundred kilometers away to the northeast, and the ocean he was riding along didn't face it, never touched it, was only ocean all the way down to the rocky south pole.

Homaj caught Zhang's eyes and pedaled harder. Then harder still, boosting his natural speed with the bike's underpowered engines. Zhang kept up. Of course she kept up. And they ended up far past the commercial beaches, past the people, at a broad outcrop of red rocks overlooking the waves a few meters below.

Homaj set the bike down and sat hard on a decent looking rock, breathing hard. Zhang did the same and passed him a water bottle from her pack. Adeius, he'd forgotten to bring any water himself. He took it and drank gratefully. Drank again.

He looked out over the water, and with his heart still racing, felt something rising up inside him, something he couldn't shove back down. Something he'd been shoving down for years, so many years, and he was too tired to shove it down anymore.

"I think," he said, "I've had enough."

He looked over at Zhang, and she at him.

She took a breath, nodded.

He tried to take another sip of water and found the bottle trembling in his hands.

Truthspoken Rulers didn't retire. Not and remain Truthspoken, they didn't. And how could he even be thinking this, with the kingdom on the edge of crisis, with the Bruising Sleep becoming more of a problem, and the nobility scheming as always, and the Kidaa becoming less of a mystery and more of a threat? How could he think of this when he wasn't sure at all about his heirs, or who would rule, or if they even could? He'd promised Arianna he'd look into the circumstances of her illness. But . . . but he had so very little left with which to do anything.

His breath caught and his eyes flooded with a sudden sting. "I fucked up, really fucked up with framing the magickers. And not because I knew it was wrong, but there's not enough of me left to know. I don't know anymore, Zhang. I can't see through all the tangles. My mind is just . . . I'm just done. I can't do it anymore. Not and do it in a way that's good for the kingdom."

She shifted to sit beside him. Twined her hand in his, pressed her shoulder against his.

"Are you sure you don't just need a rest? You haven't taken a rest in . . . over a year, at least. I can't remember when—no, no it was two years ago, we took three days in the city, holed up in that dingy safe house, and you decided to crack a crime ring."

He pinched the bridge of his nose with his free hand. "It needed doing."

She squeezed his hand. "There's a lot of stuff that needs doing. I don't think it all has to be done by you."

A larger wave crashed against the rocks below, spraying a fine, tingling mist over his face.

"But I can't—"

"No," she said. Quiet, firm.

"But Dressa—Adeius, Zhang, she's hardly fit to be the Truthspoken Heir, she can't rule."

"She's every bit as capable as you were when you made your bid to rule."

He waved an impatient hand. "That—is hardly high praise. I was young and entirely a fool."

"Not how I remember it." Zhang let go of his hand to take another sip of her own water. "And if Dressa's not ready, there's Iata."

He shook his head. "I can't step down now. I just—I'll rest this week, or try to, I promise I won't root out any crime rings. Not that there are any in Qoriale. But I can't, not now, when Arianna just publicly abdicated, and now everyone will be watching Dressa. She's going to have to dig herself out of the persona she's set for herself. She's been too good-natured, setting herself up as vapid—"

"You did it," Zhang said. "Everyone thought you were the laziest player. They didn't think that long after you made your bid to rule."

"Iata has it in hand. I don't have to decide now."

He gripped his knees. He shouldn't have said anything. It couldn't be truly over. He just had to rest a bit, catch another wind, go back into the fray. He could do that. He could.

"Maybe." Zhang watched him, the lines around her eyes deeper than usual, visible even under the heavy cosmetics. "While you were debriefing with the Green Magickers the other morning, I was with Iata as his guard. He cut a meeting with the admiralty short for no reason I could discern. Then I followed him into the antechamber, and right after I shut the door behind us, he *glowed*. Not just a little, not his usual aura. He was in physical pain. He's said before that suppressing his aura is like holding his breath, and I'm not sure he can continue to hold it. Maybe in the short run. Maybe he's stressed—we're all stressed, that's not going to go away."

The wind gusted past them, and Zhang shoved loose hair out of her eyes.

Was Iata losing control of his magics? That . . . was another worry Homaj just couldn't add to his already towering pile.

"Iata can hold it together," he said. "He has motive. He likes being the Seritarchus."

"Yes, he likes it. It's his birthright. And I know he'd rather rule as himself than as you."

Homaj pressed his lips tight. And here it came, of course they'd circle back around to this. Zhang hated—had hated since the start—that Iata, who was absolutely Homaj's equal in every way, could never live outside his shadow. She didn't understand their dynamic. She couldn't see that Iata was fine with this, and that it was the only way he could ever rule.

"It's not possible, Zhang. Just not possible. There are only ever three Truthspoken. There are never four, and if the nobility learns there have been four all along—"

"Officially. Truthspoken have retired. Your uncle retired and is still out there."

"Yes, but not and remain Truthspoken. My uncle foreswore

Change and went into exile." Which he would have to do now if he retired. And he would have had to do anyway if his father had never been assassinated all those years ago, and his older sibling had taken the rulership in their time, and their heirs taken up the mantle of Truthspoken in turn. When the number of sanctioned Truthspoken increased, one had to step down. That would have been around this time for him, anyway.

"That's not the same thing as suddenly revealing a second Truthspoken sibling," he went on, "while there are already two Truthspoken heirs. If people would accept Iata as competent enough to be their ruler, then they'd also have to accept that he's been fully trained and active all this time. That's as much as admitting we train extra Truthspoken, and that will upset the whole balance—"

Zhang made a frustrated noise. "Maja, can't you see I'm trying to give you an out? You are a shell of the person who took the rulership those twenty-three years ago. You keep going now, there will be nothing left at all. You can't hold us together anymore. There's nothing left for you to hold with, so it's either Dressa, or Iata. And I'd back Iata right now as the most stable ruler, but he can't do it as you. You can't expect him to just be you forever."

His fingers dug hard into his knees, and he rocked forward. "I don't expect that. Just long enough for Dressa to be properly trained—"

Zhang stood. "And I'm telling you he doesn't have that long. He'll burn himself out, like you've burned yourself out, just trying to conceal his magics."

He stood, too. "What would you have me do? I can't order him to not be a magicker, and I promise you, the kingdom is not ready for the revelation that Homaj Rhialden is secretly a magicker."

"You aren't," Zhang said. "He is. Have the Truthspeaker and

the First Magicker confirm that Iata is Truthspoken by birthright. And the eldest. It's not even that hard."

Not that hard. Adeius. She thought like a guard, a soldier. She saw a problem, she found a solution.

"But your argument is that he can't contain his magics. Or his aura. Whatever. So the nobility, and the General Assembly, and the general public would all have to accept that he's been a hidden Rhialden heir all along, that he was once a bloodservant, that he—Adeius, Zhang, he's good, but can he possibly fake not having met and worked with every single member of the court so far? He's been partly running the kingdom since as long as I have, and *that* can't get out. That would topple everything. And above all that, he's a magicker. He'd have to be publicly sealed as a magicker, and then everyone would see his rank's not low, because of course a Rhialden would have to excel at damn near everything!"

Zhang caught his waving arms, and for a moment, he fought her. He needed to fight her, to have something solid to resist against.

His eyes were running. His nose was running. What the hell was wrong with him, that he couldn't pull himself together? He was trained for this. He was trained for everything, every scenario. He was supposed to be infallible.

He stilled, closing his eyes, dropping his chin so she wouldn't have to look at him. Not directly, not and see him like this.

29

FAMILY

> *Family is transient, and eternal, and not always the people who were chosen for you.*
>
> — NIN HADI IN THEIR SHORT STORY "*FRIENDS OF THE LARK*"

"Maja," Zhang said softly, her voice almost lost in the crash of the waves, but not quite. "This is what I know, because I know you. You are strong, you are so strong, but you've given all of it away. Yes, I know you had to. I know that. But you can't run the kingdom anymore. You said you've had enough. I've heard you say that before, but I heard you mean it this time."

Homaj shook his head, still not looking up at her. "I have to find a way. I just—have to."

"No. If Dressa has a lot of learning to do, or if Iata goes public and takes the rulership in his own right, even with all of the pitfalls of those scenarios, they are still better than a scenario where the person holding the kingdom together is out of fuel."

"I can hold out another few months. At least until Ari comes back. Then—"

But the marriage document. He'd seen the marriage document. Dressa had married Lesander Javieri. There was no going back on that, or the kingdom would truly destabilize under the weight of Javieri pressure.

Adeius, why had she done that? Couldn't she just have held on for a few months more as Arianna? He'd thought that had been the best plan.

He'd been wildly wrong. Like he'd been wildly wrong to send Iata as a magicker to Arianna's engagement ball.

He shook his arms in Zhang's grasp and she let go. He scrubbed at his face, turned back to the ocean. It was maddeningly stable, just a thing that endured. Unlike him.

He was the one who'd opened this conversation. Why had he spent the last minutes arguing against this decision that . . . truly . . . he'd already made? He felt the weariness to his very bones. He could not go on with the weight of everything on his shoulders. His shoulders just couldn't bear it anymore.

He had to step down. He'd been running on fumes so long he didn't know what vitality felt like anymore, and that was no way to steer a kingdom through the times ahead. So, Dressa or Iata?

Iata would mean change, and certainly some political upset—even if Homaj stepped down so there were still officially three Truthspoken, there would be no hiding that Iata had, for a time, been an unsanctioned fourth. Even the Truthspeaker might need to weather that storm, because no one would believe she didn't know what was going on.

But Iata, being Iata, would find a way to use that for his advantage. For the kingdom's advantage. He'd find a way to navigate, and with him being a magicker—well, maybe it was high time the magickers integrate fully into the kingdom's governance, anyway. That was a big step for the ruler to be a magicker, but. With the right spin, it wasn't impossible.

And Dressa? She'd be publicly married soon, and she'd be able to start her own heirs. Maybe Arianna would come back fine, if intensely pissed—as she certainly had a right to be—and she'd be able to help Dressa run the kingdom until she herself would need to step down when Dressa's heirs were old enough. No, that wasn't the future Arianna had envisioned for herself, but then, futures didn't always work according to plan.

Futures seldom worked according to plan.

Zhang squeezed his shoulder. "Twenty-three years, Maja. You've been at this—we've been at this—twenty-three years."

Exactly half of his life. Those years had all been a blur of people and personalities.

And who was he, really? Who would he even be if he stepped down? All he knew how to be was the Seritarchus and every identity that encompassed. If he stepped down, he'd have to legally give up Change.

Yes, there could only ever be three Truthspoken. One to rule the kingdom, one in training to rule, and one for just in case the other two didn't work out. There was no room for a retired Seritarchus, at least not one who still Changed, not even if Dressa became the ruler now and Iata stayed in the shadows. No one would take away his abilities—those were innate. He could still heal himself. He'd still know evaku, and he'd be able to shift sex if his sense of gender required it. But he'd pick a genetic profile and then stay within it.

Could he even do that? He was too many people. He didn't know how to be just one. He didn't know which one he actually was. Over the years, he had felt less and less like the person everyone else knew as Homaj Rhialden. Right now, he wasn't even that—Iata was.

Zhang stepped to one side and picked up her bike.

Not knowing what else to do, he picked up his as well, and

they began walking the bikes down the rocky incline to the level of the beach.

"If it was my choice," Zhang said, "and I said this before, I'd put my money behind Iata. Dressa is still young. Maybe she doesn't have to bear so much so soon."

He rolled his shoulders, trying to shake out the tension. "But what of Dressa, then? And Arianna. If Iata becomes the Seritarchus in his own right, then his own children should become the heirs." This, too, was something they'd discussed before, and not to any meaningful conclusion.

"They're not fully trained."

"No, not as fully as they'd need to be Truthspoken, but they have the capacity for it. They're his children, as Rhialden as Arianna and Dressa. People might find out, or they might speak out—if their father is legally acknowledged as the Rhialden ruler, the Seritarchus, they'd have that right."

They didn't know that their father was sometimes legally the Seritarchus now.

"So talk to Ceorre, Maja," Zhang said with some exasperation. "See about the possibility of a provision that Dressa and Arianna remain Truthspoken and the heirs, as Iata's heirs. They have far more experience, and they are both trained for this. I can't imagine Iata wouldn't agree to that, not with everything riding on it. He'd explain to his children, and they'd have to abide."

He slanted her a look. "Iata's not without his own ambition. And it's not a small ambition."

They reached level ground and Zhang paused, hand on her seat but not yet mounting the bike for the ride back. "He's a magicker. He can't do violence, not without seriously disrupting his own self. And he understands the power of continuity. He's not going to make a huge wave of change himself and then change everything else stable around him. He'll need Dressa's continuity to support him. Dressa supporting him would be the difference between success and a failed bid to rule, I think."

Homaj shook himself out, his spine crackling. "I'll think about it."

"You're going to sleep on it, then you're going to declare that you're fine after all, and you'll just get back to ruling the kingdom." Her eyes bored into his. "Not this time." She shifted her weight, leaning the bike against her hip.

Adeius, could they just go already? He was done with this conversation.

He could get on his bike now and ride away from it. But he respected her too much for that.

"Iata told me you came back two days ago, covered in bruises."

Homaj barely suppressed a flinch at all the layers of hurt and reproach and concern in her tone. "I'm fine now. You saw that, you saw all of that last night, I have no more injuries—"

She stepped forward into his space, tapped his heart. "No. Not this time."

He closed his eyes, breathing hard, ears ringing.

Making the decision to do this was one thing. Actually going through with it was another.

Was he actually going to do this? Did he have no other choice? Was he going to give up his power, everything that he was, and throw his kingdom to the winds of whatever would happen next?

Was he the reason the kingdom was now on unstable ground? He'd thought he'd been holding it together, but maybe him running past his endurance had tipped everything out of balance. Maybe Iata was the only thing holding everything together.

"Maja," Zhang said, and he heard the plea in her voice. "Please. Don't fold in on yourself. Let it go."

He took a hard breath. Nodded.

"I want—we'll stay here five more days. The end of the week. I just want five days, before all of this happens." Because it wouldn't be easy. Nothing ahead would be easy.

He looked at her suddenly. "Will you stay on and guard Iata, then?"

She glanced aside. "I don't know." Then opened her hands. "If you want me to come with you, wherever you go—"

"No, I couldn't ask it of you."

But she was shaking her head. "You're my family, Maja. That won't change."

He turned away, because his eyes were stinging again.

Then he did get on his bike and push off into the sandy gravel, pedaling hard, throttling the motor. She'd catch up, he knew. She was always with him. And he thanked everything that wouldn't change.

His stomach tightened as his thoughts churned. But also . . . a weight in his chest eased. The world around him looked a little clearer.

He was going to get out. Adeius and all the holy stars, he was going to get out.

30

SUN AND STARS

> *Pageantry is society's attempt to not recognize itself in its own mirror.*
>
> — HOMAJ RHIALDEN, SERITARCHUS IX, AS QUOTED IN *THE CHANGE DIALOGUES*

Lesander wore a single, pea-sized diamond in each ear. Just one, and a single, thumbnail-sized diamond in a simple gold setting on a simple gold chain. Her flame-red hair was swept up in a simple knot, and she wore a clean-lined floor-length gown that seemed blue at first glance but then darkened into bottomless depths.

Like space, Dressa decided. Lesander looked like the sun and stars in space. And if she hadn't already been married to her, she'd want to do it all over again.

Of course, she'd have that chance too, wouldn't she?

Lesander lightly gripped her arm as they glided into the Lilac Hall, one of the smaller social halls over which the residence wing sat.

Dressa's breath caught as forty or fifty pairs of eyes turned her way, and the room collectively rustled into a deep bow.

She wasn't used to this. She still wasn't used to this level of attention. That deep a bow was usually reserved for Arianna.

She spotted her father, one of the only ones who hadn't bowed, near the back of the room with a knot of older courtiers. Well, Iata as her father, but inhabiting him so perfectly it was like the same thing. He raised his glass with that crooked, ironic smile, and gave her a shallow nod. His continued public approval was high currency for her in the palace right now.

And beside him was Dressa's mother.

Haneri also didn't bow but nodded to Dressa, with almost the same degree of approval.

Dressa's heart kicked into her throat. How long had her mother been with Iata so far tonight? Had she noticed anything off?

Her gaze flicked back to Iata, but if Dressa hadn't known it was him, she would never have known it wasn't her father.

She felt the barest tug on her arm from Lesander. She'd been standing in one place for too long.

Dressa spread a smile across her face, but reminded herself not to show it too widely. Not as widely as she might have a week ago. She was still Dressa, yes. She couldn't discount the years of openness she'd cultivated, her more wild reputation at court, but she was the Heir now. And the faces around her seemed just as hesitant on how to navigate those distinctions as she was.

But she spotted one of her oldest co-conspirators in social events—could she call them a friend?—Count Ajim, coming toward her, the widest grin on their face. They'd completely buzzed their hair since she'd last seen them briefly on the night of the ball and dyed their eyebrows and lashes phosphorescent blue. Ajim had always been more striking than the current courtly standard of beautiful, with a personality like lightning. She had to admit the glow did good things to their vibe.

Dressa had been too focused on driving attention from Arianna at the ball, and Ajim too focused on picking up a new hookup. She thought she'd seen them leave into the courtyard and likely the guest wing beyond, with its complimentary third floor rooms for just that purpose, before everything happened with Arianna.

"Dressa," they cried, hands out.

She reached her free hand back to them, feeling some of her tension ease as she spotted no hesitation in Ajim's posture. But then, they'd never been particularly sensitive to rank, and that was one of the reasons she'd kept them around.

"Ajim," she said, moving with them further into the room. "Have you met my—"

She was about to say "wife." Dressa jolted herself out of whatever stupor had led her to that word, because no one else could know that. Not yet.

"—fiancé, Prince Lesander Javieri?"

"I did—well, I saw you, Ser Prince, the night of the ball." Ajim's gaze flicked to Dressa's. "I'm so sorry I wasn't there to help when the commotion started."

Something flickered in Ajim's eyes as they said this. Not quite a contradiction to their statement, but more a commentary on how they weren't sorry for her benefit, or even sorry at all that events had pushed Dressa to the place she was now. The Truthspoken Heir, who could almost call Ajim her friend.

"Excuse us, Count Ajim," Lesander said graciously, "it would seem we're being summoned."

Dressa looked up. Who would summon her here but one of her parents? She met Iata's eyes briefly, and he made the smallest suggestion of a question.

He hadn't, then. Had Lesander heard what she'd heard in Ajim's tone, too?

Her hand found its way into Lesander's, their arms more closely intertwined as they made their way through the guests toward the Seritarchus and Seritarchus Consort. Not particularly where she wanted to be, but her stomach was sour as she took in everything in her peripheral vision, all the stares. So many people whom she'd normally talk to with social ease now looked down when her gaze swept toward them.

Was that better than the blatant ambition of Ajim?

She'd expected this, yes. She'd had some taste of it that first day after she'd been confirmed and the engagement contract publicly signed, when she and Iata and Lesander had greeted all the well-wishers in the Reception Hall. But she'd thought it would fade. That she'd still be seen as approachable, because she certainly hadn't taken major strides to change her entire persona in a few days. This was the mantle of her new title. And maybe, probably, it was for the best.

She watched Iata surreptitiously as she approached, watched him smile politely, gesture expansively, fire off some cutting remark that also happened to be charming. He was masc-presenting tonight, hair neatly braided down his back, wearing a deep jade jacket and flowing black trousers. His many rings caught the light of the holographic fire in the large hearth behind him, including her father's signet ring.

He wasn't completely unapproachable in this crowd, but Dressa didn't miss that only the more established members of the court had gathered around him. Could she be like that? Could she maintain that bubble around herself where she was both in the same room as everyone but also not quite in the same universe? The Seritarchus seemed to play by different rules of physics.

"My daughter." He reached out to clasp her hand.

31

SABOTAGE

> *A subtle word in the right tone in the right ear can build empires. Of course, a subtle word in the wrong tone can as easily end them.*
>
> — LORD ESARA TEOH MÉRON BRINT IN *A GUIDE TO ETIQUETTE AT THE PALACE RHIALDEN COURT*

Dressa's training kept her from startling when she felt something jolt through her with Iata's brief grip. A sense of, what—of more than herself. Of more than her own thoughts. A sense of . . . concentration?

What the hell?

Iata blinked twice, for the briefest moment his expression shifting away from the usual lines of her father's, so subtly she was sure only she could see it.

Then he blinked once more, and he was completely her father again.

Her heart sped up. She hadn't imagined that, had she? No.

Had she accidentally triggered one of his callbacks? But then, what about that jolt? She was sure she hadn't imagined that, either.

Had her mother seen Iata's lapse? But her mother was looking away and only now just turning back.

Lesander, beside Dressa, now read to her as more wary, though she didn't know if that was cued from her or from Iata.

She thought about him running out of his study earlier. He didn't want to tell her whatever was going on with him, but if that was what had made him lapse in public, that was absolutely her business. And what *had* that jolt been? Adeius, what could that possibly have been?

Had it been her own response to seeing his lapse? Had it been a shock, her shoes on the thick carpet?

The Seritarchus studied her, look sardonic, lips still quirked, just that shade of mocking. Absolutely her father.

Dressa's throat tightened. That look made her want to crawl inside herself. Made her want to turn and immediately start another conversation with anyone else. She'd certainly done that before.

"Seritarchus," she said. "And Mother, it's so good to see you here. I absolutely love your hair wrap."

She'd only, truly, just noticed it. It was a shimmery, holographic thing, holding up her mother's elaborate weaving of braids, which plumed up from the back along with thin crystal spikes.

Haneri was not exactly approachable tonight, either, not that anyone here was doing much more than staring and gossiping about her. And not that anyone would dare do much more with the Seritarchus also present.

The Seritarchus's posture, Dressa realized, was protective of her mother, and not in a superficial way. His arm was as tightly wound in Haneri's as Dressa's was in Lesander's. He was absolutely on alert for anyone who might comment on Haneri's sudden presence after five years of seclusion.

Dressa blinked and saw shades of Iata again, not just her father. This time, she was sure, it wasn't a lapse but something only she would notice at all. Would her father be so concerned for his consort's wellbeing? Was her father ever concerned for anyone's wellbeing? Except maybe Arianna's?

"Thank you, Ondressarie," Haneri said graciously, as if Dressa's compliment had been due. "Ah, Lesander. Such luminous diamonds you're wearing tonight. Puts all of these overdressed fuss-plumes to shame. If only everyone else had such impeccable taste." Haneri cast a baleful look around her, and Dressa saw at least one of the nearby nobles wince, another take a timely sip of their wine.

And . . . there. That was the reason why Iata was hovering so closely to her mother, not out of any sort of concern. He was trying to keep her from steamrolling over weeks and months of subtle social manipulations.

Or . . . or had her mother just shifted the attention away from Iata? Had her mother noticed something was wrong and had been doing that all night?

"Thank you, Ser Consort," Lesander said, but only just before Haneri went on:

"And Dressa, that's far too much eyeshadow, you're looking quite as ill as your sister—"

What the hell.

She'd done her own makeup, of course, with some light help from her bloodservant, Pria. She knew the trends. Half the time, she helped set the trends.

That wasn't even the point. Haneri shouldn't have brought up Arianna being sick at all. Had her mother even seen Arianna before she'd left? They all needed to get past that night, not bring it up so blatantly. Iata had spread around that

Arianna had retired to a country estate—though no one had said which estate—to recover. It had plausibly gotten her out of the eyes of the court, at least, and no one was eager to bring up the matter again, at least in public in front of the Seritarchus, while Dressa's position was still so new.

Dressa leaned in and said, "Thank you, Mother, that was quite the effect I was going for." With a smile. With absolutely no barbs in her tone, though everyone who heard it would tell everyone else just how on the mark she'd been.

Haneri herself gave a small smile.

Really, what the hell was her mother playing at? Her mother wasn't by any means dysfunctional at court. She'd always had a barbed tongue, but she'd never been unthinking in her words. Her insults were fully calculated. Had she thought she was giving herself some edge by putting Dressa down? Had she thought she was helping Dressa, because no, it was not in fact helping.

She glanced at Iata again but saw nothing amiss. For now. She would corner him later, in private, and they'd have to talk.

As Dressa and Lesander retreated from her parents, more people approached them, and not quite as stiffly this time. Dressa looked around her, keeping her bewilderment well in check, until she thought again of her mother's insult, and her own very subtle insult back. Had that been the moment of this social shift?

It was as if that exchange had caused a subtle rearrangement of the power structure, with the Seritarchus and Consort being a representation of old and stifling power, while Dressa was a fresh and subtle push against that. Dressa, a force in her own right.

Dressa caught Lesander's eye as they chatted with a middle-aged triad—a lord, his husband, and their wife. Lesander's expression was thoughtful beneath the amiable front she showed to the guests. Dressa was sure her own was, too.

She glanced back at Iata, but his back was turned now as he and Haneri engaged with a more diverse group of guests than they had before. And what in that exchange had made the both of them also seem more approachable? Was it simply that they'd all seemed a bit more Human than what their titles made them out to be? Was a family squabble the best sort of icebreaker?

Lesander leaned in to kiss her on the cheek as they moved on from the triad, heading toward another group.

Dressa smiled, and understood the kiss was partly for show, as she heard some suppressed "awwws" around them, but it warmed her all the same.

"What do you think?" Lesander asked. "Are your parents conspiring for or against us?"

For, Dressa would think. Iata had been nothing but helpful so far, beyond his oddities today. Iata had no reason to sabotage her at all beyond being in the personality of her father. And maybe that was reason enough.

But the way he moved in sync with Haneri made her uneasy, even beyond whatever that brief lapse in personality had been. She wondered if others here would note his ease around Haneri, too, and wondered if Iata even noticed it himself. It seemed a wholly unconscious thing, and one her father had never gained with his wife.

Maybe people would think that was the reason Haneri had come back to court, that she'd somehow found a better rapport with her husband.

Dressa's thoughts drifted back to the kiss Haneri had given him earlier outside the Reception Hall, and Iata's very obvious surprise and not a little distress. And then . . . him kissing her back.

Was there something going on there? Was it new, or was it . . . something else?

Were her parents conspiring for or against her, as Lesander had asked?

"I don't know," Dressa said softly, still watching her parents, not Lesander. Whatever else her mother was trying to accomplish, whatever Iata had going on that he wasn't telling her, none of it was making Dressa's life easier.

32

CHILDREN

> *Everyone in the kingdom can have contract children, except for Truthspoken.*
>
> — ARIANNA RHIALDEN, MELESORIE X IN *THE CHANGE DIALOGUES*

"I want children," Zhang said as she placed her laundered clothes back in her duffel. They'd decided to only stay in Qoriale a few days and instead were going to take a biking trip up the coast, stopping at towns along the way to rest for the night. Or just enjoy the day. They'd decided because he was going stir-crazy not being able to do something productive in the safe house and the town at large, and Zhang wasn't too keen on helping him to stamp out petty crime.

But you couldn't suddenly stop a life of motion.

Homaj was rolling up his socks and slowed, stopped. "What?"

"I wasn't born a guard, Homaj," she said and rolled her eyes. "I do want children. I want to raise two, or maybe three—don't give me that look. I'm hardly too old to chase after children. You either. You're not old. You're not even fifty, not even half of your lifespan, or a third, if you live long enough."

His breath caught, and she held his gaze.

"You—you want children with . . . me?" He pointed to himself, as if there was any other himself in the room. He noticed the gesture and scowled, closed his hand at his side.

Then opened it again, because he was done with control. Absolutely done with control.

She stepped around the bed, approaching cautiously. "I love you. You know that."

He watched her coming, watched every nuance of her guarded anxiety. Her cautious hope.

Would he ever be able to stop watching people? Stop knowing their every mood almost as surely as Iata, as a magicker, could read them with a look or a touch?

Zhang stopped in front of him, leaning on the edge of the bed, watching him with as much intensity as he knew he was watching her.

He fumbled for something to do with his hands, ended up crossing his arms. "You know I just don't . . . I don't love people that way, not romantically. I can do flings, and I love sex, but—"

She snorted. "And I don't tend to want to sleep with people. Not even with you, most of the time. Yet here we are. I'm not asking for exclusivity, Homaj. I'm certainly not asking for more than you can give, and I'm not giving it, either. I just want children with my friend. Whom I love."

She reached and gripped his hands, pulling his arms out of their knot, and he let her. A brief moment, a brief anchoring before she let go again.

"You're my truest friend. I think I'm probably yours as well," she said. "I can't think of anyone else I'd want to have children with."

He shoved a hand through his hair, turned a tight circle. "But—but—"

If he took the oath not to Change, he would no longer be Truthspoken. But could he even legally have children and pass on the Rhialden line? He'd never looked into it. He'd thought he'd be in his seventies when his Heir's second born was old enough to assume the duties of a sanctioned Truthspoken, and then he would step down. Surely he wouldn't want more children then. He'd hardly been able to think of holding the kingdom for that long. He'd hardly been able to think past the next day or week when it came to his personal needs and desires.

"I asked Ceorre," Zhang said. "She told me that, if there's ever a point at which you retire, when Arianna or Dressa would fully step up, and have grown children of their own, that there's no legal reason why you couldn't have more children. You wouldn't be Truthspoken anymore. Your children would be Rhialden, of course, but not Truthspoken. They'd never be trained."

"You asked Ceorre? But—but they'd know they were Rhialden. They might resent not having the position of their older siblings, or the training."

She shrugged. "Sure. Siblings tend to resent each other. But they wouldn't have any less power than any other lesser sibling of a high house."

That didn't fully explain away that problem, but more urgent questions were on his mind. "Are you asking for my DNA, or would you want me to help raise these children? I'm pretty sure I've molded Arianna into a copy of myself and I'm absolutely sure that's not a good thing. Dressa dislikes me so much she hardly speaks to me unless she has to. What makes you think I wouldn't do the same again?"

She sighed, sitting more fully on the bed.

He came around, sat down beside her, the mattress springs creaking.

Zhang. He loved her, yes. Not romantically, not in any way

he could define. But she'd been there since the start of his rule. She'd always been there. He wanted to be there for her in this, too, if she really wanted it.

"I'm certainly not sure I'd be a good mother," she said.

"Yes, well, we have proof that I'm not a good parent. I don't think I'd like to bet on those odds."

She took his hand again, squeezed. "Maja. Just . . . think about it?"

"Do you want to get married?"

"Adeius, no. I don't want anything to change."

He looked at her incredulously. "Seriously, Zhang. Everything, absolutely everything's going to change. Everything."

Her hand tightened around his. "I know."

They sat in the silence, listening to the birds outside the windows. The low hum of the refrigeration unit in the kitchen.

"I'm fucking terrified," he said.

She nodded. Not in agreement, he thought, but in her own statement of terror.

His back was tightening with tension and he arched it, feeling the vertebrae crackle. He didn't try to smooth away the tension, or the lingering ache from his stretch. Soon, he wouldn't be able to. Like a normal Human. Like everyone else. He wouldn't be above pain anymore—oh, he could heal himself if the need was dire, but not unless.

That thought more exhilarated him than terrified, though.

This biking up the coast—he was going to feel the strain in his calves and thighs, he was going to collapse into whatever beds they found in true exhaustion, not the weary soul-exhaustion each day from ruling the kingdom.

He'd have the chance at a normal life. Well, maybe not normal, he was still Rhialden, and still the father of the next ruler, or at least, brother, if Iata stepped up.

Children. Would he want more children? And with Zhang? He'd never given that any thought at all, though he also couldn't think of anyone he'd rather have them with than her. If, hypothetically, he even wanted that. It would hella complicate everything, wouldn't it?

But a chance to start over? Maybe to not make the same mistakes? To raise children, actual children who were allowed to just be children, not Truthspoken? He hadn't treated his children as children, not even when they were young. He hadn't been able to, knowing the weight they would carry someday. One of them, anyhow. Maybe both. He hadn't been able to ease on their training, knowing that his own life could end at any time, assassins could get through his guards, or people he trusted turn against him, like what had happened with his own parents. He couldn't leave them unprepared, with himself gone and a kingdom weighing on their shoulders.

He wished he knew Ari was okay. And Dressa—yes, he knew Iata wouldn't let her fall, but he was sure he'd failed her in teaching her how to adequately rule a kingdom.

But he took a breath and tried to let go of his need to control it all. It wasn't, truly, in his nature. He didn't need to. He could let the competent people in his life be competent. He could move with his own flow, his own life. Ialorius, not Seritarchus.

And if he was no longer Truthspoken—well, he didn't have to be either of those things. If he was no longer a ruler, he didn't need a style of rule.

"I'll think about it," he said softly to Zhang.

33

PERSONALITIES

> *I know myself. I have to know myself, because that's the anchor I always return to.*
>
> — ARIANNA RHIALDEN, MELESORIE X IN *THE CHANGE DIALOGUES*

Jis stood with faer arms crossed as Imorie tried on yet another set of clothes and discarded them. "It's an afternoon back country estate party, not a Valon City ball."

"Well, there's a duke," Imorie said, scowling at a black silk jacket with artfully slashed upper sleeves. She pulled it on over her aqua swoop-necked tank. In the mirror, the holographic swallow next to her eye fluttered.

Jis snorted. "You don't care anything for dukes."

"Well, maybe I do. Maybe this is my one chance to make some sort of an alliance, get out of this social purgatory that's too high for low nobility and too low for high."

Jis narrowed faer eyes. "I've never known you to care about that, either."

Imorie cut a glance sideways.

"And don't you think you're overdoing it?" Jis went on. "You get one good day, one really good day for you walking around the garden, that doesn't mean you have all the energy in the world. The physician said you needed to not push yourself right now. The treatment's working, it's helping at least. Maybe stay in this afternoon and catch the next party, and if you're still feeling better then—"

"I'm going." Imorie side-belted her tan trousers and tied a white sash around her waist, draped in tinkling gold ornaments. She leaned forward, grabbed a lipstick tube off a side table and dialed the color to the same blue as her hair.

Yes. That worked. She'd need to go heavier around her eyes —or maybe not. Blue was good. Blue was excellent.

Jis shifted, biting faer lower lip. Imorie knew that look. That was faer "What's gotten into you?" stare.

"What? I'm here on a vacation planet. I want to have a vacation. It's sunny, it's not too hot today, the party will probably spill over into the yard, and I can get on with the business of not looking like I've been shut up in my rooms for three days. The physician also said the gardens are good medicine."

Jis didn't contradict this, but Imorie felt the silence growing thicker.

"Anyhow. I'm going down. Follow if you want."

Jis followed as she strode toward the suite's door. "I'll escort you."

"No, I'm fine."

Jis caught her arm, and—

Ari gasped as she was slammed back into herself. She gripped Bettea's shoulder, holding tight until the vertigo passed. It was another moment before she had enough possession of herself to keep her persona squarely as Imorie, for the benefit of anyone who might be watching.

She glared at Bettea. She'd been doing fine. She hadn't been submerged for more than a day, and as herself—as herself, the panic started curling up again, all the little fears and frustrations that had been building until they felt like smothering vines.

She'd spent too much time in the gardens yesterday. Imorie had. Ari would never have spent so much time with one of the staff. Eti was diverting, yes, and his own puzzle, but Imorie was far too obsessed with him. He took her mind off of . . . well. Everything else.

Which maybe wasn't a bad thing.

Which maybe was entirely a bad thing. It was far, far too easy to lose yourself being someone in truth if it was more appealing than being who you actually were.

Ari closed her eyes, breathed, opened them again to meet Bettea's much more speculative stare.

Bettea tilted faer head—a gesture eerily like her father's. And that had absolutely been intentional.

Adeius. Was she losing herself? It had only been a few days, and Jis—Bettea—had been calling her back whenever fae could. Whenever fae dared. Truthspoken were cautioned not to submerge themselves for more than a few hours at most, though, and days submerged were strongly discouraged, even if there were breaks in between.

But she did have more energy now than when she'd first come to Hestia—the only reason she'd submerged was to protect her identity while she had no energy to do that on her own. Did she have enough now?

Ari probed through her body, sensing all its various aches which had not gone away, but had maybe returned to the state they'd been in before she'd left Valon. Before she'd collapsed at the ball.

Her mind was sharper, if not what it should be. Sharp enough, though.

"All right, maybe I do need an escort," she said, leaning on

Bettea. This was the act now. And she was so exceedingly glad that it could be, even if only in part.

"You're still going down?" Bettea asked. "You know you don't have to go to this party."

"I told Duke Kyran I would be there," she said, swallowing her distaste into Imorie's more open pragmatism.

She felt into Imorie's emotions and motivations just before Bettea had called her back just now. Imorie had wanted to go to that party to, foremost, get out of this suite—and with that Ari wholeheartedly agreed. But why had Imorie been thinking of Duke Koldari? She had been. She'd seriously been thinking he could be a path to a better life. That—that was more than a little troubling, and another danger of remaining as someone in truth for too long, especially when that personality was crafted, and not someone Ari was trying to impersonate. Personalities could diverge quickly and take on lives of their own.

But Imorie was hardly more attracted to Kyran than Ari was, which was not at all. Not even to his power, truly. Was Imorie seriously that desperate to get out of her mediocre life?

Or maybe that lonely. Ari suppressed a shudder.

As herself, she wasn't nearly as interested in going to the party, although the thought of getting a feel for the people around her in her own mind and not Imorie's was appealing. She didn't want to spend yet another afternoon in this room, no matter who she was. Maybe she shouldn't have taken that garden excursion with Eti yesterday, but—well. The weather was ideal, and Imorie wasn't wrong that the sunshine was good for her stiff muscles, her aching joints.

Imorie hadn't just been thinking about the duke in wanting to get out, either. Imorie's thoughts had been increasingly consumed with Eti. Not attraction—Ari had built Imorie's persona to be just as indifferent to physical romance as she was, and with her being ace, attraction could only ever be simulated, regardless of persona. But Imorie felt a draw toward Eti nonetheless. Maybe only curiosity, but maybe that was best stopped now, too.

Ari wasn't as obsessed with finding out Eti's situation as Imorie was, but she did share Imorie's dislike of how he'd been treated by Ryam, the head gardener. And Eti had gone out of his way to help her more than once. So call it paying back a favor, or call it boredom, but she'd see what layers and nuances she could find there. Likely, most likely, she'd just find a nest of petty estate politics.

And with the rest of the estate and its guests, she'd certainly find a spillover of greater Valoran politics—you couldn't have a gathering of any two nobles without some sort of politics. But she doubted she'd find anything as intricate as what she dealt with regularly in the palace.

Yes, she could handle this today.

And maybe if she could handle this today, she was on her way back to being able to Change again. She wanted that so badly the need felt like it would swallow her if she thought on it too long.

Bettea sighed.

"I'll be fine," Ari said. "Really."

"Yes, fine. Let me just make sure I'm suitable to escort you down. I'll only be a minute."

Ari didn't see what could make Bettea more presentable—Bettea, as Jis, was always presentable, just now in plain but well-made cream pants and a tunic jacket, light gold hair pulled up in a high bun.

Ari stared after faer. Bettea was only two years older than she was, and yet she usually managed to think of faer as much older than that. Bettea was Arianna's bloodservant, and they'd both been raised to that relationship, but here—Jis Ameer was a personal servant, and also a friend. It wasn't a dynamic she was foreign to, but it held a different context here.

If Bettea didn't have to worry about Ari, would fae want to go to the party faerself? If fae wasn't here as a servant?

Imorie's different view of the social ladder was getting into her head.

Bettea swished back, and the only difference Ari could see was gold hoops in both ears, another in faer septum. That septum ring was new today. Fae must have pierced it when Ari had been sleeping. Had Bettea been bored? Was that Bettea's way of coping with this ridiculousness they'd both been thrust into?

Bettea saw her looking, but didn't comment. Fae held out faer arm.

"All right, Ser Rhialden méron Quevedo, we go down."

34

INFORMATION GATHERING

> *So what if you had a friend for years, you saw them once a month or so, but they were dependable. They treated you well, you did things together. And what if one day you learned they were Truthspoken. What would you do? Would that mean your entire friendship was a lie?*
>
> — ANONYMOUS37494-J9 IN THE CHATSPHERE *HELP I THINK I MET A TRUTHSPOKEN*

Duke Koldari had told Imorie at dinner the night before that parties on this day of the week were reserved for more sedate and genteel dances. He'd said it with absolutely no irony, as if it was a perfectly normal thing to have enough parties that you could, in fact, reserve some for those who didn't like the livelier crowd. If Ari hadn't just spent days inhabiting a lesser Rhialden unused to a courtly social scene, maybe she might have said something like that without irony, too.

Even this apparently slower music was still uncomfortably

loud. She stepped into what only on Hestia could be called a ballroom—hardly larger than the estate's dining room, if a bit more ornate. The current song was a rock ballad from a few decades ago, the music synced with holographic bokeh spheres floating around the guests.

"I'll leave you," Bettea said in her ear. "I'll be in the staff room or right around there if you need me."

Ari nodded, started to square herself to enter, but then, no, that wasn't how Imorie would meet this current challenge. She'd had more practice in the last few days in *being* Imorie than playing the role of Imorie, and that was a very different thing.

Ari stood uncertainly just inside, holding one arm in what she knew was her own nervous gesture that she almost never let anyone see. She surveyed the guests around her. Some she recognized from the few estate dinners she'd attended, or from having seen them around the grounds. She spotted Kyran Koldari across the room, wine glass in hand, laughing with a small group of nobles. He looked as well-polished and confident as ever, a natural gravitational point for this party. Near his group, but not even remotely in the same social hemisphere, the group from the Onabrii-Kast Dynasty swayed to the music while they held their own animated conversation.

There were many guests she didn't recognize. Locals? People coming in from other estates? She didn't honestly know how many other estates were nearby, a vast oversight on her part, though she did remember the number of cars parked outside the day she'd arrived. There had to be enough neighbors for that kind of traffic.

Cautiously, she stepped further into the room and made her way toward a long table set to one side, heaped with plates of refreshments. A quick scan of the offerings found food barely on par with Valon standards, but, well, she wasn't on Valon.

She was Imorie. She was a contract Rhialden. She wasn't supposed to have those standards.

Ari wasn't hungry, but she grabbed a plate, grabbed two pink and green pastries from a stand, and hovered back into the nearest corner.

Her hand was just slightly shaking as she brought a pastry to her mouth, and she chewed quickly and swallowed hard.

She was panicking again. Why? Oh, Adeius, why? She could play a role in her sleep. She knew how to be Imorie, she knew how to work a crowd, she was Truthspoken. She shouldn't have any problems here finding out what she wanted to know about the estate and its current residents. And hopefully that would inform her more about Eti and his situation here, too.

Her eyes stung, and it galled her that she couldn't reach any kind of trance to smooth the unwanted response away.

She saw someone approaching to her left and turned, tensed.

Eti waved, balancing a tray of used pastry plates in his other hand.

She relaxed.

Imorie hadn't seen him that morning, though she'd looked out her windows, hoping to. Today, he was dressed the same as the household serving staff. She was coming to think his place on the estate was to fill in wherever he was needed.

"Hi," he said. "Are you okay?"

He didn't look at her, not quite. At least, he didn't meet her eyes.

"Fine," she said, and forced another bite of the pastry.

No, that wasn't fair. He'd purposely come over to check on her, she knew that.

She wiped the edge of her mouth. "I thought I felt a little better than I do, honestly. But it's good to be out of my room.

Uh, you weren't in the gardens today?" She nodded at his house staff clothing.

His cheeks reddened, and he studied the floor. "Yeah, earlier. I was tending to the new grafts again."

Ari had the distinct impression that was a lie. And why would he lie about that? Was he embarrassed about the run-in with the head gardener, Ryam, the day before?

Before she could pursue that, or sort through Imorie's memories or her own thoughts, Ari sensed a shift in the room. There was a barely perceptible rearrangement of social awareness that prickled at her Truthspoken senses.

She looked up to see Kyran Koldari sauntering her way. Oh, Adeius. She truly did not want to deal with him right now.

Her instinct was to reach for Imorie and submerge herself again, but as she thought it, Eti hovered a little closer, his shoulder almost touching hers. Protectively? He'd done that the first night she'd come down, too. Was he trying to ward off Kyran because he knew the duke to be a boor—which was true —or was he simply moving with her own tension?

Did he have any evaku? Was that even possible for him, a gardener and a servant, who'd fled some shadowy past on Kalistré? A Javieri vassal world. There was some minor nobility on that world. Could that be part of why he was so reluctant to talk about his past or his family? Or was she so trained in court intrigue that she was now spotting it where it didn't exist, and he was just one of those rare people who genuinely cared about those around him?

She didn't have time to study Eti's face now.

Duke Koldari captured her hand, bowed over it, and tucked it into his arm before she had the chance to jerk it out—and by then, she knew the best course was to let him feel like he'd won whatever victory he was angling for at the moment. As much as him touching her made her want to change her clothes, Imorie didn't have enough clout here to safely deny him overstepping her bounds. Not in this context, not in public. And maybe hovering around Kyran would give her the insight into the dynamics here she was increasingly sure were important.

Why had he only cut toward her when he'd seen her with Eti? Had he only just seen her, or was this some weird possessiveness like he'd demonstrated a few nights before at her first dinner here? And why was Eti so bent on protecting her from him, at the risk of his own position, even? Beyond the obvious fact that Kyran was a domineering ass?

"I'm sorry he's bothering you," Kyran said. He snapped his fingers at another nearby servant and pointed to Eti.

"No, he wasn't," Ari protested. "I was feeling faint, and he asked if I was all right."

"You should have come to me," Kyran said.

Ari didn't point out that he'd been across the room, and if she was feeling faint, how was she supposed to get to him?

She glanced back toward Eti to see the other servant hustling him toward the kitchens.

35

THE FIGHT

> *Yes, sadly, there have been times when magickers have used their abilities to exploit others. We are still Human, after all, and subject to all the Human fallacies as any of you. But far more often, magicker abilities have been exploited by others.*
>
> — FIRST MAGICKER MARIYIT BRODEN IN AN ADDRESS TO THE GENERAL ASSEMBLY

Herded by Uralin, one of the meaner house servants, Eti stumbled just inside the kitchen threshold and barely caught the tray of plates before it slid out of his hands.

"Clumsy fool!" Uralin thwacked the side of Eti's head.

"Hey, hey!"

Eti looked up to see Imorie's personal servant, Jis, storming down on them. Fae had hastily set down a tray heaped high with sandwich rolls and squared up to Uralin.

"What the hell do you think you're doing, hitting the staff?"

"You're not a Windvale employee," Uralin said, leaning into Jis's space.

"I'm an employee of one of the guests—"

Eti backed away, setting his tray down on the nearest counter.

He looked around him, hardly taking in the kitchen and the staff that had stopped to watch the confrontation. He headed toward the door that led to the pantry, then beyond it to the back service entry and then—outside.

Oh gods, he needed air. He'd seen too much. He'd been trying to avoid Imorie that day, but Ryam had co-opted him again into serving at the party, saying it would be a good information gathering opportunity, seeing how Eti wasn't doing his job so well lately.

Eti was doing his job just fine.

But he'd seen Imorie hovering near the corner, the sense of her soul so unraveled that he couldn't help but draw near.

She'd looked at him, and before he could stop it, and without even meeting her eyes, he knew she wasn't Imorie. Not the same person who'd been with him in the garden the day before. She was—she was a person Ryam and his other handlers would want to know about. And he had to forget. He had to go find a tree now and forget again, before they got the information out of him.

A hand clamped over his wrist, squeezing hard.

"Where are you going, Eti?"

He froze, looking up into Ryam's smugly triumphant grin.

"I knew you would try to sneak off," Ryam said, sounding winded. "Saw you on the security feed with the contract Rhialden. Knew you'd try and go do whatever magic you think you can to hide what you owe me."

His fingers dug into Eti's arm and Eti grunted, his shoulder twitching with the need to break free.

"So what did you find out? What's so important that you'd risk—"

The thoughts came too quickly, too easily to the surface of Eti's mind. They were still too fresh, the need to be rid of them too strong.

Truthspoken. Imorie wasn't just a Rhialden, and not even a minor one. She was Truthspoken.

Ryam sucked in a sharp breath. "Oh, fuck." He stared at Eti in growing horror. "You're sure?"

Eti closed his eyes. He tried to fold in on himself and disappear, but of course it wouldn't work. He might flicker a little, but Ryam knew he was there.

"Stop that," Ryam said, shaking his arm. "You're sure, Eti? Was she sent to investigate us? Does she know about you, and our operation here?" He shook Eti again, harder this time.

"I don't know, I don't know!"

"What the hell!" another voice called. Jis again, now storming outside. "Why is everyone out to get this man!"

"Back off!" Ryam shouted, with a vehemence that made Jis pause. "This is estate business and none of yours. Eti—come with me." He dragged Eti toward another door, one of the side entrances back into the house.

Eti looked back at Jis, and for a moment, just a moment, let his aura flare.

Jis, who'd started to step after them again, froze. Eti watched as first realization and then terror dawned. If Jis was regularly around Truthspoken, he had to trust fae would know what it meant for an unsealed magicker to be in a household such as this.

Jis turned, tensing to run back into the house for Imorie.

But Ryam, still holding Eti's arm, felt Eti's intent and the flare of his aura. He stopped, pulled a slim stun pistol from inside his jacket, and shot Jis before fae got more than three steps away. Jis crumpled, falling into a heap on the ground.

"No!" Eti shouted. But the muzzle of the pistol pointed his way now.

"I'll shoot and drag you inside."

Would that be better? Would it take him longer to wake up, and then he wouldn't be able to tell them anything more?

But he also wouldn't be able to help if he could. To divert them if he could. Oh gods. If he saw Imorie, he'd yell for her to run, and pray to She Who Runs that she could.

Ryam resumed dragging him toward the house, and he didn't resist, because he knew he couldn't win that fight.

36

THE MESSAGE

> *Truthspoken must be ever watchful, not just because it's our holy mandate to watch over our kingdom, but because so many see it as theirs instead.*
>
> — ARIANNA RHIALDEN, MELESORIE X IN *THE CHANGE DIALOGUES*

Duke Kyran led Ari to the group he'd been talking with before, only half of whom she recognized as guests of the estate.

A young masc person reached up and kissed Kyran on the cheek, and Kyran smiled.

"One of my partners, Iwan, newly arrived on Hestia. They and them. Iwan, this is Imorie Rhialden méron Quevedo."

"A Rhialden," Iwan said, delighted. "Oh, and a contract Rhialden. Kyran, what a treat. You don't see too many of those."

Ari's lips tightened into a smile. "That's because there's not that many of us to go around." She carefully pulled her arm from the duke's grip and put just a bit of space between herself and him.

Kyran smiled down at her, as if he knew exactly what she was doing. As if he'd planned for her to react this way.

She would stay for two minutes. She would indulge him that far, just long enough to not stand out more than if she turned around and left now.

"And a Quevedo," another of the nobles pointed out. "Imorie, your family are the Quevedos that work in antiquities, correct? From Gray Moss?"

"Correct," she said tightly.

"You very much look Rhialden," an older person with a thin mustache said. They pushed back a strand of pink hair. "Except, you know, a little less bottled up. Have you met any of your more famous cousins?"

Who the hell did these people think they were that they could interrogate a Rhialden, no matter how lesser a Rhialden, about the Truthspoken?

"I have," she snapped. "It was a singular experience."

Kyran rested a hand on her shoulder. "Forgive my friends, their manners are lacking, as always." He shrugged. "But honesty can be refreshing. Imorie, would you care for wine?" He snatched a glass from a nearby servant's tray and handed it to her.

She took it, and took a sip, just enough to wet her dry throat. What did Kyran want from her? Surely not to add her to his rotating roster of partners. His body language wasn't truly that way toward her, not sexual in nature so much as possessive. Did he want to add her connections, then, no matter that they weren't that functionally high?

Iwan said, "Imorie, as a Rhialden—"

"Contract Rhialden."

"Yes, contract Rhialden then, what do you think of these Kidaa attacks? Do you think they're actually from the Kidaa?"

Ari's brows knit as she focused fully back on the group, who were watching her closely. "Kidaa attacks?"

Had there been? And no, there couldn't have been. There were sometimes rumors of strange things happening on border worlds, but every rumor always checked out to be something other than the Kidaa, because of course it did. The Kidaa had never shown much interest in their Human neighbors.

But was this in the news that she hadn't read for the last few days? Even as Imorie, she had wanted to set the things from the capital aside. And was it a wild rumor, or related to some other problem?

"I haven't been paying attention to the news, sorry," she said, and shrugged, taking another sip of her wine. "What happened?"

The music changed from a slow pop melody to a more rhythmic lounge beat. Ari's head stabbed with a headache.

Iwan and the pink-haired person launched into an overlapping account of three separate attacks on worlds near the Kidaa border, one of them being on Sangor Brec, Duke Kyran's homeworld.

Kyran seemed less troubled by this than he should have been, his face remaining mostly neutral, creasing in angst at all the appropriate times.

"We don't know it's the Kidaa," Kyran said, holding a hand palm down in a quelling gesture. "And of course, I have my people looking into it."

"Yes, but, a Javieri world was attacked as well," Iwan said. "Maybe the Kidaa—or someone who wants it to look like the Kidaa—is targeting high houses. Who will be next?"

"Most worlds in Valoris are owned or protected by high houses," Kyran said. "That hardly means anything here. But if it is an attack on my person and my land, I will of course seek the fullest justice." He took a drink, as if he was bored with the subject. "Imorie, have you seen the latest episode of *Nova Hearts?* The one where Olun and the prince finally, Adeius, *finally*, get—"

Iwan swatted at him. "No, Kyran, you'll spoil it!"

Kyran grinned, stepped out of reach.

Ari sighed inwardly and glanced toward the other side of the room. She no longer saw Eti. But she did see Count Badem striding toward them, posture open and smile wide. There was something tight around her edges, though, that set Ari's nerves on end.

"Good evening, my guests," Badem said, inclining her head. "Imorie, it's good to see you—and oh, you must be Iwan?" She reached a hand toward Kyran's partner. "I've heard so much about you. Make sure to give me a dance tonight, hmm?"

Iwan agreed enthusiastically, but Ari's attention was caught on the very subtle interplay of body language happening between Kyran and the count. Kyran's mannerisms had gone just that shade stiffer, and the count seemed impatient and agitated. They glanced at each other only once directly, but that look held a mutual distaste, though neither of them seemed inclined to step away from the group.

"I'm actually here for Imorie," Badem said. "A secured message came in on the estate channels for you. Will you step outside with me, and I'll take you to my office?"

Ari's sense of unease heightened. A message? No one but Bettea and her father knew she was here, and her father wouldn't send a message unless the circumstances were truly dire. He would have received the network pingback of her new identity—there was enough time for that to have reached him, messages on drones traveled much faster than ships with passengers and crew. But was there enough time for him to have sent a message back? Maybe just possibly. Adeius, was this going to be his confirmation that she was officially out of the line of succession? That she wasn't just no longer the Heir, but no longer Truthspoken?

Count Badem's tightly contained body language, though,

bothered her. The count wouldn't be so agitated if this was just a secured message reaching a guest.

She had a moment's hesitation in following the count—but really, what harm could come to her in Badem's office? Here, where there were multitudes of guests? She'd read the message, she'd leave.

Should she ask for Bettea? But that could be read as insulting, and she didn't want to insult the host.

"Excuse me." She dipped a bow to Kyran and his crowd. "Pleasure to meet you all."

"And you, of course, Contract Rhialden." Iwan grinned, twittering their fingers at her.

Kyran gave her the smallest bow. "I'll save a dance for when you return."

Then Ari followed Badem out of the ballroom.

37

TEA AND CONVERSATION

> *The abdication of a ruler is always a turning point.*
>
> — TRUTHSPEAKER CEORRE GATRI, AS QUOTED IN *THE CHANGE DIALOGUES*

They sat in his study, sat in chairs and on the couch around the central table, because they all knew this wasn't going to be a short talk.

Homaj, Iata, and Ceorre. Homaj had wanted Zhang there as well, but she'd adamantly, and probably wisely, refused to be a part of this one.

Iata, across from him, poured the steaming tea, the whole pot Homaj's usual preference. Iata poured with a sardonic bent to his lips, and he was doing absolutely nothing to drop his mannerisms as the Seritarchus.

Homaj watched him warily, trying to unpack the layers. But —but he was exhausted. And not even the days of not being the Seritarchus himself had left him energy enough. Biking up the coast had been fantastic. He'd let the wind whip his hair from his face, take away his struggles for a time. If he kept moving, maybe everything else wouldn't catch up to him again. And then there was Zhang, and what she'd asked of him. He hadn't been able to stop thinking about it.

That was, until he and Zhang had slipped back through the underground tunnels, back into the palace and into the back corridors of the residence wing. Then, it was as if all the air had gone out of him. He'd felt any warmth of the last few days draining away into . . . this place. This state of being. This enormous weight he wasn't sure he could cast off, and he wasn't sure he should try.

And still they were all here, everyone but Zhang, and he found himself intensely annoyed that she'd dodged out of this. No matter that Iata and Ceorre might not appreciate her presence as much as he did. No matter that she absolutely could not be seen to have any influence over him, even here, among the rest of his family. She was still the captain of his guard for a little while longer, and it wasn't appropriate at all for a guard to decide the fate of the kingdom.

He was about done with doing the appropriate thing.

Well, and that was why they were all here.

Iata handed a steaming cup, and the milk and syrup, to Ceorre—she had never liked Homaj's favorite teas. Why hadn't Iata used the infusers? Was making the whole pot Homaj's preference a subtle dig at Homaj's authority here, or meant as a kindness?

It was the sort of thing he himself would do. That tiny detail, just one detail, to set the entire meeting off. To set the person he was meeting guessing.

With Iata still so very palpably and purposefully Homaj Rhialden, Homaj felt the person he was inside himself freeze.

He didn't know who to be here. It didn't feel like any other time he'd been around Iata as the Seritarchus. This felt like nothing else at all. So he leaned back into the persona he'd adopted around Zhang the last week—he was still wearing that face and body—and swiped his hair out of his eyes. And yet that felt wrong, too, because that persona had started to blend into—into he didn't know what. Into something that was maybe not a persona at all, but also wasn't an absence of one, either.

He watched Iata pour a cup for him, mercilessly drawing out the moment. Why was Iata trying to provoke him? Iata knew he'd had a rough week—but, ah. So had Iata. And Iata had been the one cleaning up Homaj's messes.

He decided he had no energy left not to get to the point.

"I want you to be the Seritarchus," he said.

Iata looked up mid-pour, then swore as the cup overflowed. He sat back, scrambling for something to wipe up the spill, grabbing a ridiculously expensive throw off the back of his chair to sop up the tea before it fell on the ridiculously expensive rug.

"Augh!" Iata scowled at the throw, holding it dripping over the table. "Ambassador Mura will not be pleased. This was on loan, wasn't it?"

Homaj sat back, feeling numb.

He had decided in favor of Iata this last week. He and Zhang had argued it long into most of the nights, whether he should step down in favor of Dressa or Iata. Both choices had come with risks, but in the end, he thought Iata was much more able to handle the complex mess of issues the Seritarcracy was currently plagued with. Even if Iata might have to—at least eventually, and hopefully after he was already confirmed as the Seritarchus—admit he was also a Green Magicker. Even if, up front, they'd have to admit that he was Homaj's full older sibling, and that would add its own mess into the mix. But the alternative—throwing a very young and unprepared Dressa into the fire—was not better. And there was still the problem, the unknown, of Lesander.

Ceorre eyed him, reaching to help Iata clean the mess.

"Homaj. Maja," she said. "Are you saying you want Iata to be Seritarchus for a while? Do you need an extended break?"

He knew that she knew he'd meant more than that. But he sensed, too, that she needed time to process.

"No, Ceorre. No. That's not what I'm saying."

Iata cleared the tray on the table, wiping up more spill as he set cups and pot and snack plates aside.

"Here," Ceorre said, reaching for the sopping throw. She strode from the room with more force than necessary. And was back again, swinging the door wide before Homaj worked up the nerve to meet Iata's eyes. Iata wasn't trying too hard to meet his, either.

Ceorre headed straight for him, accusing finger out. "You. You want to quit."

The words hit him like a fist to the gut. "I'm done, Ceorre. Truly done. I don't think rest will change that. Not even a lot of rest."

The last week hadn't—it had only deepened his resolve. It had only shown him how dry his well really was. He'd wrung himself out, squeezed his soul for every last drop of himself and then invented more when he was truly empty, for too many years.

Iata didn't ask why. Iata knew why. Iata had dealt with the strain of holding together an entire kingdom this last week, and so many weeks before then.

Ceorre's face rippled through emotions, which was rare enough, but settled squarely on determination. She nodded and sat down again with a slow release of breath.

38

WITNESS

> *While we can only observe Truthspoken from a distance, history has told us that Truthspoken will seldom protest the requirement of abdication and swearing off the use of their trained abilities when a fourth Truthspoken comes into play. One can only wonder if this cessation of duty is a relief, and not the loss of power it would at first seem.*
>
> — DR. IGNI CHANG IN "DISCOURSE ON THE HUMANITY OF OUR RULERS"

Iata wiped the last of the spilled tea from his hands. "So you want me to continue to be you? I can do that in the short term, even a few months. But after that, I'll have to arrange for Dressa to make her bid to rule. I can't be you indefinitely."

"You're not me now," Homaj snapped. He waved at Iata. At Iata being Homaj Rhialden. "This isn't me. You know this isn't me, it's a role I've played for so long I thought it was me, but it isn't."

"It's not me either, Maja. I'll train Dressa as well as I can. I can wait at least until after the wedding. And then—" He ran a hand through his hair. Homaj's gesture.

Iata caught himself, sighed, and eased his hold on being the Seritarchus, relaxing back into his own mannerisms.

Part of the knot gnawing at Homaj's insides eased. And then it was like looking at his brother again, his twin who was not truly his twin.

"Then what," Iata continued, "do I fake my death? Do I abdicate? Abdication could be disastrous after Arianna just did so."

Homaj couldn't quite hide his flinch. Iata paused, but didn't apologize.

"No," Homaj said. "Yan. I want you to be the Seritarchus. Not Dressa, she's not ready."

"More ready than you think. She's done excellently this last week. I have been training her every spare minute I have, catching her up on everything she needs to know as the Heir. A few months, and I believe she could be ready to rule, if one of us at least helps from the sidelines."

"If it was Ari, maybe," Homaj said. "But—no. I want you to be the Seritarchus. Iata byr Rhialden. No—just Iata Rhialden. The 'byr' is a fabrication of our father, anyway."

Ceorre, who'd let them talk, held up a hand. "Maja, that isn't possible—"

"It is possible—"

"—wait, wait—and you know why. Iata can't hide his aura indefinitely."

"I'm struggling to do so now," Iata said, and to the point, let his forest green aura flare around him. He grimaced in the relief that gave him. "If I do have to be the Seritarchus for these next few months, I will likely be close to your own state of burnout."

"Which is why you need to be yourself," Homaj said,

spreading his hands, a gesture very unlike his own that he'd given himself this last week.

Iata's cheek twitched. "Will you stop that? You're not—just be yourself, Maja, we're alone here—"

"And who the fuck would that be, Yan? I don't know who I am."

Ceorre stood now, still holding up her hands. "It's not possible, because if you bring out that bloodservants are fully Truthspoken, you topple the whole house of cards. The balance between Truthspoken and Truthspeaker and the nobility and the common people is so delicate, you both know that. Iata can't be himself—"

"Maybe there don't need to be bloodservants," Homaj said. "Maybe it was a cruelty to begin with."

Iata scowled at him. "I'm not upset that I exist, Brother."

"But that's just it. You're not a bloodservant. You never should have been a bloodservant, you should have been the Seritarchus from the start."

"Adeius." Iata dropped his face in his hands, scrubbing hard. "Maja. I appreciate the sentiment, but—"

Homaj stood from the couch, wove around the center table, and knelt down in front of his brother.

Iata was shaking his head, eyes widening in horror. "No. What are you doing? No, Maja, get up." He tried to pull Homaj up, but Homaj braced against the table.

"Ceorre," Homaj said. "Witness. Systems: record, highest security encryption. I, Homaj Rhialden, abdicate—" He dodged Iata's palm aimed at his mouth, jumped back, fast-stepped backward to put himself behind the couch. "I abdicate in favor of Iata Rhialden, born a full Truthspoken heir to the Kingdom of Valoris. He is my brother, fully, by blood. He is the eldest of us two."

Iata lurched to his feet, face dangerously red, and strode toward him. "Homaj, I swear—"

Homaj danced back again and said quickly, "I'm not Truthspoken. I've never been Truthspoken."

Iata stopped. "By that logic, Maja, neither am I! Our two eldest siblings would hold those roles, and they are both gone!"

"Then it falls next to you," Homaj rasped, "then to me." He was still backing, and Iata finally pinned him against the wall, an arm on each side.

Iata stared at him, panting. His face twisted in rage, in anguish, in . . . hope? He was trying to suppress the hope, and Adeius, Homaj saw the war going on there.

"I witness," Ceorre said quietly, and Homaj sagged, his knees giving out.

Iata, after a moment, followed him to the floor to sit across from him. Staring at him, looking blank. "What the hell did you just do? Maja, what the hell did you just do?"

39

RULING THE KINGDOM

> *We can plan, we can discover, we can manipulate. We can do everything in our considerable power to make sure events go forth in the way we wish them to. And sometimes it works.*
>
> — HOMAJ RHIALDEN, SERITARCHUS IX IN A PRIVATE LETTER, NEVER SENT; PUBLISHED IN *THE CHANGE DIALOGUES*

Homaj's heart was racing so fast he couldn't talk.

It was over. The worst of it was over. Was he free now? For once in his life, free?

Ceorre came over, dragging the desk chair so she could sit nearby.

Homaj glanced up, and she looked down, brows pinched.

"Maja. You know that abdicating means you will have to swear not to use your Truthspoken abilities from here forward. There can only legally be three Truthspoken."

"We've hardly been following the law these last twenty or so years," Homaj said.

"Even so. It is something everyone will expect, because once you've abdicated, and Dressa and Arianna are still the heirs, I'm not able to balance you any more as Truthspeaker. The people will want reassurances that you won't go rogue and spy on them for the new ruler—that's the deal we have with them. Only three. Enough power, but not too much."

That was the part that had kept him up at night these last days, after he and Zhang had spent themselves arguing and testing various strategies into the night. He'd wanted—very much needed—to sleep with her again one of those nights, but whatever gave her that occasional desire, it hadn't come again. So he'd found a nearby tavern, found a gruffly handsome man who smelled a bit too much of stale beer. He'd made the first move and had lost himself to that sweet oblivion for a while.

He would no longer have that power of anonymity. Whatever he decided he'd Change himself into as his final form—and he didn't think it should be who he'd been all these years as the Seritarchus, but was unsure of exactly who he should be—that was it. That was who he would be forever.

He wasn't sure if the thought was terrifying or horribly liberating.

"I get one last Change," he said, "I know that much. Then, I'll take the oath."

Ceorre closed her eyes, breathing out. "All right. All right. Iata?"

Iata was staring into the space beside him, slowly kneading his hands together. His aura rippled around him, and Homaj could almost taste Iata's distress from where he sat. He wasn't sure if that was his own evaku, or Iata's magics.

Iata's attention snapped back, his aura stilling.

"Maja. I'm a magicker. The people—the nobility—will not accept me. And someone will put my rank seal together with Sodan Iseban, they'll have to. It's not a hard leap."

"So we'll get the First Magicker to make you a new one, and

use that one in public. It would be a very small thing when he's getting a magicker in control of the kingdom."

Homaj tilted his head back, stared up at the ceiling. He had the strangely disorienting thought that soon this room wouldn't be his anymore. This study, where he'd spent so much of his time it was almost more familiar than the room he slept in. This apartment wouldn't be his. This palace wouldn't be, either.

"Didn't say it would be easy," he went on. "But it is your birthright." He looked down. "I abdicated. You are the Seritarchus."

"Not yet," Ceorre interjected. "He'll need to make his bid to rule and wait out the ten days of any challenge to his claim. And Iata, if you intend to lead with your magics, there will be many challenges. There will be so many questions. The high houses could see this as a bid for magicker power and fight that for all its worth. A Seritarchus who can read the lies in anyone around him?"

"I can do that now," Homaj said. "Evaku is remarkably close to Green Magics in that capacity."

"But the nobility don't see it that way. Evaku is a thing that can be learned. It takes skill, yes, and requires mastery, but it can be learned. Green Magics are random. It might be easier, and better for the kingdom, for Dressa to make her bid instead."

"She could be ready enough, in a few months," Iata said.

But Homaj saw the look in his eyes. He knew Iata wasn't going to let the idea of ruling as himself go that easily. As much as he'd protested, as much as he'd fought it, it was, truly, what he'd always wanted, a thing he'd never thought he could have.

"But," Iata said, sighing again, "I don't see Dressa being able to hold down this kingdom on her own for several years yet. She needs training, and that requires one of us—and I do not trust she has her bearings yet around Lesander, either. One or both of us need to be here to watch what the Javieri prince intends to do."

Yes, because the Javieris wouldn't go through all the trouble of training an illicit Truthspoken, and marrying her to the Heir, if she wasn't meant to do something with those abilities.

Iata waved his hands, weaving through the thought. "If Dressa's the ruler, there's no good excuse for either of us to be around—you won't be able to, and my position as bloodservant will be severely demoted if there's no Truthspoken for me to serve. I'm expected to go with you and fade away from court politics. You realize you're putting yourself in voluntary exile—even if you don't leave, which you'll probably end up having to do anyway—you'll at very least be in exile at court. You'll hardly be better than Haneri—"

Iata stopped. His mouth pulled tight, a curious heat coming into his eyes before it faded just as quickly. Adeius, what was that?

"You'll need to talk to Haneri," Iata said. "I think—isn't the marriage contract nullified on abdication?"

"Yes," Homaj said softly, watching Iata's reaction. But whatever had crossed his brother's features before was carefully guarded against now.

Iata nodded. "As mother to Truthspoken, she can keep her position at court, but it will also be drastically reduced, especially with Lesander now in residence. It's already been reduced."

Homaj felt the details piling up, trying to overwhelm, but he pushed back for all he was worth.

He held up both hands. "We'll work it out. I've abdicated, that's done, but it's not fully official yet until I take the oath not to Change, is it?" He turned to Ceorre.

"No, it's not. Not the Truthspoken part of it." She didn't look happy about any of this. And truly, though he felt relief on the horizon, he wasn't happy, either.

"We need to tell Dressa," Iata said, tapping a finger on the floor. "She needs to know all of it. She knows about you and me, she's seen the book. But she doesn't know I'm a magicker."

It was on Homaj's tongue to order Iata not to tell her yet, not until they'd all thought through all the angles, but no, that wasn't his place anymore. He was still Truthspoken for the moment, but he wasn't the Seritarchus. He'd never be the Seritarchus again.

That thought hit him with a surprising pang of loss.

"And we'll need to tell Ari," he said, "when she returns."

"When," Iata agreed. "And we need to talk to the First Magicker. He might have ideas on how to best present this, present me. And when that revelation might be best. Maja—we're going to have to think everything through so carefully. And when we have decided on the best course, set it all up over time. The wedding is in two months—less than, now—we can't make any large move publicly until that's accomplished, and Dressa and Lesander are seen as stable in the eyes of the people. Then, if this all backfires horribly, the kingdom has someone to fall back on. I can continue to be you until that time, and we'll all have to seed things during that time, set everything up in the eyes of the people to have a positive—or at least, not overly negative—reaction to me making my bid. As myself, and likely also as a magicker."

"Agreed." Homaj ran his hand through his hair, the same gesture Iata had used earlier. He scowled at his hand.

It wasn't over yet. There was work to be done yet so that the kingdom he was leaving would remain standing. And maybe, at some point, it would thrive again like it couldn't under his care.

"Yan, you understand that if this works, this will do everything we've been trying to accomplish to bring the magickers up to parity in our society."

Iata's face showed more skepticism than hope in that regard. "Some. It will do a lot. I will have to very carefully watch myself, though. People will know that if I'm attacked, I can't use violence to defend myself."

Homaj wanted to counter that yes, Iata could use violence if he absolutely had to. It would just . . . cost much. And for a Green Magicker to publicly use violence—well, even what he'd done as Sodan Iseban had stirred the panic over magickers into a frenzy. If Iata used violence as a Green Magicker and also the Seritarchus, the cost might be the kingdom.

He met Iata's eyes. Iata well understood that truth.

With a groan, Iata pushed himself up, then bent down to pull up Homaj as well.

"Thank you, Brother," Homaj said.

"I want you here," Iata said. "I want you to train Dressa, too, if you can—you have different insight into all this that I don't. She's not a Seritarchus, I know that. I thought maybe Melesorie, but now I'm wondering if she's Ialorius. She's remarkably adaptable. She's a lot more like you than I think you realize. And help me strategize all of this—I'm not as good at the long game strategy as you."

Homaj stiffened. He'd been hoping to just walk away tonight. Talk it all out, or even leave that to Iata and Ceorre. He'd wanted to remove himself from the palace life so he could fully breathe again, to find out who he actually was, but . . . but, well. He'd known that wasn't as likely as the longer, slower transition, no matter how much he'd wanted it to be.

"I can't resume being myself, if that's what you're asking. Not as—" he waved at Iata's general Seritarchus-ness. "Not you as Iata the bloodservant, either. It's too close to all of this."

"You can be a speaker," Ceorre said, standing as well. "It would be ideal—people don't typically notice the lower-ranking speakers as more than set dressing. And you'd have access to me, to the Adeium, and to privacy. You already know most of the liturgies."

And she'd be able to keep an eye on him, he knew. He didn't like that idea. But also, it made the most sense at the moment.

"What about Zhang?" he asked.

"What about Zhang? If Iata's still you, she'll need to remain as his guard. At least until your abdication is public."

Well, yes. He nodded. She would have to wait a little while longer, too. He'd try to convince her to become more religious in the next two months as an excuse to visit the Adeium. He needed her stabilizing presence. But he could also think of no one better to help Iata conceal his growing trouble over his aura—of his guards, only she knew that Iata was a magicker. Not even Commander Jalava knew that. That absolutely couldn't become public before any of them were ready.

"Fine," he said. "I'll do that. You can send Dressa to me there."

40

CRUMBLING

> *To detain a magicker, you will need to contain them completely in a cell made of plastic, particularly the Denerive-Xiao type. There should be no metal, stone, or wood within five meters around this cell. No guard or any other person should also be within five meters. The locking mechanism, the lights, the facilities must all be plastic. Even then, stronger magickers can still circumvent this material with time.*
>
> — ONARAWUL DRINA IN *METHODS AND MATERIALS FOR MODERN LAW ENFORCEMENT*

In Count Badem's office, Eti stared at the door. He'd stepped toward it and away again at least ten times now. His hand had actually touched the doorknob twice, lingered on it once before he'd backed away again. Didn't they know this lock wouldn't actually hold him? He could crumble the metal, he could crumble the doorknob and the wooden door. The strength from the metal, or the residual strength from the wood, could be called to him as easily as he brushed against the strength of his plants. He could be out again in seconds.

But a crumbled doorknob wasn't something anyone could hide. It would be around the house in minutes that there was an unsealed magicker here and would only take so much longer to trace everything back to Eti. His handlers wouldn't spare the blame. They might not even now if everything went sour.

Still, he reached for the handle again. When Ryam had brought him in, Badem had been finishing the last of the day's paperwork. Ryam had explained the situation in a jumbled tirade, and Badem glared at Eti before she'd stormed out, Ryam on her heels.

"Stay here," the count had said on her way out. "Do not unlock this door. You know the consequences."

Not just his freedom, but his family's freedom, too. If they could call any of this freedom.

But Imorie. He knew they'd be going for her, and didn't know what they'd do after. Surely they wouldn't try to kill a Truthspoken? Surely, whatever reason she was here—and she was sick, he knew that, she had that particular feel of the Bruising Sleep in her energy field—she was still known to whoever was waiting for her.

A name surfaced in his thoughts. He'd been trying, since he'd heard it again, to shove it back down.

Arianna. Ari.

Was Badem going to bring her back here? He'd thought she would, but it had been a while now. The desk displays were off, and he didn't have his own comm on him—he didn't know the time, but it had been more than the few minutes he'd been hoping for, and dreading.

This not knowing was almost worse than if Badem had dragged Imorie back here.

The door burst open and Eti jumped back as Ryam barreled

in, looked around, saw him nearby. Ryam grabbed his arm, and Eti tried to shake him free.

"I'll come. Ryam, I'll come with you."

Ryam didn't let go, didn't say anything, just dragged Eti out into the corridor, then down toward the door that led outside at the end. Several of the staff peered into the corridor, wondering at the commotion. They scurried away just as quickly. You didn't work at Windvale without knowing there were certain things you just did not see.

Ryam let the door slam shut behind them and pulled Eti onward toward the large garage to one side of the house. Ryam had one of the apartments above the garage, a lot nicer than Eti's over the shed, he suspected, though he'd never been inside it.

Ryam finally let go and slowed his pace as they passed two of the other grounds keepers, both Ryam's people, guarding the side door to the garage.

Inside, Eti followed Ryam past the mostly empty rows where estate cars were usually parked—most of the cars were parked outside just now, having been used to shuttle guests from other estates and needed to shuttle them back again.

Ryam led him into a storeroom at the back of the garage, then pressed the back wall to activate a hidden door. Down a narrow, steep set of stairs, then into a basement room where Eti had only been once before and hoped to never come again.

Imorie was there, gag tape over her mouth, arms and legs secured in the center chair's cuffs, the chair bolted to the tile floor.

Eti trembled, meeting her eyes.

One small thing he could do, one very small thing, was to warn her at least of what he was.

He glanced around him. Badem was here, which was unusual—she typically kept herself out of the messy parts of all of this. And Ryam, of course, who seemed to enjoy the messy parts more than he should. And Dr. Lin, who was laying out what looked like surgical instruments on a side counter.

Eti's stomach clenched.

He didn't have to hide his aura here, everyone here knew he was a magicker. So he let it out, freeing it from the claustrophobic confines he was forced to keep it in all day, every day.

Imorie's eyes widened, flicked between his own. Down to his hands, which had touched her, back up to his eyes, which had looked into hers. He hadn't meant to find out what he'd found out, truly. Well, no, it was his job to find things out about people. He hadn't meant for it to get so complicated. He hadn't meant for it to threaten someone he knew it shouldn't threaten. Someone he liked.

Her eyes flashed with rage. She understood that he'd betrayed her, though he doubted she got that he'd tried not to. He'd tried so hard not to, he'd made himself forget what he'd learned, even though the trees had protested, and his own soul had protested this subtle violence against himself. He'd risked so much to keep this moment from happening, but they were both still here.

Dr. Lin rolled up his sleeves, a careful and methodical gesture.

Eti looked away. Gods, he didn't want to watch. Whatever they planned to do to her, he couldn't watch.

Badem crossed her arms, her face tight, but the sense of her soul was determined.

The doctor stepped forward and carefully peeled the tape from Imorie's mouth.

41

NAMES

> *A Truthspoken's name, the name that anchors them back to themself, is just one facet of who they truly are. As with all of us.*
>
> — ARIANNA RHIALDEN, MELESORIE X IN *THE CHANGE DIALOGUES*

Eti watched as Imorie winced and spat as the tape came off, but she didn't say anything.

Her eyes went back to Eti, and her look seared. Her look, he thought, meant something, but he wasn't Truthspoken, he didn't know what she was trying to say to him. He couldn't read her body language, only her soul energy.

Then, from one moment to the next, her soul changed. She was still multi-layered, yes, but the vast portion of her was shoved away somewhere else, like he did with his own aura.

Imorie. He absolutely knew he was now looking at Imorie, who'd been with him in the garden the day before.

"Magicker," the doctor said, "please take her hand and take Ryam's. Witness her truth."

The doctor held to courtesy no matter who he was around, and that had always turned Eti's stomach. He knew what the doctor really was beneath all the pleasantries.

Eti carefully knelt in front of Imorie, holding eye contact, though he had to strain to do so, acutely feeling her fear. Closer now, he had a better read of her emotions. When his hand touched hers, she flinched, but kept her eyes locked on his. He still felt her rage, yes. Different, he thought, than a moment ago. And her terror and confusion. Her resolve not to give these people what they wanted, whatever they wanted.

Ryam grabbed Eti's other hand. He would be sensing Eti's emotions and Imorie's through Eti, verifying everything that was said.

"All right then," Dr. Lin said. "Are you Truthspoken?"

"No," Imorie said.

True.

Eti's breath caught. Ryam shifted, glanced at Eti, then at Badem.

"Why would you think I'm Truthspoken?" Imorie asked. "Because I'm a Rhialden? I'm so, so far down the hierarchy I'd be surprised if the Seritarchus remembered my name."

True.

"Eti," Ryam growled. "You said—"

"I didn't say anything," Eti hissed. "You felt what I felt."

Count Badem stepped forward. "I've heard Truthspoken can suppress their own personalities in favor of another. Ryam, did you retrieve the servant?"

"Yes, but fae's still unconscious. I put faer under guard in the library. Didn't think it would look good to our guests to be dragging an unconscious person to the garage."

Badem nodded and squatted down in front of Imorie. "Imorie, dear, we know you're Truthspoken, whether you currently know it or not. I promise, this will all go a lot easier if you cooperate with us. We only wish to know why you are here, and who sent you. Are you a Rhialden Truthspoken, or are you from one of the high houses?"

Eti shifted. There were more Truthspoken than the Rhialdens?

Imorie was shaking her head. "I'm not—I'm not even trained in evaku. Just a little bit of social training. Eti—if you're a magicker, you know I'm telling the truth."

True. It was all true. And yet he knew it wasn't. And from him knowing, Ryam knew, too.

"It's this Truthspoken act," Ryam said. "How do we snap her out of it?"

Badem stood again, making a humming sound. "We could keep her here and wait until the servant wakes up. The servant would surely know. But either of them might also have sent a signal to whoever sent them—we don't know what tech they have implanted, if any. We don't know what tech the servant has been around."

"I shot faer before fae had a chance to do anything," Ryam said.

"You don't know that. They might have alerts set to go out if they're incapacitated."

"Do Truthspoken do that?" Ryam asked.

Badem shrugged and tucked at a few loose strands of hair that had come undone from her knot. "Do you truly want to find out?"

"So what do we do with her? If we know she's Truthspoken but we can't make her talk, because she's, what, literally a different person?"

Badem winced, glanced at Eti. "Magicker, is there anything else you can read, anything that would be helpful? Can you see how to bounce her out of this, or do it yourself?"

He wasn't sure he could, but he wouldn't do that anyway. That would be a violence against Imorie.

But her thoughts flickered, a subconscious thing that surfaced and was gone in an instant, but he still felt it.

Her arm. Something to do with her arm.

Eti swallowed. Even this intrusion into her thoughts was a violence, and his gut churned with it.

"What was that?" Ryam asked, starting. "What was that you just felt?"

Eti swallowed again. He couldn't refuse to answer. He couldn't deflect, Ryam would know. Ryam, and the Javieris who kept his mother and sibling under close watch, just waiting for him to mess up. Just waiting for him to refuse to do something like this.

"Her arm. There's a special trigger."

His words surfaced a ghost of that subconscious memory for her. Her only link between this self and her other self.

He knew Ryam would ask, or would try to do it on his own, so Eti leaned forward, meeting Imorie's eyes again. She stared back, terrified, trying her best, he knew, to trust that he might be on her side. Though she could probably also sense that wasn't true.

He reached for her wrist and hesitantly made the three movements he'd seen in her thoughts—two longer, one swift—she took in a shuddering breath, her eyes darting around.

"Ah," the doctor said. He'd pulled out a scanner sometime in the last minute and was now staring at the screen. "Different brain pattern. That is truly fascinating."

"Truthspoken," Badem said. "Now that we actually have your attention—your name, please, who sent you, and why you are here."

The glare Imorie gave Eti could have scorched him, but she just as quickly looked back to Badem.

"I have absolutely no reason to give you any of that information," she said, "and I'm under strictest orders not to."

Then she shut her mouth, and Eti, back to kneeling again beside her, felt her iron resolve.

"She needs encouragement," Ryam reported.

The doctor nodded. He turned back to the counter and picked up a gleaming scalpel, rolling the handle slowly in his hand. The blade spun, glinting in the overhead lights.

Eti felt Ryam's anticipation building, and so, through Eti's link with both of them, did Imorie.

Ryam suddenly turned to Eti. "You know her name. Don't you?"

Eti stilled. "I did, but I forgot it."

That was true. He had remembered it again, but it was true that he'd forgotten it once before. Several times, probably. He was doing his utmost to forget it again now.

"Etienne," Ryam growled. "If you can just tell us what we need to know—"

"I can't," Eti said. "I don't remember—"

Ryam crushed his hand in a tightening grip. Eti hissed, bending to try and stop the pain.

"Tell us!"

"I—"

"Etienne," Badem said, "remember the terms of our agreement."

He didn't have an agreement with her. He had an agreement with the Javieris, who'd insisted his mother come with them to serve them as a magicker. And he'd gone in her place. He'd volunteered, so his mother would be safe and could still watch over his younger sibling. So his mother wouldn't have to do . . . things like this. Though he hadn't, truly, known things like this would be a part of it.

That the Javieris had decided he would best serve them here didn't mean he was beholden to Badem.

No, that was exactly what it meant. He didn't have a way out of this. He couldn't look back at Imorie, couldn't ask her to understand.

But he felt her squeeze his other hand. Not gently, but not calculated to hurt like Ryam's grip.

"Ari," she said. "My name is Ari."

42

INTENT

> *We can act like we're always in control, we can impress and intimidate our power onto those around us, but as Truthspoken, we're hardly invulnerable.*
>
> — HOMAJ RHIALDEN, SERITARCHUS IX IN A PRIVATE LETTER, NEVER SENT; PUBLISHED IN *THE CHANGE DIALOGUES*

Ari hardly dared to breathe as the room itself seemed to pause for breath.

"As in, 'Arianna?'" Badem asked.

She watched a dangerous glint come into the woman's eyes. Well, more dangerous than before. Adeius, her father had told her not to break cover, never to break cover. But Eti would have pulled it from her anyway, wouldn't he? She'd felt him straining not to do so, and also straining under the head gardener's grip. None of this was what Eti wanted, she knew that. She could absolutely feel that from him. That didn't make her less furious that he'd outed her to Badem and the rest of them.

These, what, criminals? With an unsealed magicker among

them, and an estate promoting discreet treatment of the Bruising Sleep for the nobility, it wasn't a stretch to get what sort of criminal enterprise they were running here.

"Just Ari," she said.

"True," Eti said.

"And your father?" Badem asked.

"Maja."

Badem leaned forward. "Is he the Seritarchus?"

"No."

"True," Eti said, and his brows drew together.

Maja wasn't the Seritarchus. Maja, the private person, was merely her father. The title of Seritarchus was reserved for Homaj. Which was all shaky and a matter of separating the technicalities in her mind. Would they believe that?

"It's another game," Ryam said. "It has to be."

Apparently not.

How would she get out of this? What threads could she pull here—what did they want, and what did they actively fear? They feared their little information brokerage would be found out, surely. How could she use that?

Ari leaned back. "If you're not going to believe anything I say, even if it's verified by a magicker, then why bother asking?"

Badem narrowed her eyes. "Why, indeed? Tell me, Ari, why were you sent here?"

"I'm sick," Ari retorted. She looked to Dr. Lin, the fucking slime. She'd been starting to improve—had her treatment been real? Had it been prolonged? Had he tampered with any of the meds? She keenly felt the med patches still on her left upper arm. "You know that."

She sent her awareness down through her body, trying to find the edges of a healing trance that she could gather into herself. But of course it didn't come.

Had any of these people found a way to give her the Bruising Sleep in the first place?

But no, they seemed entirely dismayed that she was here.

Had her father purposely sent her into this den of criminals?

But he'd been upset enough, and seemed worried enough, that she couldn't see that as true.

"She is sick," Dr. Lin confirmed. "She has the Bruising Sleep, like the rest." He held up her silver medical bracelet, which they'd taken off her when cuffing her to the chair. Oh, and did they *not* want a record of her heightened heart rate just now?

"A Rhialden with the Bruising Sleep," Badem mused. "Forgive me—this was big enough with a contract Rhialden, but a full, Truthspoken Rhialden—well."

Ari watched as subtle emotions flickered through Badem's face and body language. Would Badem dare to try and blackmail her for that information? Is that how she'd get out of here alive?

She felt a flicker of trepidation from Eti, a sense of familiarity with this whole farce. Was this where Badem usually gave a pitch to the nobles whose secrets he stole for her? How much is your good name worth to you? How much would you be willing to give to never let anyone know why you were here?

Ari tilted her head. "What's it worth to you that I never tell the Seritarchus what you're doing here?"

"That," Badem said, "is a given. I feel the strength of our information in this outweighs yours. Why are you here? Why come here? There are other retreats for recovering from the Bruising Sleep. Why Windvale?"

Ari smiled, tight and cruel. "I came for you. The Seritarchus knows what you've been doing here. He wishes to include you in his network of informants."

There. That might do something, or at least give them pause.

"Not true," Ryam the gardener said.

Ari flinched. She'd forgotten that the information would be shared with Ryam as well. He'd called her bluffs before.

She swallowed, wishing for water, wishing she'd tried more than a sip of the wine at the party. Badem had taken her down the corridor, past her office—when Ari had questioned that, Badem waved it off, saying her office was being used by someone else at the moment, but Ari could use her personal comm. They could just step outside onto the patio.

The brute Ryam had seized her as soon as they'd stepped out and shoved the muzzle of a pistol into her side. "Walk with us cordially, Truthspoken, and no one has to get hurt."

She hadn't known what else to do but walk with him. She'd been too startled, too disoriented from this sudden shift, and by the time they reached the garage and her mind caught up to her screaming instincts enough to think to fight back, she found out he only had a stun pistol—when he shot her with it. And then she'd come to here, restrained to this chair. Why would the managers of Windvale need a chair like this?

Well, she knew that now. She'd gone to that party hoping to get a few threads of information to pull, but she'd wound up tangled in the whole tapestry.

Badem tsked and waved at the doctor, who'd put down the scanner again and reclaimed his scalpel.

"Is it true Truthspoken can regrow severed limbs?" He asked this in a tone of genuine curiosity. "I've always wanted to know."

She wanted to strain against her bonds but knew that would do nothing.

She felt Eti's fear spike, and she reflexively gripped his hand tighter as he gripped hers.

He wasn't her friend in this, not after he'd betrayed her. Not before, either, if he was an unsealed magicker on this estate. But she didn't think he wished to be her enemy, or that any of this was what he wanted. He'd said he'd tried to forget her name, and she felt his remorse and misery at his betrayal through their touch.

Adeius, she'd played her only card, her identity, because she'd known it would be forced out of her anyway and hadn't wanted to see Eti in pain. Hadn't wanted to feel his pain while it was happening to him. She'd thought she could talk her way out of this, somehow, or spot an opening. But how could she bluff and bluster when nothing was possible but the truth?

"Yes, I'm sick," she said. "The Seritarchus sent me to get well, it wasn't anything to do with all of you. I'm not here for any reason but that."

They could destroy her. They could certainly extort money from her, and she didn't know if there was anything her father could do short of sending in an assassination squad—which wasn't unlikely, and with the way Badem's expression was growing more pinched, she seemed to know that, too.

They could do nothing and let her go, but then still risk that she'd tell the Seritarchus, and he'd hunt them down.

They could kill her and also risk the Seritarchus's wrath, but if they made it seem an accident, that might be their safest prospect. They'd still, of course, need to flee for their lives.

Did Kyran Koldari have a hand in all of this? She'd felt the tension between him and Badem earlier. Did he know what was going on here? Was he here because he was sick, like her, or because he was gathering information? Was he the mastermind, was he a client, was he an innocent who just happened to dislike Badem? If he was involved, it wasn't hard to see his motives. The Koldaris were the least of the high houses, but they'd always fought viciously to both get and maintain their status.

"What does Koldari think?" she asked.

Badem blinked, licked her lips.

There, Koldari knew something. But maybe wasn't in rapport with Badem, by the souring look on Badem's face.

"Koldari is at the party and doesn't have any opinions on any of this, because he doesn't know," Badem said.

A lie? A partial truth, at very least.

So. Where could they go from here? If Ari got out of here alive, they were all at risk. If they killed her, they were still at risk, though maybe that risk was more diffuse. She couldn't, currently, see a way for her to kill them, and that would cause its own problems, too, especially if Koldari was involved. He had ties to both the Javieris and the Delors.

If they killed her, they'd have to kill Bettea, too. Adeius. No.

And Eti?

Had these people yet realized, too, the information bomb she'd dropped in their laps? The timing for Arianna abdicating and the timing for Imorie showing up on Hestia didn't add up if you factored in the travel. The Truthspeaker could be questioned on if her witness was true, and that would call the whole power structure into question.

That could topple Ceorre, that could topple Dressa, and topple her father.

She could not leave this room knowing these people, and all they knew, were still alive.

Adeius, why had she given them her name? But, Eti still would have given it to them anyway. Eventually.

She glanced over, catching Eti's eyes.

She felt his agitation through their touch, growing, widening into panic. How much of her thoughts had he tracked, and how much had gone through to the gardener as well?

Eti's breaths were coming faster.

"Etienne," Ryam warned. "Calm down."

He wasn't calm. He had no intention of being calm, Ari felt.

Ryam swore, holding up Eti's hand, but he didn't let go.

Badem was eyeing Eti now. "Is it safe to assume our magicker is compromised?"

"Yeah," Ryam said, "and pissed."

Eti took a breath, straightening. "I'm not. I'm fine. I'll do what—"

"That's a lie," Ryam said, and let go of Eti's hand. "He's good and truly smitten. Has no interest in helping us anymore."

Eti jerked, but his grip on Ari's hand only tightened. "I'm not. I'm sorry—I'll help however—"

But that was so blatantly untrue Ari could sense it without trying. He was conflicted, yes. But his was not a soul built for violence, and what Badem and company were doing here was definitely violence.

Badem sighed, pinching the bridge of her nose. "Well, the Javieris won't be happy to lose their magicker, but—"

Eti was controlled by the Javieris?

Ari's thoughts darted. She was mostly sure that her stumbling into this scheme here had been an accident, but if the Javieris were behind this information racket, and presumably the Koldaris and maybe even the Delors—Adeius, that was a significant portion of the power of the high houses right there. That had to be stopped. Were they trying to run their own Truthspoken network?

The Javieris could not have the information that she was sick. Oh, no. Or that Dressa's legal right to be the Heir was in any way in question. She didn't want her sister to be the Heir, but she also didn't want her to be taken down by criminals like this.

Ari glanced at the scalpel the doctor was playing with in one hand. If she could get free, if she could get the scalpel from him—then what?

Yes, she knew how to fight, or at least to defend herself. But her body was still weak, and the stress of the last hour had drained what little energy she'd gained for the day. She was struggling to keep her breaths steady again.

And Eti would be no help, not when he was a magicker.

Her thoughts snapped back to what Badem had just said. Eti wasn't going to leave this room alive either, was he? He knew too much, and having just proven his disloyalty, he was a liability.

Ari gripped his hand hard, nails just biting into the skin. The roiling sense of his thoughts flattened, if that was the right word, became more attentive.

The restraints, she thought at him. *Do something about that.*

She knew, of course, magickers could crumple and degrade almost any materials other than plastic, and even that wasn't impossible. This fact was the subject of many rumors and fears, but seldom demonstrated. Did Badem know that? Did Ryam? She had to believe, working with Eti, that they did.

One of Eti's fingers crept around her wrist to touch the cool metal cuffs.

And then nothing happened. If he was doing anything, she couldn't feel it.

"Etienne, step away," Badem said, and pulled a small pistol from one of her skirt's pockets.

43

WHAT MAGICKERS CAN DO

We've never had intent to harm anyone.

— FIRST MAGICKER MARIYIT BRODEN IN AN ADDRESS TO THE GENERAL ASSEMBLY

Badem's pistol, Ari saw, wasn't a standard stun pistol. It glowed with the ominous orange light signaling a loaded energy charge magazine.

She was going to shoot Eti now? And then, presumably, also Ari? Or would she try to wring more information out of Ari?

Whatever else Eti had done, or been forced to do, he'd still tried to protect her. He was still trying now, as she felt a gritty tickle of degrading metal on her wrist. Finally.

He'd tried to protect her that first night with Koldari at the ball. He'd hovered around her, and he'd said he'd forgotten what he'd learned about who she was. How, through his magics?

If he was being coerced, and all the signs pointed toward that, he was also the victim here.

And he was the only one who could get her feet out of their bonds.

My feet, she thought, and he seemed to lose his balance, bracing himself against the floor by her feet.

This time, she felt a warmth as the cuffs rapidly crumpled. These people had their own torture room, but they hadn't thought to use anti-magicker cuffs, had they?

"What—" Ryam said.

Ari launched herself upright at Badem. Badem was a brawny woman, but Ari knew how to make the body fail even a strong person, and she planned her first jab directly at one of those points.

But her limbs were slow. Her legs couldn't move fast enough. The room spun, she couldn't catch her breath, and her aim was off.

Badem raised the pistol before Ari had a chance to stop her, or move aside, and aimed the muzzle squarely at her face.

Ari, horrified, watched as Badem's finger twitched on the trigger, the count's brows drawing down with concentration.

Then she watched the exact moment the life left Badem's body. One moment, there was a person behind those eyes, bristling with intent. The next, it was like looking at an empty shell.

Badem fell, with no attempt to catch herself. She couldn't. She was already gone.

Ari froze.

Ryam and the doctor—Ryam had been moving to stop Ari, and the doctor had retreated toward the counter—also froze, watching as Badem's body hit the ground.

Ari hadn't touched her. She hadn't been close enough yet, and that fact was obvious. At least to her.

"You killed her!" Dr. Lin screeched.

But Ryam was still looking between Ari and Badem's body. Searching Ari for any unseen weapons.

A sound made them both look at Eti, who was huddling on the ground, shivering.

Ari almost, almost, couldn't see him, though she knew he was right there. His aura was a shuddering black-gray, hardly any green at all.

"Y—you," Ryam said. "Eti, you killed her?"

Ryam took a step toward Eti, then stopped, and stepped back again.

In the pause, not daring to take time to think through what this all meant, Ari stumbled forward and grabbed Badem's pistol.

Ryam turned just as she raised it high enough and shot him in the chest.

The pistol was semi-automatic. She'd only meant to fire one shot, but got off three.

Ryam screamed, and Ari looked away as he fell, his scream dying off.

Another dreadful pause.

Then the doctor screamed and ran at her, scalpel raised.

Her arm was so heavy, and if she hadn't been able to get enough breath before, she was struggling to get any now. Spots didn't just dance in her vision, they closed around her. She fell to one knee, struggling to raise the pistol again and keep it steady. The doctor blurred in her vision, and she knew her rapidly draining strength wouldn't be enough.

Eti raised his hands, and this time, she saw the slight jerk he gave with them, like pulling on invisible strings. This time, she saw everything in the moment it happened. Like he'd yanked the doctor's soul right out of his body.

The doctor fell.

Silence.

Eti sat shuddering, fading in and out of her focus, and she didn't think it was her eyes failing her there, but him pulsing through visibility.

Her other knee collapsed, and she caught herself from falling onto the tile floor. But her arm was shaking, too. She couldn't breathe.

Eti looked up, eyes locking with hers.

His eyes were almost as dead as those he'd just—he'd just—

But magickers couldn't kill. She knew that to be fact. Magickers couldn't kill without also harming . . . themselves.

He scooted toward her, holding out his hand.

She didn't want to touch him through that murk surrounding him.

"Please," he said, his voice a rasp, like it was coming from a different plane entirely. Like it was coming from a ghost. "I'll help."

She was about to pass out. So she extended her arm as best she could and felt his hand take hers, cold but solid. She felt a trickle of warmth breathe into her before it stopped.

Had it done anything to help? She didn't know. But she hadn't passed out yet.

"Have to get up," he said. "Can you stand?"

She was sure she couldn't. But as she watched his own efforts to stand, she knew she had to try.

He helped her up, supported her with an arm around her back.

The sense of his touch was so viscerally repellent that she almost flinched away. Why? Was it because of his murky aura? Was it because of what he'd just done?

They moved, slowly, toward the door, which was unlocked.

They shuffled toward the stairs.

She had little left but to concentrate on one foot in front of the other.

She made it halfway up the stairs before she blacked out.

44

SPEAKER MURIAN

As a speaker, my role is to help the petitioners of the Adeium, to perform scholarly research, and upkeep the Adeium so everything runs smoothly. But truly, my role as a speaker—as with any speaker—is to support the authority of the Truthspeaker, and thus the authority of Adeius. The Adeium would hardly be the Adeium without its speakers.

— DR. SPEAKER AVA HAYAT IN *EVOLUTION OF A SYSTEM: SPEAKERS THROUGHOUT HISTORY*

The Seritarchus had summoned her, not to his study as he had for the last week, but to Ceorre's office in the Adeium. So Dressa, passing Lesander bent over a desk they'd temporarily relocated to the prep room, collected her guards and made her way down and across the palace courtyard. With every step, her curiosity and anxiety grew.

Did this have to do with the now-rampant rumors of Kidaa attacks? Was it something to do with her public wedding, now a week less than two months away?

She was also aware, so very aware, that a week had passed since her father had left. Iata had said he'd return in a week.

Had it, in fact, been Iata who'd summoned her?

She allowed herself the brief flexing of her hands before stilling them, and settling a pleasant expression back on her face.

Dressa left her guards in the Adeium courtyard, since no weapons were allowed into the Adeium proper.

She was expected. An indigo-robed speaker she didn't know met her at the entrance to the Adeium and escorted her straight to Ceorre's office beyond the front of the sanctum, the hologram of Adeius barely flickering as she passed.

Iata, standing with his arms crossed in front of Ceorre's desk, turned as she entered. And it was Iata—she was growing more and more familiar with the barest subtleties of who he was when he was being her father. Those tiniest differences that had only registered to her as "off" on the day of her confirmation.

Adeius. Not her father, then.

Dressa's gaze darted to Ceorre's desk, but Ceorre herself wasn't there yet.

"Close the door," Iata said to her escort.

The speaker shut the door quietly, but then, they didn't leave.

Dressa blinked. With her senses so finely attuned to parsing the nuances of her father's tells that Iata was projecting, her eyes caught on the body language of the speaker.

Their dark hair was braided down their back, long-lashed eyes watching the floor. The only thing remarkable about them was the amount of effort they seemed to be expending to make themself fade into the wall.

She saw it in the twitch of their cheek. And something that she couldn't define in the way the speaker held themself. Not anything close to how Iata was standing now—deliberately so. Adamantly so.

Dressa swallowed on a dry throat. Her father.

What the hell game was he playing now? Being this low-ranking speaker, demanding she meet him here. So the summons had been from him after all.

He looked up, met her eyes. And she saw something that froze her in place, froze anything she might have said on her lips. His eyes were open, far too readable, and they held fear. Fear of her?

Had she been wrong, was this possibly not her father after all?

"This is Speaker Murian," Iata said softly.

Her father wasn't here as himself, that was clear. Iata hadn't introduced him that way, and Iata was still the Seritarchus. Iata was radiating Homaj Rhialden in absolutely everything he was.

Sudden bile burned in her throat. How dare Iata. How dare they *both* summon her here to play these games, but truly, she'd thought Iata had grown to know her better than that this last week. They'd been working so well together. Yes, she was Truthspoken, and yes, she lived and breathed in subtlety, but if this had anything to do with a Truthspoken mission, or some elaborate test of her skills—

"Be gentle," Iata said, and headed for the door.

Dressa opened her mouth in protest—but had he meant that for her, or for her father? He'd been turned in her father's direction, but eyeing her. And her head was spinning, with one of them so very much being her father, while the other, this speaker, projecting the opposite.

The door shut behind Iata. And if Iata, or her father, had orchestrated this meeting here in Ceorre's office and not the Seritarchus's study, they certainly had a purpose.

So her father wasn't the Seritarchus right now? All right, then, she wouldn't treat him as such.

She rounded on him. "Why are we here?"

Speaker Murian waved at the door. "You might want to lock it."

She stared. It took two heartbeats before she decided that yes, that was probably a good idea. She pressed the old-fashioned lock plate beside the door, waiting for it to read and accept her palm. As the Heir, it should, and did. She heard the deadbolt thunk into place.

She'd been dreading his rage this whole last week, but maybe . . . maybe, he should have been dreading hers. He was the one who'd put her in an impossible situation. He was the one who'd forced her to act, forced her to disobey him. Forced her and Ceorre both to commit that minor but deeply significant treason.

He hadn't thought she could be the Truthspoken Heir on her own, as herself. But she was doing it. She was the Heir. And she knew she was doing it well. Iata had told her that, more than once.

Unless Iata had been pushing her toward this moment? Was Iata only a means to her father's ends?

But, Adeius, she couldn't believe that. That was the curse of her father, of the actual Homaj Rhialden, that made her distrust everyone he came into contact with.

Whatever had been in his eyes before, his expression was more guarded now. He walked to the desk and pulled both chairs in front of it to face each other. Then he sat in one, and, after a long hesitation in which Dressa was contemplating walking out the door the same way Iata had, she took the other.

He hadn't tried to fortify himself behind Ceorre's desk and glare at her as he normally would at his own desk, in his own study. She wasn't sure if she was relieved or alarmed. *More* alarmed. Her knee wanted to bobble with nerves, but she absolutely kept it still.

He wore a light layer of makeup, more natural than

anything, and his mannerisms at the moment were on the edge of femme but not quite over. Medium-brown skin, wider eyes. A large mole over his left eye. Fairly ordinary, and his posture was, again, much more open than she was used to.

"You really do look well, Dressa. How was your first week as the Heir?"

The question was framed so innocently. The tone ordinary, like ordinary parents and children might say over a dinner table. Not, you know, what the conniving bastard of a ruler would say to the daughter he'd so recently condemned to masquerade as his favorite daughter instead.

"Thank you, and it was fine."

He gave a small smile and looked down. His posture, all of it, suddenly struck her as overwhelmingly . . . weary.

She didn't understand. She did not understand what he was driving at. She didn't understand the trap. There had to be a trap here.

"I'm pleased, truly, that you stepped up as you did," he said.

What the hell? Was he going to pretend that this had been his idea? That her being the Truthspoken Heir, his heir, was something he'd planned all along?

She'd been reigning herself in, holding her anger back, but this was too much.

His voice went hoarse around the edges. "And I'm sorry, Dressa, for putting you in the position I did."

Dressa tried to swallow on a dry throat and gulped loudly instead. She looked around for a pitcher or glass, spotted a half-filled water bottle on Ceorre's desk. The Truthspeaker would forgive her for using it. Her father might not forgive her that lapse in control, but she didn't care.

She sat again, replacing the cap but keeping the bottle near her. "Okay, but why?"

He couldn't truly have just apologized to her. Her father didn't apologize, not with words that actually meant something.

"Why?" He tilted his head. "Why did I ask you to—"

"No, why this, why here, and—are you apologizing to me? Can we please, for once, for just once, Father, stop playing these games? Can you just tell me how bitter of a disappointment I am to you, so that I know, and you know, and we can get on with things?"

She sucked in a breath and sat back. She hadn't meant to say that. That was cutting too close to her own skin.

He turned his palms up on his knees, his brows knit, watching her. Warily, she thought—there it was again. Was he actually afraid of her?

"Dressa." He swallowed audibly. His turn. An affectation? Nothing with her father was ever what it seemed.

Except she had the horrifying, dizzying impression that at this moment, this was real. There was no pretense here.

"Dressa," he tried again, and his voice firmed. "I'm abdicating. I've already abdicated except for the final oath forswearing Truthspoken Change—"

Dressa was out of her chair again. "What! But—no, you're the Seritarchus—"

She stopped, because in the small space of the office, she had little room to pace.

He couldn't have done it. She didn't believe it.

But on his face, there was no lie.

45

COMPLICATED

> *A Truthspoken can study, and they can prepare. They can even come into their rulership naturally, when their parent abdicates. But nothing can prepare them for the reality of actually ruling the living, chaotic mess of motivations, problems, and triumphs we call the Kingdom of Valoris.*
>
> — ARIANNA RHIALDEN, MELESORIE X IN *THE CHANGE DIALOGUES*

Dressa shook her head. "No. *No.* I'm not—I'm hardly ready to be the Heir, I'm not even remotely ready to be the ruler—"

Her father, sitting across from her with a weariness she didn't think was feigned, narrowed his eyes. "I'm well aware of the insufficiencies in your training."

Strangely, that calmed her. That was more like the father she knew.

He grimaced. "No, sorry. I'm not myself."

"Well that's blazingly obvious."

He glared up at her. "That's not what I meant. You've talked to Iata. You know I'm not really a Seritarchus personality. And even before then, I did what you've been doing the last few years, crafted a personality at court that was close to who I am, but not really myself. It was useful, and it was satisfying to defy what people thought a Truthspoken should be, but it was not who I am."

Dressa shifted. Yes, she did understand that, not that she'd admit it now.

Her father sighed, rubbing his face in his hands.

She came back around to sit, because she wasn't sure she could puzzle him out standing up. Something was very, very wrong. Beyond the fact he'd just said he was going to—Adeius, that he already had—abdicated.

It had to be a test. A trick. Something.

"Take it back," she said. "It's not public, so surely Ceorre can—"

"Dressa, I'm not abdicating in favor of you. I wouldn't do that to you, because no, you're not ready for that yet. Maybe soon, but not yet. And we'll take care of that, but—I'm abdicating for Iata."

"But—"

"As himself.

Dressa's chest clenched. Iata, as himself?

Was that even possible?

"He's been partially ruling the kingdom for years—you do know that? Good. Iata knows all the complexities of what's happening in the kingdom right now and how to navigate. Dressa, I know we've had our differences, but—"

"But you don't think I'm ready."

His lips gave a frustrated twitch. "I've already said as much, and I don't mean because you don't have the training—which you don't have all of it, not yet—but you don't want the weight of the kingdom. Not yet. Not before you're ready for it.

It fell on me before I was ready for it, and it almost —almost—"

He made a nebulous gesture, stopped, cleared his throat.

She crossed her arms. "So, what, you're just giving up?"

His eyes flashed. "Look at me, Dressa. Do I look in any fit state to keep ruling a kingdom? When the nobles are snapping at our heels, and there are these attacks that may or may not be the Kidaa, and my Heir has become sick, and the magickers are scrambling for their rights, which truly they should have anyway—I'm not handling it well *at all.* I would absolutely abdicate in favor of you right now if that was my only other option, but it isn't. Iata will hold the kingdom steady, if he can, for the next however many years until you raise your children and they are grown. And then he'll step down, and you'll become the ruler, and your children will become the heirs. Or," and he sat back, looking deeply tired again, "the people will reject Iata, and you'll get to rule anyway. It's a possibility, and in the next weeks before the wedding, Iata and I will both prepare you for that as best we can."

"I—"

She was struggling to keep up. Whatever had happened, whatever this was, he'd already discussed it with Iata, that was clear. And if they were meeting here in the Adeium, in Ceorre's office, that meant Ceorre knew what was going on, too. Hadn't they thought to bring her into this conversation? She was the Heir and absolutely needed to know this.

But then, maybe that was what they were doing now.

She ran everything he'd just said through her thoughts again, snagging on the last part. He was going to train her again? But she'd asked Iata to. Had he talked to her father about that, amongst all of this?

His lips twisted in a mocking smile, as if he knew what she was thinking. But the smile didn't seem aimed at her this time, but himself.

Dressa shivered, looked away. "So, I'll still be the Heir? If Iata becomes the Seritarchus as himself? Not Bettea or Pria?"

"Ah. Well, yes. They're not fully trained as Truthspoken. That training would take several years at least to bring up to parity with your own, and then there's the alliance with your mother's family to consider, the Delors, and now the Javieris, too. Lesander is already married to you."

There was a note of reproach there, but Dressa decided to ignore it.

"It will, of course, be made legal that you and Ari will remain the heirs."

Dressa sat back, mind racing. Iata. Iata was going to rule, and she'd gotten to know him well enough this last week to think that was a good thing. She was absolutely sure she wasn't ready to rule the kingdom. She hadn't, truly, wanted to rule to begin with, but this last week as the Heir hadn't been as bad as she'd thought. Dressa hadn't been trying to present herself all stiff-laced like Arianna did, and that had made the difference. She didn't have to be Arianna's sort of Heir, but she could be her own.

And if she could mostly deal with Iata as his Heir, and not her father? Wouldn't that be all the better? Hadn't that, truly, been where her mind had wandered ever since she'd learned of Iata's and her father's ruse?

"Why wouldn't the people accept Iata?" she asked. "I mean, yes, there's the fact that he's a full Truthspoken and a full royal Rhialden that they didn't know about. But we can spin that, make it all fairy-tale-like. The people will love a good sensational story, it might even boost his approval ratings."

Her father twisted one of the few rings he wore—a comm ring, she now saw. He held it to his lips and murmured what sounded like a code word.

"What are you—"

The door clicked and Dressa stood as Iata entered again.

Then he hadn't gone far, maybe just outside the door—he'd only been waiting for her father's signal to return. A callback to a ruler, not a summons of its own.

Iata was still very much the Seritarchus. And her father was still very much not.

He and her father shared a look, and she did not at all like the sense that they were ganging up to decide her future.

"Seritarchus," she said, lifting her chin. "What do you think of all of this?"

Iata considered her, and let his mannerisms, finally, shift back to some of his own. He pressed the door plate and locked the door once more. He stepped further into the room, the third point of a triangle between Dressa, her father, and himself.

"I think, in the end, we'll all do what's best for the kingdom. And sometimes what's best for the kingdom is making sure that those who rule it have the most ability and capacity to do so."

That was maybe half a response, and half a dodge. Dressa started to challenge him on it, but he held up a hand, stilling while he closed his eyes.

She frowned. What was he doing? Had he injured himself, was he trying to attempt a light trance here?

She shifted uneasily, taking in his tensing posture. This reminded her too much of the time he'd come into his study and abruptly had to leave again, and the time he'd had that brief lapse at the party. She hadn't seen him lapse since, or do anything else odd like that, and hadn't yet found the right timing—or really, the nerve—to challenge him on it.

This last week had just been too busy, especially with trying to quell people's fears around the Kidaa—the maybe-attacks had become a vicious rumor and they hadn't been able to do anything to stop it. Maybe originating at the palace, or maybe from outside—there'd been another attack. Iata had shown her the damage, and the rune carved into a suburban parking lot, the night before.

Whatever had been going on with Iata before hadn't happened again, so she'd just been hoping it wouldn't. She had too many other things to think about.

Cold sweat rippled down her back as she waited for what he'd do next. Was he going to tell her what was going on with him? Is that what her father had meant about people not accepting him? Was there still something going on, and had he just gotten better at hiding it?

Iata opened his eyes and met her father's gaze again. Iata's face was pinched in some emotion she couldn't identify.

The moment was dragging out, and her sense of dread grew deeper.

"What?" she asked. "What else do I need to know that you're both not telling me?" Because she was sensing the shape of the hole in this entire conversation, and she was so tired of being left out.

Iata hesitated, then held out his hand.

She stared at it. Why could he possibly want her to take his hand, and what would that solve?

But he raised a brow in just that way her father had of making her feel like a child, so she ground her teeth and took his grip.

His hand tightened briefly, then—green flared around him, a deep forest aura.

Dressa jerked back but caught herself, didn't allow herself to let go. Because—because if that meant what she thought it meant, he would be sensing her reactions.

As she thought this, she felt a trepidation that wasn't hers, and a vibrant, dancing sense of self. That sense was him, wasn't it? That sense was Iata.

Oh, Adeius. And Dressa began to understand.

She watched, still clasping his hand, as he reached into an

inner jacket pocket and pulled out a rank seal, holding it up. The metallic edges, the holographic swirls, caught and shimmered in the room's overhead lights.

And then she got it. She really, truly got it, and just how much shit they were all in. That hadn't been her father with Arianna at the ball. It had been Iata. Iata was, for real, a Green Magicker.

So if her father said he was no longer able to rule the kingdom, and she wasn't yet ready to rule it, and Ari was still away getting treatment, that left Iata, who was absolutely capable and ready to rule. Iata, who was also a magicker.

Dressa waved at his face, which she'd viciously clawed that night at the ball. "Sorry."

He snorted, the sound almost embarrassed, and slipped the seal back away again.

Yes, he was embarrassed. She felt that from him. And regretful, so deeply regretful that night at the ball had happened at all. He didn't blame himself for Ari's illness, but he did blame himself for how much his calling it out had affected the kingdom.

This sense of him, this glimpse into what he actually felt, and thought even, was dizzying.

He cleared his throat, gave her hand a squeeze, and let go. But the aura remained. The aura pulsed gently, and she wondered if it was to his heartbeat or to some other rhythm.

"Yeah," she said into the silence. "Yeah, this complicates things."

46

DRIVE

We surf on the plains
while we run
while we drive.

— ANTI-SPIN CONNECTION IN THEIR POPULAR SONG, "DRIVE"

Ari woke up shivering. She must be lying in front of an air vent, she thought, as the wind caught at her hair.

She blinked, trying to rapidly assimilate her surroundings. No, not an air vent. She was in the back seat of a car. The same back seat of the junky hovercar Eti had used to pick them up on that first day. It didn't have a top. And by the near scream of the engine and the buffering of the wind, Ari thought they were going fast.

Eti's hands were on the yoke, fingers in a death grip, eyes firmly planted ahead.

She tried to sit up. Pain lanced through her from no definable place—from everywhere. She gasped and lay back down again.

Eti, finally, looked back, though he swerved the car as he did so. He quickly returned his attention to—the road? The field? She couldn't see over the doors from her vantage on the seat.

Fragmented visions of what had happened in the basement of Windvale's garage came back to her.

The doctor and his scalpel, the edge gleaming in the light.

Badem's tall body hitting the tile floor, her dark hair fraying from its knot.

Eti's hands upraised, face blank and tight in concentration.

Her hand on the trigger. The gardener.

Bile rose. She'd killed someone—she'd killed the gardener. She'd shot him. He was very dead.

And Eti—Eti had killed the others.

She registered his aura now, faint around him, like a gray mist. The haze around him wasn't the wind, as she'd first thought. Was he trying to suppress it again and failing?

Green Magickers couldn't kill. Her father had told her that multiple times. She'd even heard First Magicker Mariyit Broden say it once. It was absolutely a known thing, because if a magicker could hold the kind of power they did, being able to take the truth from anyone, and both take from and give strength to various organic substances—if they could do violence, they would be horrific. They would truly have to be feared.

At the moment, Eti almost seemed like an apparition. She looked at him and wanted to look away. Like his very presence resisted hers.

"Where?" she called—or tried to call—over the howl of the wind. "Where are we going?"

Eti glanced back again. "We'll go where it's safe!"

She almost didn't catch the words. They were also flat, also shifted away from where they should be. Like her ears didn't want to hear them.

She strained, managing to push herself up enough to prop against the back seat, swing her legs around to sit.

"Are you hurt?" he shouted.

She tried to focus inward, but even that sense of herself faltered. She went back to shivering. Her fingers felt numb, though the air wasn't cold.

Then she sat bolt upright. Bettea. Bettea wasn't here, was fae? She looked around frantically—not in the back seat with her, surely, and not in the front, either. Certainly not in the trunk.

She pounded on Eti's seat. "We have to go back! Bettea —Jis—"

"We can't! I took the car. They're following!"

Ari twisted to look back behind them. They were on a road, and she couldn't see any other traffic behind them. Green fields to either side.

She pounded his seat again, though it sent wracking pain up her wrists and forearms. She yelled through her teeth. "Eti! We have a ship!"

"You were out! I couldn't fight anyone else. I took the car, it was in the garage—"

She pressed her hand to her mouth to suppress her scream of frustration.

She couldn't leave Bettea. Not in that den of criminals—except three of them were dead. Were they the leaders? Were they all that mattered? Apparently not, if Eti said they were being pursued.

"Are you sure there's someone after us—"

But she saw it now, a silver spark in the distance behind them.

She sat back down, winded, just trying to breathe. Every breath was pain.

Adeius. She reached for her strength, the strength she'd

always had, that she'd been trained into, that was her birthright, and it wasn't there.

"Where are we going?" she asked again. And then she had to ask it *again* because her voice wasn't loud enough. She couldn't make it loud enough.

"Racha. The city. There's a spaceport—"

And what was he expecting to do there? She was a mess, and didn't have any identifications. She couldn't even reveal herself to be Truthspoken if she wanted to and request help from the authorities. No one would believe that without some proof of Change, not when there was sharp evidence that she and Eti had murdered three people. No matter if it was self-defense, mostly, and how would she explain that without having to explain why they'd detained her?

And she couldn't break her identity further, anyhow. The three people here, besides Eti, who knew Arianna Rhialden was actually on Hestia were now dead.

She sat a moment, straining again, reaching for a deeper well of—something. Some reserve, some source of Truthspoken ability that had to be there, because she was Arianna Rhialden and she had never been trained to give up. There had to be a reserve. She just hadn't tried hard enough. Hadn't wanted it badly enough.

Change, damn you. Change, heal, get out of this mess!

She reached. She reached with all she had in her.

And she found something.

The world around her *popped*. Her ears rang, and her head crowded with a sudden rush of . . . what?

She shook her head. Had she damaged something? She tried to inventory herself again, but even the thought resisted her.

She felt strange. She felt . . . she could almost hear a song on the wind, like chimes.

Ari held up her hand, waving her fingers through the wind

rushing toward her. Reveling in the taste of it against her skin. It was warm, nourishing. She touched the lace of it and drank it in.

Only then did she see the green.

Her hand, rimmed in a halo of solid forest green.

Ari shrieked and jerked back against the seat, shaking her hand.

Get it off, get it fucking *off*. It was Eti's aura. He'd put it around her somehow, he must have.

It didn't come off her hand. And it wasn't just on that hand, but the other as well. On both of them. Up her arms. Around her legs.

Eti turned around, and the car swerved sharply, shuddering as its buffers ran over the rougher ground at the side of the road.

Eti bared his teeth and got it back on the road, fishtailing as he fought to steady it.

Ari had enough presence of mind to look behind them—the silver glint was larger, closer.

"Drive," Ari hissed. "Drive!"

47

FOG

> *We don't yet know how or why someone manifests Green Magics. We only know that once they do, the change is permanent, immune to genetic therapy, and inheritable after.*
>
> — DR. M. OYALA, INTERVIEWED IN THE POPULAR VID ZINE *VALON CITY SUNSHINE*

She was a magicker. She was a *magicker*. And Eti knew with absolute certainty, even suppressed as he was, even with his magics twisted and painful as they were, that she hadn't been a magicker five minutes ago.

"Drive!" she screamed.

Gods. He couldn't deal with this. He could barely hold on to the edges of himself to keep his soul from imploding under its own weight.

He gripped the controls and pushed the yoke as far forward as it would go.

His mind was fog. It was like trying to gather the air just to focus his thoughts enough to aim toward the city and keep driving. He didn't know how to handle a newly manifested magicker.

Except he did. His younger sibling had manifested when they were three. He'd manifested when he was five.

Eti checked the flickery dash screen. They were nearing the city. He could see the low tumble of buildings up ahead. No tall buildings on Hestia, it would mess with the garden mystique.

When he'd manifested, he'd just gotten a paper cut, and it had hurt enough that it had triggered whatever happened to bring Green Magics out. His sibling hadn't had any manifestation trigger that he knew of—one day they'd just awakened with an aura.

Green Magics manifested randomly in those who'd never had it in their families. But once it was in a family, the children would often manifest, too. Magickers were discouraged from having families.

And when he'd manifested, he'd been panicked enough that he'd crumbled the wooden floor beneath his feet and sank halfway through. His mother had caught him, dangling from one arm, her own magics flaring.

That was also the day he'd learned his mother was a magicker.

He glanced behind him again.

Imorie—no, Ari, but that name held too much anguish—"Imorie" was safer. Imorie sat staring at her hands, eyes wide, mouth pinched. If he didn't help her, she could bring the car down around them.

"Imorie," he said, and she looked up.

Eyes searching him. Panicked and accusing.

"You did this!" she shouted.

"I didn't! You know I didn't."

Not that she could trust him. Not that he hadn't so deeply betrayed her.

He tried to care about that as much as he should, but his soul was so numb. His soul was unraveling.

He gritted his teeth and looked around himself, spotted a wrench on the floor of the front passenger side. It was sometimes used to pry the trunk open if it refused to open all the way on its own. He grabbed it, feeling the car sway at his sudden movement, and handed it back to her.

He steadied the car and then watched her hold the wrench in bewilderment.

"What—"

"Pull strength from it. Just, just a little."

"What? I can't— How do I do that?"

But she was staring at the wrench. She'd figure it out. It was as natural to magickers as breathing, sensing the strength in everything around them. Metal was one of the simplest sources of strength.

And he had to keep the car steady on the road.

The city was closer now. He could see individual windows on the buildings ahead.

The screen flashed a red warning and the car's speakers crackled.

"Welcome to Racha's traffic grid. Warning. Unsafe speeds detected. Please slow down or be subject to forced shutdown."

Eti swore beneath his breath. He'd forgotten about the traffic grid. He'd never taken the car—any car—by himself into the city. The few times he'd come before, he'd been with Ryam, getting supplies for the gardens. Ryam had been driving.

Ryam. The only one that he hadn't—

He swallowed the thought.

Imorie leaned forward. Gods, her aura was so green. Vibrantly green. He hoped whoever was chasing them couldn't see it, but then, they'd probably just think it was his.

"Is there a place to input a security override?" she asked.

"Don't know."

She stretched and started tapping at the screen. She held the wrench tightly in one hand. Fine tendrils of rust were forming around its otherwise shiny metal.

Imorie pushed herself further toward the screen and kept jabbing at the controls.

Then she said a short, "Yes. It worked."

Eti blinked hard to keep his concentration on not dissipating. It was taking so, so much effort. But Imorie needed him to drive. He felt the darkness all around him and kept shoving it back.

"What worked?"

"The Racha traffic grid accepted my code. There's a mandatory—" she paused to catch her breath "—code sequence installed into every government system. I have . . . um. I have a code. But the Racha system won't know it was used, or at least, won't tell anyone. I shut off any monitoring systems in this car, too. And wiped the recent logs."

And then she seemed to deflate and fell back again, as if that many words, or what she'd done with the city system, had drained her.

The wrench crumbled into dust in her hand.

That was too soon. She'd used it up too fast, and he knew she'd be unconsciously searching for more strength to pull.

Eti frantically tried to look around him, while keeping an eye on the road and the traffic they were heading into. He had to slow, at least enough to weave around the other cars, only just barely missing some of them.

Multiple grievance alerts pinged on the screen from drivers around them.

Metal. He needed metal.

"The seat harness—the buckles. Pull strength from them," he said.

She didn't question, and he chanced a glance back to see she was holding both of the backseat buckles in either hand.

His shoulders eased the tiniest fraction.

But his vision was tunneling. And the world was starting to waver around him again.

"What's wrong with you?" she asked. "It is because you—"

He couldn't hear what she said. His ears, what little soul he had left to him, filtered it out.

He slowed the car further as they reached the outer limits of the city. They were among the buildings now. He needed all his attention just to drive.

"We're invisible," Imorie said. "The grid won't show us to anyone."

"But we have grievance alerts—"

"Yes, they're local only, and aimed in our direction, not sent directly. People can see us, but the system can't. Keep driving."

He could turn himself invisible, and his clothes and any small objects he was carrying, but he didn't think he could make the car invisible. Not, certainly, in the state he was in now. Not and bring it back again.

He checked the screen's map display and spoke in the destination: Racha's spaceport. The map glitched, froze, then rearranged itself to show a route to the port.

"Eti, I think I still see our pursuers."

He couldn't look back. He'd hoped they'd lose them, somehow, weaving among the other cars. Was it Ryam's groundskeepers chasing them? They'd shouted when he'd surged the car out of the garage, but he hadn't looked back then, and had only noticed his pursuers later. They had to know that he and Imorie would be heading to the spaceport. It was the only logical place for them to go.

Could they hide in the city, though? Hide somewhere else on Hestia? Wait for all of this to cool down and then leave?

But . . . but Eti had to beat the news back to his family, or at least try. Not that it was possible. Interstellar comm drones were much faster than even the fastest military transport, he thought, and that much faster than civilian ships. He couldn't afford to think that the three who'd been—

He couldn't think of it. Could not think of what had happened in the garage basement room.

But he couldn't afford to hope that the Javieris wouldn't know what had happened. That someone else wouldn't be in contact with them and send a message.

They'd take it out on his family. A breach of agreement. Worse than that. He had *killed*—

"Eti, you're fading! Eti!"

Imorie pounded on his seat, and it jarred his thoughts just enough to regain his slippery grip on himself.

He bit his lip. He had to drive. Just had to drive.

He felt pressure on his wrist and looked down to see her hand. She was bent forward again, this time twisted to look up at him. A fierce concentration on her face.

He felt, beyond the darkness closing in, a faint flow of warmth. She was giving him her own strength.

It was a moment before he could bring himself to jerk away. Her face had a sallow tinge, her eyes bloodshot.

"Ari, no."

She flinched at his use of her real name. But he had such a strong sense of her from her lingering strength that her other name wouldn't form in his thoughts.

"Sorry," he said. And the name came back. "Imorie. Sorry."

He became aware of their surroundings again—they were coasting toward an intersection, drifting, and the screen was pinging with grievances again.

He sped up in the gap he'd caused in traffic, steered them back on course, and glanced at Imorie.

Her aura was a light of its own, and the car was open. He looked wildly around. People were staring. People were pulling out their comms, because Imorie very visibly did not have a magicker's seal. Neither did he, and he'd been fading.

"Imorie, get down. Get on the floor."

He didn't know if it would help, but he sped up anyway.

48

RUN

Yes, when a person first manifests Green Magics, they must be given the help and guidance of other magickers as soon as possible, as they can sometimes endanger themself or those around them with their magics, though never directly. This is only a byproduct of their new abilities, and swiftly learned to be controlled with guidance. The best possible thing you can do to help a new magicker in crisis is to help them stay calm.

— FIRST MAGICKER MARIYIT BRODEN IN A QUESTION-AND-ANSWER SESSION AFTER HIS ADDRESS TO THE GENERAL ASSEMBLY

Ari didn't hesitate, dropping down behind the front seats as best she could as Eti swerved the car down a side street. She'd seen the people pointing. She'd seen the naked fear on some of their faces. She'd seen their raised comms. Alerting the authorities that there were rogue magickers on the loose? Taking images or vids?

She'd be identified as Imorie, surely. Tied back to what had happened on the estate. And tied to . . . to . . . the Green Magickers. Imorie Rhialden méron Quevedo, a contract Rhialden, visibly a Rhialden, was also, very visibly, a magicker.

Some among the lesser nobility had manifested magics before, and it had always caused a scandal, but only a very few in the high houses had ever manifested throughout history. And no Rhialden that she knew of.

Or was that also like what she'd thought about the Bruising Sleep? Did nobles just get really good at hiding it?

Adeius, how was this happening? How was this happening to *her*?

She focused back on Eti, the gut-churning sense of his self-implosion still buzzing in her mind.

He'd been so translucent he'd hurt to look at. She couldn't let him just fade. Not and leave her here alone, not knowing anything about any of this.

So she'd gripped his wrist, which had still been solid beneath her touch, though deathly cold. She'd tried to do the opposite of what she'd done with the wrench and the seat buckles—using whatever essence was inherent in them for her own strength—but even then, she didn't know how she'd done that. She didn't know if her trying to give some of her own strength to Eti, just a little, had worked.

But something, at least, had jarred him back to being corporeal and present. He was still driving. Which was good, because the way her heart was pounding, the way her every breath was a strain, she wasn't sure she could drive on her own.

She looked in the cramped space between the bottom of the seats for metal—yes, she'd caught what he'd been doing. The wrench was gone, the buckles on the seat harnesses had rust flakes all over them now. She could sense the strength in the metal of the car, but she was absolutely not going to try and use that. They needed the car.

But she'd need strength from somewhere. She was dizzy, and her vision was hazing again.

"Take a back route to the spaceport," she called.

"I know!" He jerked the car down another, narrower alley.

Out of the main flow of traffic, she pushed herself up far enough to see the map on the flickery dash screen. They were, at least, headed in something resembling the right direction.

She looked behind them.

Shit. She'd been too pre-occupied with keeping Eti with her, and then keeping herself hidden.

But they had been seen, widely seen, and two cars had followed them, people with their comms held up. Were these civilian vehicles co-opted by the city security grid until actual law enforcement could arrive? Overzealous residents? People tended to get weird when new magickers manifested, like it was a plague that had to be contained. Was Racha a large enough city to have magickers in residence? The city guards would certainly have protocols for dealing with newly manifested magickers, like everyone else.

Ari had heard that sometimes the captures were brutal. Sometimes the magickers tried to fight back, and were felled by their own attempts from their new aversion to violence.

She was in no state to fight, but could she fight even if she wanted to? Just the thought sent a queasy flame through her gut that didn't feel just physical.

"Eti! Behind us!"

He looked back, swerved. Then braked and skidded the car, the engine protesting, down yet a narrower alley. This one only allowed space for one vehicle at a time.

"I know!" he shouted, and they sped up again.

The engine hadn't stopped protesting this time, and that wasn't good. More wheeze than whine now, a couple more undernotes added in. How much longer would it last? Truly, she should be surprised it had gotten them this far at this reckless speed.

She checked behind again. The second car had followed them in, though it wasn't driving as recklessly as Eti and was much farther back than it had been. The first must have overshot the turn.

Ari gripped the edge of the seat, still hunkered down as much as she could be and still see behind them. If she'd just gained the ability to turn a wrench into rusty flakes, could she do the same to the car? Do it at a distance, without touching?

The thought sent a shuddering pain through her gut and she gasped at the urgency of it. Adeius, was this what magickers felt when they thought anything resembling violence? But she'd only wanted to stop the car. There was a chance, though, that stopping the car might hurt the people inside it.

"Eti! Can we stop them?"

"No," he said. Hard and unequivocal.

She hadn't, as herself or as Imorie, seen this side of the quiet, normally awkward gardener before. He was braced against the yoke and she saw, with both evaku-trained senses and this new explosion of senses that he was sliding away from his truths toward a maw that wanted to devour him.

Oh Adeius, what was that? She'd felt it when she'd touched him, and tried very hard not to look at it in case it could latch onto her, too. What was that sludge in his aura? He was still fading in and out of visibility, and she didn't think he had any control over that.

"Can I stop them?" she asked, because she wasn't sure if he'd only meant that he couldn't.

"It's violence."

But he'd killed two people. She'd watched that.

Her stomach churned.

He'd outright just . . . just plucked their souls out of their—

"Ahh!" Ari doubled over, gagging, trying not to vomit. Just

thinking about what Eti had done was like razors skimming over her soul.

She clamped her mouth shut, closed her eyes, and fought to keep the acid down.

She needed strength from somewhere—it had helped before. She looked around again, with both her eyes and these new senses that overlaid meshes of . . . strength? . . . energy? . . . all around her. There was a metal frame inside the front passenger seat—that wasn't essential to the function of the car, was it?

She placed her hand to the plastic seat cover, but was able to reach beyond it to pull at the strength of the metal within.

A beeping alert went off in the car.

"Ari, what are you—"

Sirens blared in the distance.

"Eti, you need to find somewhere to pull off, where we can hide or let them pass."

"I don't know—Ari, I'm barely holding on."

She knew that.

She glanced behind them again—and they'd picked the second car back up again. She was fairly sure neither of them were the pursuers from the estate. Should she be glad of that, or terrified that these new pursuers had decided to help with the chase of a rogue magicker?

The sirens doubled their wails.

49

THE SECRET

> *Truthspoken are trained deeply in many skill sets, but also trained to adapt their skills for every scenario they might encounter. Circumstances people find themselves in often run in patterns, and skills in one area can be adapted for others. And still, of course, there are scenarios for which Truthspoken find themselves unprepared.*
>
> — ARIANNA RHIALDEN, MELESORIE X IN *THE CHANGE DIALOGUES*

Sirens. Ari might have hidden them from the traffic grid before, but that was definitely not working now. She looked all around—and, heart pounding, looked up.

Oh, Adeius. What if the city guards had aircars? There would be much less chance of escape if the guards could follow them across buildings and streets without obstacles. But then, why hadn't they already done so?

"Eti! Does Racha have aircars?" Had she seen any on the

way into the city? She didn't think so. Everything had been hover vehicles, ground-based.

"No?" But he didn't sound sure. "We don't have aircars at Windvale."

It had to be another of Hestia's rules, like no industrial exports, or no skyscrapers in the cities.

She looked up again. But what about drones? Had she seen any drones?

Eti turned the car down a wider side street, and Ari braced herself for whatever might be ahead. Brick and metal walls blurred past them. There were a few cars on this street. No city guards yet, though.

Eti sped through an intersection, barely missing a freight truck, and beyond it, turned down another long alley.

Ari looked behind them. Their pursuers weren't there—could they possibly have lost them? No—no, there was the first one, just turning into the alley after them.

Where were the sirens coming from? Where could they possibly turn that would give them enough time to hide? This alley tunneled out ahead, dotted with cross streets, any of which could hold danger.

The sirens were louder, they had to be closer.

Ari pushed up to reach the dash screen again, keeping one hand pressed to the passenger seat. It wasn't much use trying to stay hidden now. Could she feed her Truthspoken overrides into the city system again, telling the guards to disengage—but no, it was far too late for that, and the worst kind of overplayed hand. It would only tie Imorie further to the royal Rhialdens.

The screen was glitching with the alert from whatever she'd done to the front seat.

"Eti! How do I get it back to the map?"

"I don't know."

"This is your car—"

"I don't know, I don't usually drive it!"

She pressed buttons, and when nothing worked, pounded the screen. Which also didn't work.

And she was running out of strength again. The passenger seat had sagged, and there was little strength left in its metal for her to pull.

The back seat, then. If it sagged, it sagged. She twisted so one leg of her pants pushed up and her bare shin could touch the seat. A trickle of strength flowed into her.

She couldn't get the screen to work. How were they supposed to navigate without it?

Eti made another turn, making her stop and brace herself on the center console.

She saw flashing red and golden lights ahead.

Shit.

There was another alley halfway up this street, but the guard cars with their flashing emergency lights were turning toward them.

Their car might make it to the alley, it might not. Or there might be other guard cars on the other side of that alley, and then there were the cars chasing behind them, too, though those cars didn't seem interested in stopping them so much as keeping tabs on them.

Ari bit her lip, fatigue and too much to handle making her eyes sting. She'd been taught a lot of things as a Truthspoken, but she was short on education for how to evade law enforcement in a ground car chase when there was nowhere else to run and she couldn't Change. She couldn't fucking Change—if she could, that would make all the difference. Even a few minutes were enough to do . . . something.

Ari blinked, shifted her leg on the back seat to pull more fully from the strength of the metal inside it.

She couldn't Change, but that wasn't the only set of abilities available to her now.

"Eti. How do I become invisible?"

He didn't, as she'd thought he might, immediately tell her she couldn't. She knew that was a rarer skill among higher-ranking magickers and illegal without special permits. She was so new at this, she hardly knew the terminology.

Eti slowed the car, though he didn't stop, not yet.

They'd have moments before either their pursuers behind or the three city guard cars ahead were upon them.

"Stop the vehicle and put your hands in the air!" one of the guard cars blared through its external speakers.

The guard cars had slowed, too, and the cars behind her. It seemed everyone wanted to avoid a crash, at least. Or maybe they were just afraid of the rogue magickers.

She couldn't be caught. They couldn't take her in. She'd be connected to what happened at the estate, yes, but when someone scanned her to genetically seal her as a magicker, it would go much deeper than the surface scans. And a magicker would sense her untruths.

Badem and her people had been bad enough. But if the magickers found out that she, Ari Rhialden, was a Green Magicker, that would be a disaster. Adeius, especially after she'd been attacked by a magicker at her engagement ball.

She had to get some control of this situation.

"Eti! How can I—"

He turned and gripped her arm. His grimace was so tight the muscles on his neck stood out. His eyes were bloodshot, dull as stone.

Despite her revulsion of him—no. It wasn't her revulsion of him, was it? It was his own. A self-loathing so intense it was folding him in on himself, threatening to consume him.

Because of what he'd done? Oh Adeius, Eti.

He was flickering again.

He braked the car to a stop. They were four meters from the crossing alley and a possible escape.

But at that moment, she was focused only on Eti. She

choked on a sob, she couldn't help it. So this was the secret of the magickers' ability to go invisible? A self-repulsion so intense it spread to those around them, making their senses not want to see. Fading from the world.

She'd felt it from him before in the basement room, before she'd had these new senses. And with her new senses, she felt it so much stronger now, though she couldn't not see the spark of his own self at his core, the part that was still centered in his own truth. It was the self-loathing that was the lie.

And still.

She let go of his hand. She understood.

"Get out of the car and put your hands in the air! Any use of magics will be considered aggression—"

She took two painful breaths, pulling the last of the strength from the back seat as she braced herself and then reached for . . . everything.

Everything that had gotten her to this point, every mistake, every failure.

It hurt. Oh, Adeius, it shredded her up inside, this violence. But she looked at her hands and could barely see their outlines. And then she couldn't see them at all.

The guards were shouting, but their words were indistinct, coming as if through a haze.

She looked up and couldn't see Eti, only sense that small but pulsing sense of his inner truth.

And now that they were going to run, she reached for the metal of the car and pulled on as much strength as her body would let her.

She staggered after Eti, through the disintegrating rust of the door panel, as they ran for the alley.

50

INVISIBLE

> *I was right there. I was standing right there when you kissed them. You didn't see me, because you're not a magicker. But I am.*
>
> — DENA OLEGANI IN THE VID DRAMA *NOVA HEARTS*, SEASON 7, EPISODE 5, "REGRETS"

Ari's legs burned with every step. Her lungs burned with every attempt at breath, but she didn't stop running. She was sure that if she stopped, she would collapse.

Shouts came from behind her, but Ari didn't dare spare the time and effort to look back. She concentrated everything she had on running and keeping herself invisible.

And with every pounding step, her thoughts pulsed with, *failure, failure, failure.*

It wasn't true. Her core was repulsed by the idea. But the more vocal part of her, the part that had pulled those words around her like a shield, could not shake it. And she couldn't shake it, anyhow, if she wanted to remain invisible. She just had to run.

The end of the alley tunneled in her vision ahead. She still couldn't see Eti, and a growing panic was rising that maybe it hadn't been a good idea for him to make himself invisible. He'd been straining so hard just to remain visible earlier. Would that let the darkness consume him? Would he fade away and not come back?

But she still sensed him dimly ahead of her.

She definitely heard shouts closer behind, too. The guards were following.

The strength she'd gathered from the car, all that strength she'd taken at that last moment, crumbling the door, ran out. She was left gasping on her own strength.

Adeius. How was she supposed to make it to the end of this alley, let alone however many kilometers yet to the spaceport?

But she had no choice. She did chance a look back now and saw a handful of city guards behind her.

Strength. She'd found reserves before. She had to do it again. It meant saving the kingdom, she told herself. Keeping her kingdom safe from those who would discover her identity and use that against the Truthspoken.

That she was so close again in so many hours to giving her identity away, to breaking her father's express command, to utterly failing at what she had been born to do, only fed the numbness within.

How was she supposed to push on and give this her all when she was actively making a case against her own abilities?

Her legs were cramping, but she breathed through her teeth. She would not cry out. She would not betray herself. If she failed, it would be because she hadn't measured up, not because she hadn't tried. Dammit, she would *try*.

Ari reached the end of the alley, paused a breathless moment to try and sense which way Eti had gone, and then veered right. This street was more pedestrian, commercial. A raised sidewalk ran its length, and she charged down it.

Could her pursuers hear her footsteps? Hear her wheezing? She hadn't had time to ask Eti if sound would carry through this magicker trick.

Trick? This was hardly a trick. This was like folding herself into a box and forcing down the lid.

It wasn't true that she had failed. She had fucking tried! With everything she had, she'd tried. She'd completed her Truthspoken training. She'd done everything her father had ever asked of her—except, maybe, for insisting on using her public name in private, too, and that was hardly an unforgiveable offense. Unless it was? Unless that was the one weakness in her perfect armor that had cascaded down the years to lead her to this moment.

What if the Bruising Sleep was punishment? What if Adeius had seen that flaw in her, a Truthspoken, or some other flaw she hadn't even seen yet, oh, and what would Adeius think of her now, using heretical magics? Unable to Change? Unable to run fast enough to free herself and keep the kingdom safe? She was a hazard. She was a wreck. She wasn't fit to be a Rhialden at all.

Ari stumbled on her sob and caught herself against a brick wall. She had to stop running soon. Had to. The world was starting to tilt again, and she slowed, brushing against a brick building as she fought to catch even a little bit of breath.

She needed, desperately, to not be invisible, too. Oh, Adeius. And she dared not ask the god she was supposed to serve for strength, dared not recite or even think of the supplications for aid in time of need, for fear of the response.

She felt a touch on her arm and nearly shrieked, but with it came that self-repellent sense of Eti. Was she that self-repellent, too?

No, she thought, whatever he had going on was more. That, at least, calmed her a little.

"Hey," he said quickly, under his breath. "We should go into a store. Hide."

But they weren't nearly far enough away from the guards. Three guards were rounding the corner from the alley just now. They would certainly search every store and building. They'd set up a perimeter in the meantime—maybe were even doing so now—and could this invisibility fool bio-tracking scanners?

She could not get breath. Eti pulled her into the store just ahead of them, a small clothing boutique. They ruffled racks of shirts as they passed on their way to the back, but no one made any sound of alarm. If the store had bio-alerts on their front door, they hadn't sounded.

They reached a door in the back and Eti tested it—unlocked. It led to a crowded store room filled with overflowing shelves and piles of boxes on the floor. A bathroom stall sat to one side. Eti tested the door at the back—it led to a short hallway and another door with a translucent window showing sunlight. Did that lead into another alley, or a courtyard?

It didn't matter. She had to sit now.

They returned to the storeroom and Eti overturned a bucket. Ari sank down onto it, shivering. After a moment of poking around, Eti shoved a pair of scissors into her hand, putting a cloth on her lap with his other hand. Both objects swiftly disappeared into her own personal invisibility distortion field. And the cloth was a good idea, because she'd crumbled the scissors in moments.

He came back again with more tools and a metal measuring rod.

"I think that will be enough," she whispered.

She couldn't hear him nod, but felt her sense of him settle just that tiniest bit.

In seconds, she had an invisible pile of rust in her lap, and just enough breath to think again.

The metal hadn't stopped the shaking, though. That wasn't just her fatigue.

She eyed the door back into the shop. The guards could come through it at any moment, but she had to sit. She absolutely needed a pause.

What the hell were they going to do? If the whole city would now be looking for them, where would they go? They couldn't remain invisible forever. It was eating her up now, a gnawing pain inside her stomach and chest, a burning in her veins. A tearing at her soul.

"Eti," she said, as quietly as she could, "what was your plan? When we reached the spaceport?"

There was a pause. The silence rang in her ears, and she frantically felt around with her new senses for the sense of him—yes, he was still there beside her.

"Become invisible. Stow away."

She stared at the empty space where he should be beside her.

"Become invisible? What if I hadn't been able to do that?"

"I knew you would."

Because he'd sensed just how much of a failure she was?

Fuck.

She was still holding the depth of all of that failure, and it didn't hurt less than when she'd started. It hurt more. It had grown new layers, new reasons to possibly be true.

But she didn't know if there were cameras in this room, and they might have to run again.

"What if I hadn't—hadn't gained an aura? What then?" What if she hadn't become a Green Magicker? That couldn't have been part of his plan. That was the one thing in the universe she knew for sure was impossible to manipulate.

Unless she'd been wrong about that, too? Could she trust Eti at all? Could she trust anyone, anywhere?

Certainly not Dressa, who'd taken her life and her title. And not her father. Her father had sent her here, to that den of criminals, and left her without recourse. Had her father somehow known she'd manifest Green Magics and decided this was the best way to get rid of her?

She closed her eyes and took a long, long breath.

It wasn't true. None of that was true.

Another pause from Eti. "I was going to try and make both of us invisible." His voice was flat, wispy again, and she didn't like that at all. She wished to everything he, at least, could become more visible again. But it wasn't safe for either of them. Not yet.

"You can do that?"

"No, not really. It's dangerous. We're not supposed to try."

"But you were going to?"

"If I had to. I didn't see another way."

Adeius.

She pushed herself up. "Should we keep going? Get to the port?"

The port would be on lockdown, though, or it would likely be shortly. With two rogue magickers on the loose, no one would chance them getting away.

She wanted to scream.

She wanted to go back to Windvale, get Bettea, get their ship. Get off this horrible world. And go . . . where?

She knew a lot of things. She had been trained for so many things. But in this, now, she was completely out of her depth.

Failure.

There was a clatter from out in the main shop. Raised voices, and loud footsteps coming their way.

"Guards," Ari hissed.

As one, they dashed toward the back door.

51

CHARGES

> *When I was younger and new to the Seritarcracy, and the nobles were still testing my rule, a few of them who were brave enough and stupid enough would ask me at parties if I'd ever spent time in jail in my roles as a Truthspoken. And if I said yes, they'd want to know when and how, they'd want me to prove it. If I said no, they'd make a fuss like I was somehow not giving it all for the kingdom. I finally just learned to smile and say, 'Have you?' and let the dogs take care of their own. They didn't ask me much after that.*
>
> — HOMAJ RHIALDEN, SERITARCHUS IX IN A PRIVATE LETTER, NEVER SENT; PUBLISHED IN *THE CHANGE DIALOGUES*

Eti reached the back door first, jiggling the handle.

"It's locked," he said. And they hadn't thought to check it—at least, she hadn't. Every other door had been open.

Was this the mistake that would take them down?

"I can crumble it," Eti said, "but then they'll know we—"

The door to the store room banged open.

"Do it!" Ari hissed.

She watched as the doorknob crumbled.

She supposed she could have done it, too. It would take time to learn to adapt to these new parameters. If she had that time at all.

They stumbled out into—a closed courtyard. Well, but other doors were adjoining it. She followed Eti to the left, to another locked door.

A shout came from the shop they'd just abandoned—no time. She grabbed the handle this time and yanked on its strength.

The strength in the metal came to her, and the doorknob and lock mechanism crumbled, but her stomach churned. Had that been violence? How?

No time.

They ran into what looked like a private home, finding a central corridor that led to the front door, back to the main street. Ari heard some noise in another room—the house was occupied. But they were still invisible. And the front door, they found, wasn't locked, at least from the inside.

A shout came again from the courtyard door they'd just come through. No time to find another exit—they pushed out the front door.

They were still invisible, but the door itself could be seen opening and closing. Two guards ahead down the sidewalk pointed and started running back toward them, stun pistols in hand.

Failure.

There was no way out. Her stomach clenched again, and she really thought she might vomit this time.

Two more city guards were rushing toward them from the other direction, and the front door of the house flew open.

Across from them was a busy street. Could they possibly cross it?

No, not being invisible. Not with her legs going wobbly again. Adeius, this was so not the right time for her strength to give out.

She edged closer to where she knew Eti was also standing frozen, unsure of what to do next. Her shoulder brushed his arm, and the contact must have shown something, because one of the guards pointed and shouted, "There!"

Ari sprang apart from Eti, but the stun pistols were trained in her direction now, the guards still closing in until they were a tight box around where Ari and Eti might be.

"Make yourselves seen!" one of the guards said. "Hold up your hands. No weapons."

Had the person ever captured a rogue magicker? Did they seriously think magickers could do violence?

But, Windvale. Yes, magickers could do violence. They just couldn't do it without cost, and she still wasn't sure of that cost.

Eti was still alive. Could she possibly do what Eti had done—

The thought drove her to her knees, the pain driving into her skull, scattering that tight hold she'd had on herself and her own emotions. A sound escaped her lips, and the guards were around her, reaching until they'd clamped their hands around her arms, in multiple places.

She didn't know if she was fully visible—she didn't think so. Her stomach was still cramped and her thoughts screamed at her that this, this right here, was the biggest failure of them all. This moment right here was what would bring down the kingdom.

She couldn't, in that moment, convince herself she was wrong.

The guards pressed her to the ground, wrestling her hands behind her, locking them into cuffs. She tried to reach for the metal in the cuffs—but no, they were plastic. Anti-magicker cuffs. She was absolutely out of luck for today.

They pulled her to her feet, and one of the city guards, a lieutenant by their pins, stepped forward. They didn't quite look at her eyes. Was she still invisible? She'd felt her control of that slip, but the spiral had taken on a life of its own.

Ari glanced down at herself.

She was flickering like a bad vid projection.

"You were identified as Imorie Rhialden méron Quevedo, registered guest of Windvale Estate. Is that correct?"

She pressed her lips tight. She'd already played this game today and had zero interest in playing it again. Though she doubted the city guards would resort to pulling out a surgeon's scalpel. She'd already faced that down today, too.

No, she remembered, they'd just find a magicker to fully debrief her.

She gave her bonds another tug, even as she knew it wouldn't help her. She could refuse to let a magicker touch her, magickers wouldn't truth read someone without consent. At least they weren't supposed to—but not letting a magicker touch her was as good as admitting guilt.

"Imorie Rhialden méron Quevedo, you are wanted for three counts of murder on Windvale Estate, as well as for practicing Green Magics without a seal."

Oh, no. Someone at the estate, or maybe whoever had pursued them, had reported what had happened at Windvale to the authorities, or at least, a version that included murder. And no wonder the guards had come after them in force, even beyond the fact that they were unsealed magickers. Well, or probably because they were unsealed magickers up against a charge that should be impossible.

In the part of her mind that was still thinking clearly at all, she'd been hoping that Badem's operation was too secretive to report the deaths, at least right away. But maybe the report had come from staff who weren't as high up in that hierarchy. Had there been any innocents among the staff?

She looked around and still didn't see Eti. She was having trouble sensing around her, too, with all of the guards. Had he escaped? Had he slipped through the guards while they were concentrating on her?

She saw something glint above her and looked up, then flinched as she looked into the eye of a camera drone. The media had arrived, or maybe a private feed caster. There would certainly be more drones around, especially with the name Rhialden attached to all of this.

A magicker accused of murder. Oh, Adeius. Oh, Adeius, it would not at all be good to be a magicker after this.

She looked around her, casting about for any idea—anything—that could make this situation better. Absolutely anything.

She saw someone making their way toward her through the crowd. A masc person, fat and with the barest thin line of a beard. And—and a pale green aura.

"I'm Magicker Doryan Azer, fourth rank, they/them," the magicker said. "I have orders to take these two to be sealed."

"Ser, we only have one, and she's accused of murder—"

Doryan waved. "Yes, yes. The other is over there." They pointed, and Ari sensed Eti again. Oh, no. The guards in that area went into a frenzy and caught an invisible something between them.

Eti flickered into view, just barely, hissing through his teeth in his strain. But the guards shoved him down and managed to get cuffs on his wrists.

"I have to take them to the chapter hall to be sealed. Depending on their ranks, they may need to be sent to the capital for sealing and training. As they are magickers, we take any capital crimes committed by our own seriously, and those crimes fall under our jurisdiction."

"Our orders are to—"

"Check with your commander, please. We've been through this before. Albeit not with murder charges, but it's still the same procedure."

Doryan had cleared their way through to Ari and stopped in front of her. They paused, glancing at her aura, and maybe, she thought, at her still flickering body. Her invisibility thought spiral had unwound itself further in her panic. Try as she might, she could not fully reach for it again, though the pieces of it were scattered throughout her thoughts like needles. She couldn't think Eti was in any better shape.

"Hm," Doryan said. "Imorie. May I touch your shoulder? May I check you for injuries?"

Injuries? She looked down at herself again. And remembered that yes, in fact, she had been roughly handled into the garage basement at Windvale. With bruises, likely, but she didn't think blood. A lifetime ago. But with her illness, and with the car ride and the run, she was pretty sure she looked terrible.

But if Doryan touched her—Doryan, a trained magicker—the chances that they'd see who she was were high. Eti had.

She blinked and refocused on Doryan. Met their eyes, which were sharp and knowing.

Their aura was faint, but her sense of their magics was not. They flared bright in her awareness, steady and strong. The rank seal on their cheek was fourth rank, as they'd said—high fourth, nearing fifth, and likely high enough to be able to identify a Truthspoken.

They already knew she was Truthspoken. She was sure of that. Some magickers would know that on sight—it couldn't be helped, and those magickers knew to never give a Truthspoken's identity away.

No one had asked Doryan to do a truth read on her—Doryan was acting on their own initiative. And she knew she'd be able to sense their intentions, too.

And truly, did she have a choice? The very last thing she wanted was for everyone to think she was guilty before she had a chance to defend herself. And what could she even say to defend herself without all of the truth spilling over? This Doryan would know all of her lies.

"Is this a good idea?" one of the guards asked.

"Settle down," another said. "It's protocol."

Ari finally nodded, washing over in a cold sweat at this decision. What would her father say?

But her father wasn't here. And she had to make this decision now.

Doryan gently placed a hand on her shoulder, and with their touch came a gentle flood of calm.

"There," they said. "There, that's better. Let's check you for injuries. I'm going to sense your map of pain, that is all."

Ari swallowed, but held still. She wasn't as familiar with this function of Green Magics, and not every magicker had that skill, either.

She felt their presence near the edge of her own sense of self, their emotions calm and reassuring. How could they possibly be calm in this chaos? Knowing—knowing by now who she was, surely. Knowing at very least that she was Truthspoken. Did they know more than that? But how much farther of a leap was it to her true identity? She was a Rhialden, even as Imorie. She didn't even look that far off from herself as Arianna, and she was sure some of her feature-obscuring cosmetics were messed up by now, too.

She shouldn't be thinking of this. She'd caught hazy impressions of Doryan's thoughts, though more so their emotions. But she was untrained in the nuances—trained only to keep her mind still if a magicker was near, and there was no chance of that now.

"Ah," Doryan said. "Let's see if we can soothe some of that discomfort. May I?"

She gave the barest nod, and then her various roaring pains didn't go away so much as get . . . less urgent.

Her shoulders sagged, and she swayed forward. The guards went on alert, but Doryan caught both shoulders, steadied her. "There, now. Let me see to the other. Etienne, was it?"

"Eti," Ari supplied, and didn't know why she'd bothered in this crowd.

"Ah, thank you. Eti, may I touch your shoulder? Check you for injuries—"

Eti must have nodded, because for a moment Doryan went still, and she could read the shock in their body language, though they were trying to hide it. Could anyone else see that?

"Oh, yes, we'll need to do something about that injury, won't we? But in a bit. In a bit."

Doryan turned back to the guards, face harder now. "Thank you for apprehending these magickers. On behalf of the Council of Magickers, I accept them as my charges and absolve you of all future responsibility. These two are in my custody now."

52

FLIGHT

> *The first thing I learned when I became a Green Magicker was that my world had not, in fact, ended. But the best thing I learned was that I, like all the life around me, everything that has strength, also am a life that has strength. And that strength is innate, and that strength needs nourishing, like any plant, like any living being, even our planets, even our galaxy. Doing no violence isn't a curse. Seeing all lies isn't a curse. The ability to see past my own bullshit is the most amazing thing.*
>
> — FIRST MAGICKER MARIYIT BRODEN IN AN ADDRESS TO THE GENERAL ASSEMBLY

Some of the guards looked like they wanted to argue with Doryan. Most, Ari thought, looked relieved.

"Please remove the cuffs," Doryan said, and the guards did balk at this.

"Imorie, do I have your word that you will not try to run and will accept my temporary custody?"

They looked into her eyes as they asked this, and she knew there would be no getting around it.

"Yes," she rasped.

"Yes," Eti said, when Doryan asked him the same.

She stood with as non-threatening a posture as she could manage, but the guards were still tense as they unlocked her wrists. Eti, still not fully there, wrapped his arms tightly around himself and didn't look at anyone. Ari wanted to move closer to him, but he was still repulsing her attention. Now winding down from her own spiral, wary of her own chaos, she wasn't sure how to handle his. So she stayed where she was.

Ari glanced up. The camera drone was still there, the red recording light on. Two more had joined it.

Doryan saw them, too, and paused a moment, frowning. "Never mind those. Come, please. I have a car waiting, just a few meters away here. Guards, can you please clear the way?"

Bystanders had stopped now, too, to watch the spectacle. Some had their comms out, also recording. This was likely all over the local feeds, and the highest-rated posts would be bundled automatically and sent to Valon on the next departing interstellar comm drones.

Ari closed her eyes, the pulsing *failure, failure* still too vivid in her thoughts.

That failure wasn't true. Not all of it. But it didn't, at that moment, feel untrue.

Her vision blurred, and she realized with numbed shame that her cheeks were tracking tears again. Publicly, in front of . . . everyone. This was the sort of thing that would be everywhere. Her father would see it. Dressa would see it.

She didn't keep her head high. She had nothing high to keep it for.

The backseat of Doryan's car was thick and padded, if a little worn. The air beneath the canopy fresh and cool.

Doryan settled into the front seat, grabbing the yoke and

then flipping a switch. The hover engines started, whined, and then shifted into the lift engines of an aircar.

"Don't worry," Doryan said, "I've got emergency clearance and a special license." They lifted the car manually, a vertical lift over the rooftops, then banked and flew over the city.

And what level of emergency was this when even the city guards were confined to hovercars?

Ari followed Eti's lead and hugged her arms tightly around herself.

"So, newly manifested today," Doryan said. "That must have been terrifying."

They looked back at her, smiled. "It's all right. We've all been through it. You're safe. No harm will come to you—you're among those who understand."

Her throat closed at those words, and she didn't know why.

"I—I left someone behind. At Windvale Estate. My servant—"

But Doryan was shaking their head. "We're going straight to the spaceport. It's not safe to do anything else, and I only have leave to transport you out of the system if we go there now."

She thought that through. Tried to think that through. "Can you get a message? Can you—"

But she couldn't alert the city guards to check on Bettea at Windvale. She was already so tarnished that anything and anyone she brought attention to would likely only endanger that person further. With murder in the air, and this blowing up into a high-profile event, the guards would be all over Windvale as it was.

She dared to pray, just a small thought, not for herself at all, but to please, Adeius, please see Bettea to safety.

She shuddered and glanced to Eti. He was rocking back and forth, his eyes squeezed shut.

Her insides clenched again, thinking about why he was in this state.

He'd done what he'd done to save her. And even though she couldn't think about it without pain, and even though all of that combined might have brought about . . . all of this . . . and even though he'd been the one to tell Badem and the rest she was Truthspoken, all she wanted to do was hug him. To make it better, somehow. Especially knowing what all of that had cost.

And knowing, just a little, what it had felt like.

Bettea was trained. She had to hope fae would know to reveal faerself and get help if fae absolutely had to. Fae could prove fae was Truthspoken, or a bloodservant, at least. There was that, though Ari didn't know that wouldn't make everything worse, drawing more and more unwanted connections.

Doryan said, "I might have, possibly, looked at the camera drones a bit too enthusiastically. Their chips might have been fried."

Ari snorted a laugh, so sharp was her relief. But there were the comm images and vids from regular people, too. Those taken on the drive into the city, likely more on the chase through the alleys, more when they'd been captured. And she didn't think Doryan could wave away those.

"Are we going to Valon?" she asked.

"Yes. On a fast transport."

As they said this, they banked the aircar left, heading down. Out Eti's window, Ari saw the spaceport below, with its fifty or so pads holding ships from shuttle sized to mid-weight planetary freighters. Doryan angled toward a sleek indigo craft on an end pad, unmarked with any insignias. A rented craft? A magicker craft? She wasn't sure she should ask.

Doryan set the aircar down beside it but didn't get out right away. They turned back, brows drawn together as they looked between Eti and Ari.

"I won't lie to you. This might get ugly. There were deaths involved, and—" they took a breath "—deaths directly caused by a magicker. Not to mention using magics that require a permit without a permit. And, well, being unsealed. I will, however, protect you—both of you—as best I can. The First Magicker and the Seritarchus will absolutely be involved in whatever decisions are made."

They looked to Ari. "I need to file our flight plan and identities as soon as we board the ship. It must be done within fifteen minutes of boarding, or the craft will lock down. This is more than a standard identification process—magicker movements are all heavily watched and tracked. Imorie, I'll list you as Imorie Rhialden méron Quevedo. Correct?"

The way they'd phrased that, the very slight twitch to their eye, the question that wasn't quite a question—yes, they knew. They absolutely knew who she was.

"Correct," she said, and her voice was shakier than she'd have liked.

Doryan studied her for a moment, their lips pursed. They looked like they wanted to say something, stopped. Turned to face the front.

Turned back again and opened their mouth.

"I know you had to do it to escape, becoming invisible. I know what it does to you. Imorie, truly, there are very few things in this universe that are meant to be invisible. And even those are seen by someone or something else, in some way."

They stretched out their hand, and, her throat closing tight, Ari found herself taking it again. Found the steadying of their calm. The depth of their concern. And no judgement. Truly no judgement.

Truly? They knew who she was, they, a magicker, who had every right to distrust her and dislike her if not outright hate her for being at the pinnacle of a government that had traditionally distrusted magickers. That had certainly not done a lot to help them, had created the sort of environment where people would chase someone who was terrified of her new state of being through the city streets. That would force Eti into going against his own nature, force him to share secrets he never would have otherwise.

Doryan shouldn't be helping her at all. They were her captor, her jailer. They shouldn't be trying to soothe her.

And she'd just made it all worse. She, a Rhialden, had now planted the idea in the minds of trillions that magickers could, in fact, kill.

Doryan's other hand closed around hers. Gentle. Their eyes were shining, their lower lip trembling. As she knew her own must be, too.

They didn't say anything more, didn't try to reassure her. No platitudes, no empty promises. Just their steady presence. Their openness. Their truth.

That she was someone worth seeing. Worth knowing. Worth accepting.

The rhythm of failure that still drummed in her thoughts became discordant, exposed fully for what it was.

She didn't know what she was. But maybe, maybe she wasn't that.

Doryan nodded and let go.

"All right. Let's go to Valon."

53

NEWS

> *Urgent news is seldom good news.*
>
> — LORD PIN DRAVI IN A VID INTERVIEW FOR *THE INTERSTELLAR FEED*

Iata sat back in his desk chair, studying the cluster of open holo windows over his desk. To the right, minimized bubbles of his never-ending message queue. To the left and center, an overlapping array of text and holo images, both 2D and 3D, showing information on the Kidaa attacks. There had been five now.

Information on the last one had come in that morning—Ynasi III, the Javieri homeworld itself near the border with the Onabrii-Kast Dynasty, and that was not sitting well with anyone. Including the Dynastic ambassador, whom he'd had to reassure that morning, at length, that he was doing all he could to look into this threat.

News of this new high-profile attack, and now the others, too, was clogging up every feed he found, and he'd had to issue a statement that the Seritarcracy was aware of these incidents and was currently investigating their origin—he was not confirming or denying this was the Kidaa. He was only projecting calm authority to try and quell the panic.

This latest attack had happened over a week before it had come to his attention, but Ynasi System was far enough away that the report itself had taken that week to arrive, jumped from system to system with highest priority comm drones, as a single jump at that distance was too far.

The attack was similar to the others, this time occurring outside a minor Javieri noble's estate. No casualties, thank Adeius, though a cabbage field had been thoroughly mangled. Like the other attacks, there had been no ship detected in orbit in the range of where the attack would have come from. The rune carved into this one, as best his experts could approximate, meant something adjacent to "water."

The report of this attack had swiftly been followed by reports of rallies and riots on Ynasi III, calling for the Rhialdens to step up and help protect the Javieris.

Iata rubbed at his strained eyes. He sat back and touched a light Change trance, doing his best to smooth the fatigue over.

Five attacks now, that he knew of. There could be more, if these locations had been chosen at random—in forest areas where no one traveled, or over water, even. If they had been done by the Kidaa, he couldn't rule that possibility out. As it was, their locations on land had been . . . odd. They hadn't seemed deliberately chosen so much as . . . in the way of whatever rune had been carved into them. But all the attacks he knew about had been near people, on farms or near towns.

He'd moved the military into watchful alert status. After this last attack, publicly, he'd had to.

That two of the last three attacks had been on the homeworlds of prominent high houses, though, was troubling. Damning evidence, even, that at least some of these attacks had not been made by the Kidaa. The Javieri's homeworld was very near the border with the Onabrii-Kast Dynasty, and not particularly close to the border with the Kidaa. That, too, was troubling.

Was the expansion-minded Dynasty wanting to expand into Valoris, instead of their most recent rumblings about expanding into Kidaa territory? Were they trying to provoke a panic, or a war? Or were the attacks a repercussion of something the Dynasty had already done to the Kidaa, and the Kidaa were taking it out on all Humans in sight? Except, there were much easier and closer targets than traveling far into the Valoran interior to attack.

He hadn't been able to get an answer either way from the Dynastic ambassador, just a lot of bluster about how Valoris shouldn't endanger the Dynasty with its own problems. He hadn't let himself sense her out with more than his own Truth-spoken-trained senses, either, though he knew Maja would have thought him foolish for not using every tool he had at hand.

But he would not use his magics like that, not anymore—not for Maja, and not for himself. He kept those senses tightly contained, which itself was exhausting.

Iata sat back, staring at the runes, trying to make it all make more sense. The first rune had meant "being" or "person." The second had been something unknown, but adjacent perhaps to "galaxy." The third had also been undefined, but shared characteristics with "life." The fourth had been the same as the third, which itself had been puzzling. This fifth was adjacent to "water."

Was there a pattern? Could anyone discern a pattern from these disparate meanings? The concepts were too broad, too universal, too random.

And how, if it was the Kidaa, had they slipped in and out of Valoran space undetected? There had still been no evidence at all of Kidaa ships in Valoran space, unless one counted the attacks themselves as evidence. But no evidence of Valoran ships involved in these attacks, either.

Iata sighed, rolling his shoulders. He should get up and stretch, he'd been at his desk for hours. Light healing could only go so far when he himself was exhausted.

He couldn't keep carrying on like this—he needed someone as a second, someone who could function for him as a blood-servant as he had for Homaj. Ruling the kingdom was just not a task meant for one person alone.

And Maja himself was holed up in the Adeium, performing whatever duties he had now as a low-ranking speaker. Absolutely unimportant things in the grand scheme of things—but, that had been the point.

But it was just such a horrible waste of resources, when they were all needed.

There was a knock on the study door. Zhang's knock.

"Enter."

She stepped inside. As the captain of his—well, Homaj's—personal guards, she was one of the very few who was keyed into all of his genetic locks.

"Seritarchus. First Magicker Mariyit Broden is here to see you."

Iata frowned. He glanced at his message queue. Had Mariyit sent a message and he'd missed it? It was late, and unusual for the First Magicker to come to the palace at all, except for formal summons and events.

A thread of foreboding wound around his gut.

"See him in, please, Zhang."

She nodded, left, and a few moments later came back with the First Magicker.

Iata met Zhang's eyes, and she nodded again, backing out and closing the door, leaving Iata alone with the First Magicker.

"Mariyit," Iata said, pushing back his chair to stand, but the

First Magicker waved him back down, sitting heavily in a chair across from the desk.

The First Magicker, of course, knew who he was, and could see the spark of his magics even through his personal dampening of them. There'd been no hiding any of this from him and the other highest ranking magickers, and he and Homaj had never tried.

Iata had hid his aura when Zhang had come in—there was no use in tempting fate if anyone else had chanced to see in—but he let it bloom out again now.

"I hope you're well, Iata," Mariyit said, "but you'll want to be sitting down for this."

Iata's shoulders tensed back up again. His thoughts sped through several reasons for the First Magicker's late-night visit, landing on the fear that had been high in his thoughts lately.

"Does someone know about me?"

"About you? No."

Iata let out a breath. It had been growing harder and harder of late to contain his aura. The necessity of tamping down his own soul essence and much of his senses was uncomfortable at best, and had lately slid much farther toward painful.

"This . . ." Mariyit tapped the arm of his chair, then leaned forward to hand Iata a data chip. "This might not be much better, though."

54

THE REPORT

> *I think most people, in their deepest truths, just really want to be seen and loved for who they are.*
>
> — ETIENNE TANAKA, AS QUOTED IN *THE CHANGE DIALOGUES*

Iata took the data chip from the First Magicker and tapped the top to activate it. He set it on his desk, watching as a new window popped up.

The report was terse and text only:

Inbound to Valon with two unsealed magickers. Imorie Rhialden méron Quevedo and Etienne Tanaka. Imorie has just manifested; Etienne has been a magicker for an unknown length of time. Both were involved in an incident involving three deaths at Windvale Estate on Hestia, which are being called murders. Imorie is in better shape than Etienne. We're traveling at military speed. Recommend utmost discretion.

—*Doryan Azer, fourth rank*

Iata gripped the edge of his desk, using everything that was not centered on this report to keep his breathing steady.

Imorie Rhialden méron Quevedo was the name Ari had logged on Hestia—he'd received a pingback of her choice of identity last week.

"Who is this Etienne Tanaka?" he asked.

"Unknown," Mariyit said. "This came in minutes before I left Green Hall, and I only had time for a cursory name check. I found nineteen people with that name across Valoris, none registered as living or working on Hestia." He hesitated. "But I certainly thought you'd wish to see that this concerns a contract Rhialden. If there are murder charges involved, this could get ugly. No, it *will* get ugly. And if a Rhialden magicker is involved—"

"It's Ari," Iata said, and Mariyit briefly closed his eyes.

"I had wondered. With Hestia being known in certain circles as a treatment haven for the Bruising Sleep—and Homaj coming to me those two weeks ago, with what he wanted to test at the ball." He grimaced, and Iata carefully buried his own chagrin at that other disaster, a disaster that was just now feeling small by comparison.

Mariyit continued, "This report came in on the highest priority channel, the fastest drone. The public news reports will likely arrive within hours, and it seems like public news will be involved."

Iata stared at the far wall, his fingers drumming on his desk. That this was a political disaster was . . . an understatement. That the magicker reporting hadn't called Ari by her true name was something, but he had to assume her identity had been compromised, at least with this one magicker.

And there were deaths involved. Adeius. That thought

alone was ice in his gut, because he knew what happened when magickers killed, accidentally or not.

This magicker, Azer, had said Ari was better off than Etienne. What did that mean? Could he take from that specific point that she was not in danger of fading? That she herself had not killed?

He had seen a magicker fade once, years ago. Before he was a magicker.

It still haunted him.

"Doryan Azer. Do you know them?"

"Not personally," Mariyit said, "but what I skimmed of their record in the time I had showed a person of discretion, though I'm not sure they've dealt with anything this big before. Not that many have." An ironic smile. "But they have helped handle some more thorny manifestations on Hestia—a few with noble visitors before, too. All of those, in the end, were smoothed out."

Iata looked between his cluster of holo windows showing the Kidaa attacks and their corresponding runes, then at this new window, this intensely damning window. He didn't have to question Mariyit's security—Green Magicker comm security at the highest levels was comparable to the military's. It had to be, with the sensitive subjects they dealt with on a daily basis. Identities and secrets and truths. And the Seritarchus always had access to those comm records, too.

He smoothed back his hair—one of Homaj's gestures, and in that moment, it grounded him.

If Doryan Azer said they were traveling at military speed, their ship itself would likely be here within the day—three days instead of the usual regulated commercial five from Hestia to Valon. Every world had at least one ship reserved for fast magicker use if necessary.

So Ari had manifested Green Magics, and it sounded like

whatever had happened had been public and spectacular, Adeius help them all. And whatever had happened, the magicker involved had made a point to say that she was better off than Etienne. A reassurance—he had to take it as that. He had to hope, oh Adeius he had to hope that she hadn't been the one who'd killed. If the deaths had been from magics, or even by her and Etienne's hands at all. In this current climate, it was certainly possible the deaths had been blamed on them, whether plausible or not.

Just how much damage he'd be able to divert he'd have to see when the public reports arrived, and then the magickers themselves.

What the *hell* had happened on Hestia, beyond the fact of this manifestation? Magickers wouldn't kill on their own without drastically dire need—he of all people knew that—and even accidental deaths during manifestations were extremely rare. Hestia was a resort world. It was supposed to be a haven for discreet medical treatment.

And what about Bettea? The report hadn't mentioned anything about Bettea, unless fae was the other magicker? No, that wouldn't make sense. They couldn't both have manifested at the same time, and he didn't think this Azer would have falsified that information. This was going to be much too high profile not to be airtight.

The next few hours were bound to be torment as he waited for more information.

"You saw the part about her being better off than Etienne?" Mariyit asked into the too-stretched silence.

"Yes. Do you take that as a positive sign as well?" And likely the only reassurance Azer could give, even in that heavily encrypted message. That it was even possible for magickers to kill was a fact the magickers had worked tirelessly to suppress. Another sign as well that Azer knew who Ari was, if they thought someone who knew that would need reassurance.

"Positive for Ari, perhaps." Mariyit looked grim, and Iata

understood. If Ari was better off, then the person she was being compared to might be in danger of fading.

And—and it would absolutely not be productive to sit here worrying about that.

Iata stood. "Thank you, Mariyit. I need to speak with Maja."

Mariyit stood, too, smoothing out his day robes. Had he put them back on after retiring for the day, or had he still been working when this report had come in? Well, Iata was still working, too.

"How is Maja?" Mariyit asked. "He was . . . in rough shape when I last saw him. And I can't help but notice you haven't switched back yet."

Iata's lips pulled tight. Maja's bruises, when he'd been with the Council of Magickers after the ball, had gone deeper than the surface, certainly. Mariyit would have seen that. That Iata's own decisions that night of the ball were at the heart of this whole cascade of events sat uneasily in his soul.

"He needed some time away."

Iata hesitated. He hadn't spoken to the First Magicker yet about Homaj's abdication, and himself planning to make his own bid to rule. There'd been too much going on, and he'd been trying to decide how to frame it all. He was still trying to decide.

Mariyit Broden had been an ally and a friend even before he'd become First Magicker three years ago, having mostly been carrying out the duties of the aging First Magicker for years before then. But Iata knew they moved in different worlds. Different viewpoints and needs. Iata was a magicker, yes. But his foremost concern in everything was the good of Valoris. Mariyit's primary concern was the good of the magickers under his charge. His own kingdom within the kingdom and beyond it.

But Mariyit would need to know. Especially with what

might now be coming down, and with Iata's increasingly intense struggle to keep his own magics under wraps.

"Maja has no intention of switching back again." He watched Mariyit's reaction, both with his evaku-trained senses and his magicker senses.

Mariyit sighed, leaning on the back of the chair he'd just vacated. He didn't look surprised.

"I saw that possibility in him, yes. I don't know if I should be glad he'll get some rest, or nervous for what's to come. You—or he—will be stepping down in favor of Dressa, then? Is that what all of that was about with her becoming the Heir?"

"No, we're planning for him to abdicate in favor of me. As myself."

Mariyit's brows rose. "Well. Well, and do you also intend to tell everyone you're a magicker?"

"I've given that thought, yes."

Mariyit wiped a hand across his lined face, and he himself looked wearier than usual. Older, and worn.

"Ah, friend. And what's happening now—well, we'll have to wait and see what will even be possible in the next few days, won't we?"

It was all horrible timing, Iata agreed. But then, what was good timing for a disaster of this magnitude? If only Ari could have managed to do something, for once, without it shaking worlds.

No, no. That wasn't fair. She hardly would have asked to manifest Green Magics, and he knew exactly how panicked she must be right now. And the last time she'd shaken worlds, it had been largely his fault.

And she still might be in danger of losing her life.

When a Green Magicker killed, even by accident, sometimes their soul and body would immediately fade under the intense conflict of the violence. Sometimes they would linger for a time in a haze, holding on, and dissipate later. And a very few rare times, they would hold on and recover, regaining solidity, regaining soundness of mind and soul.

Iata waved off his desk displays, using Change to tweak his brain chemistry in that moment, to calm the fuck down. He touched the comm controls. "Zhang?"

She was back in moments.

"Zhang, please see the First Magicker out and safely to his transport." It was already becoming more and more unsafe to be seen as even a sealed magicker, no thanks at all to his stunt at Arianna's engagement ball. In the next few days, he couldn't think that situation would get better.

"Of course, Seritarchus. First Magicker, if you will follow me, please."

"I'll be in touch," Mariyit called over his shoulder.

Iata nodded. He waited for the door to close, then grabbed the chip Mariyit had given him from his desk and crossed toward the hidden panel that led into the back corridors. It was the quickest and most secure way to the Adeium.

55

DISASTERS

There is no rest for Truthspoken in the center of it all.

— HOMAJ RHIALDEN, SERITARCHUS IX IN A PRIVATE LETTER, NEVER SENT; PUBLISHED IN *THE CHANGE DIALOGUES*

On his way to the Adeium, Iata twisted the center band of his comm ring to the secure channel he had with Ceorre.

"I'm coming," he murmured into it. "Have Speaker Murian there when I arrive."

She didn't ask more of him over the comm, though he could hear the tension of her silence, knowing that something was very wrong.

"He will be."

When he emerged through a panel in one of the Adeium practice rooms, Ceorre was already there, with Maja. Her face was drawn tight, eyes searching his.

"What is it?" she asked. "The Javieris? The tensions with the Kidaa? Has Lesander—"

"No, nothing with that," he said.

Maja stood in his indigo robes, arms wrapped protectively around himself, near the corner vanity. Iata knew he'd been nervously rearranging the cosmetics moments ago. And he knew, too, that neither Maja nor Ceorre would appreciate that small flair of pageantry the First Magicker had given him in allowing him to read the report first, without explanations.

So he dispensed with preamble. "It's Ari. She's manifested Green Magics, publicly and with prejudice, and she's inbound in custody as Imorie. There are murder charges."

He did pull out the chip, then, and set it on the vanity table. He waited while they both read.

Maja stood unnaturally still. He didn't look less haggard, Iata thought, than that awful night when he'd abdicated. When he'd told them both of his plans. And this certainly wasn't going to help anything, was it?

Adeius, what a mess.

Ceorre swore softly, poking at the holo to see if there was more. She stood back.

"When will they be here?"

"Mariyit, who brought this to me, seemed to think within the day at military speed."

Ceorre nodded, but it was a rote response. Her brows were drawn together in thought, and it was a mark of her distress that she was showing that much emotion at all.

"She might have killed," Maja said, and looked up, meeting Iata's eyes. They both knew—they both knew what that could look like.

"I don't think so," Iata said. "Magicker Azer made sure to say she was better off."

Maja held up his hands, a wrenchingly helpless gesture. "Well, then, if she's manifested, it's not the end of everything. We know that, Yan. We know that from you."

Wasn't it the end of everything? Iata felt his anger rising

above his tight control and had to consciously tamp it back down. Yes, he'd managed. That didn't mean it had been easy, and he was barely managing now to keep his magics under wraps and still rule the kingdom. He'd been hoping to smooth the way to step up fully as himself, as a magicker, too. That idea had taken hold and grown until he wasn't sure he could bear to not go down that path.

He didn't know how much longer he could take it, this having to suppress most of himself every day, to walk around without the senses that had become his primaries.

He wouldn't tell Maja that, though.

"We won't know for sure what happened, or why, or how she's handling it, until they arrive," he said, and knew he was only restating what they already knew, but it was something to say. A narrative he could, at the moment, control. "And by the time they arrive, it will be all over the news. The attacks with the Kidaa are bad enough to have the Seritarcracy on shaky ground, and Arianna's engagement ball is still lingering in people's minds, there hasn't been enough time yet. People will jump on a reason to mistrust the magickers. And with her being Rhialden, even a contract Rhialden . . ."

Maja nodded. Nothing he didn't know. He sighed, looking away. Not acknowledging that he'd had a hand in this particular fear of the magickers.

"I'll do what I can to quell the panic," Ceorre said. "We should have the Municipal Guard on alert for more riots. Send some of the Palace Guard to Green Hall, if that's where this ship's going to land. Unless you direct them to the palace?"

"No, I thought about that, but too obvious. I'll go there."

"No," Maja said, his voice breaking.

They all paused. Because all of them were attuned to the pain in that break.

Maja waved them off. "No, I need to do this one." He looked up, and wasn't trying to hide his dismay, or his gathering of willpower. "One more time. Ari will already be disoriented—I know how it was after your manifestation. We can't spring this on her right away, can we? You and I, Yan? And we won't be able to hide who you are as a magicker from her, either."

Not likely with Ari being a magicker now, no. He didn't know what rank she'd manifested into as her starting point, but with Ari, he couldn't assume it would be low. His own hadn't been. He could keep his aura tamped down and mostly hidden from lower-ranking magickers—but even if she was a lower rank, if he was Homaj and she touched him, she would know.

The many, many more disasters that could come from her hesitating, from accidentally exposing him as Homaj as a magicker, bloomed out in his thoughts until he took hold of them, reigned them back in.

He nodded at Maja. "Yes. One more time. Do you want to Change now or wait for the news drones to come in?"

Maja stretched, rubbing the back of his neck under his long braid. "Now." He glanced at Iata. "Be yourself?"

Yes, he would have to Change too, change back to being Iata. Which this time felt more confining than it should be. He'd grown used to spreading out his own presence. This always happened when he was Homaj for any length of time, but this time, knowing what was ahead of him—ruling in his own right—this time, it was different.

But he nodded.

For Ari, and for the good of the kingdom.

Maja glanced around them at the practice room, at its small, neat bed. They could Change here, there was a second room beside this one. It would be quickest.

But. But they'd always done so at the palace. It was safe. It was, or at least had been, routine.

"One more time," Maja said, and led the way into the back corridors.

56

LESANDER

Any intelligence system substantial enough to be publicly known as such cannot exist in a vacuum. And while the Kingdom of Valoris itself has opposites in the intelligence systems of the Onabrii-Kast Dynasty, the Farani Protectorate, and other nearby kingdoms and nations, the largest threat to its stability has always come from within. If High House Rhialden has its own private intelligence system, even if it's used for the greater good of the kingdom, other high houses have their opposite systems as well.

— DR. LASHONDA KOJIMA, MILITARY HISTORIAN, IN *THE RISE OF THE NEW INTELLIGENCE SYSTEM*

Lesander's lips lingered on Dressa's, the taste of Dressa's honeysuckle lip gloss.

"Mmm," Dressa said, but it was half a moan, half a sigh, and she pulled back first. "I have to sleep. Have to wake up early. Everything with this mess with the Kidaa attacks." She yawned, stretched, and settled further into her pile of pillows and skewed blankets.

Dressa, Lesander had found, was not a still sleeper. And she was very definitely a blanket thief.

"*Maybe* Kidaa attacks," Lesander said, tugging one of the blankets back her way. "We still don't know that for sure."

"Well, they hit your world, too. Whoever they are. Which is part of the mess I have to deal with tomorrow."

"*We* have to deal with. Us. Let me help you, Dressa. I'm doing the research the Seritarchus asked. I found Koldari, didn't I?"

Just that night. Between his random and private trail across worlds—heavily muffled by bribes—and the time it took for comm messages to go back and forth to verify information, it had taken nearly two weeks, but she'd found him. He was staying at an estate on Hestia which didn't publicly announce its guest list and discouraged social posting while there. But one of Koldari's partners, Iwan ko Antia, hadn't been so quiet about where they were going. Lesander had sent all the information over to the Seritarchus a few hours ago and was having trouble not feeling immensely triumphant about it.

Something faint and quickly suppressed rippled across Dressa's face, a disruption Lesander could see even in the dim light from the wall sconces. Something had been bothering Dressa these last few days, and Lesander hadn't yet been able to figure out what it was. She didn't think it was just these attacks, and finding Koldari had become less of a priority than managing the full picture.

Lesander propped up on one elbow, studying her wife. Dressa's hair, which she'd made curly two nights ago, was bundled in a sleep wrap, but a few curls had escaped the edges.

Dressa had not said anything, but Lesander had watched her enact subtle changes in her appearance over the last week. A slightly different shape to her eyes. A slightly different width to her lips. And the hair, of course. Lesander certainly wouldn't protest her slightly bigger bust size.

All of these changes were farther from the body she'd inhabited as Arianna. None of them were *not* Dressa, but rather, a different sort of refinement.

Just now, though, Dressa's eyes had deeper shadows than they should have, though Lesander knew she would correct that overnight or in the morning. Her every curve flowed and fit her exactly. That she'd ever inhabited any body but this one felt . . . ludicrous.

"Are you all right? Is it your father? Is he putting too much pressure—"

Dressa snorted, making a frustrated hand wave. "It's all pressure. All from here on out."

She rolled over, staring up at the ceiling. Her hand found and locked with Lesander's, and Lesander sighed, shifting to stare up at the ceiling, too. The soft pattern of flowers.

"I'm going to redecorate. Or maybe you can. If you want."

Dressa had been complaining about the apartment since she'd moved in the week before. It was Arianna's old apartment, which traditionally belonged to the Truthspoken Heir pre-marriage. They'd be in the post-marriage apartment soon enough, so Lesander didn't see much point in redecorating in the meantime.

And she wanted more meaningful work, not relegation to aesthetics. But she'd been pressing too much for that already, and Dressa didn't seem inclined to give any further. Lesander was absolutely aware that her search for Koldari, and the various other tasks the Seritarchus had set her to, was useful work but nothing palace staff couldn't do. Dressa had to know that, too.

Did Dressa suspect what she was? Had Dressa seen something in an unguarded moment? She'd been so careful. She hadn't made any attempt at Change, not even smoothing back a blush, or smoothing away the light but persistent nasal allergies that one of the royal physicians had said was normal for someone from offworld coming into the capital at this time of year. So much of the palace gardens were blooming.

Could she give a little ground and push from a different angle?

"Redecorating would beat tracking down all the disparate pieces your father's set me to," Lesander said. "Now he's got me tracing a bunch of financial records from minor Delor estates, and a few Javieri, too. And Xiao. And a few other names that are of less consequence but apparently he thinks are important."

Dressa was quiet, not answering right away.

Lesander looked over at her. They still didn't know each other as well as they might, she still found herself teetering on the precipice of missteps.

And she knew Dressa didn't tell her everything about her life—of course she didn't. She couldn't. She was Truthspoken. She was the Heir.

Dressa had seemed less bothered by her father's greater intrusion into her daily life than she'd first made out she would be, but Lesander felt a different sort of tension around the subject of her father. She was watching Dressa take strides in her own right, too, and that—that was exhilarating, and she never would have expected it to be.

But then, she'd never expected to actually like the woman she was going to marry. She'd never expected this woman at all.

Dressa sighed. "Please, I think I'd like to not talk about the palace, and the Seritarchus—Adeius, definitely not the Seritarchus—and all of those politics and chores here, in our bedroom."

Our bedroom. Lesander felt a ripple down her spine at those words. She had an apartment of her own in the residence wing now, a few doors down, but she'd hardly spent any time there. She didn't truly wish to.

"Okay," Lesander said. "No work."

"No work," Dressa agreed. Then, "Right. I'm going to sleep."

She rolled over, facing away from Lesander.

Then rolled back for one last kiss.

Lesander bit back her own groan at the heat rising in her, knowing she couldn't sate it tonight. Not with Dressa, and not with anyone else—their marriage contract might not be public yet, but it was certainly binding, as was the exclusivity clause. Not that she truly wished to be with anyone else just now.

Lesander rolled out of bed. "My mind's still in work. I'll be in the prep room—back to bed in a bit."

Dressa made an indistinct noise into the pillow, then flopped a hand to wave Lesander off.

Yeah, they both knew if she stayed, there would be a lot less sleep tonight.

57

MISSION CRITICAL

> *Truthspoken must be ever vigilant, even within their own families. Especially within their own families.*
>
> — ARIANNA RHIALDEN, MELESORIE X IN *THE CHANGE DIALOGUES*

Lesander grabbed her comm off a nearby chair and carried it with her into the prep room, quietly shutting Dressa's door.

In the prep room, the only sound was the soft hum of the palace air system. The spacious room itself was tidy, with the two large vanity stations to her left and the doors to the enormous closet to the right. Lesander's newly installed desk also sat to the right beside the closet, and that's where she was headed.

Pria, Dressa's bloodservant, had cleaned up Dressa's daily sprawl and gone to bed before Dressa, as she usually did, their bedrooms being joined. That was something Lesander was having to get used to—Pria, she'd found, was far more than a servant in Dressa's life. She was somewhere between friend and sibling, nursemaid and household chamberlain. Pria could Change, too, and not just superficially. And Pria certainly knew evaku and was highly tuned to Dressa's moods.

There was a lot Lesander had been taught about palace life that was just slightly, and critically, off. She was sure the Rhialdens actively maintained that leak of misinformation. And should she tell her parents about that?

She settled herself at the desk. Dressa's new post-marriage apartment would have a designated study that had no surveillance, but Dressa had said in this apartment, only the prep room and bedrooms were truly safe. So a desk had been brought in here.

Lesander set down her comm and the desk amplified it, throwing up holo windows in front of her. Her comm had military-grade security installed, but she had no illusions that her activity wouldn't be monitored. They had, of course, planned for that.

She surveyed the windows she'd had open last time she'd been working on her comm, a few hours ago. She dismissed the information on Koldari—the rest of the windows were articles and responses to the latest Kidaa attack, this time on Lesander's homeworld. On one of her cousin's estates.

There would have been just enough time for news of her engagement to Dressa—and the much more heavily encrypted news of her private marriage—to have reached her family, for her family to have manufactured one of these Kidaa attacks, and for that news to have reached Valon again. Just enough.

That assumed that her parents had known about the other Kidaa attacks ahead of time. Had they?

Did they know because they were in fact behind them?

She wasn't sure if she wished that or not, or if she was manufacturing motives that weren't there. These attacks really could be coincidental. Maybe.

Lesander flicked idly through images and articles of riots

on Ynasi III. She paused on a holo of Palace Javieri, her home. Not so different in appearance to Palace Rhialden. Much, *much* different in atmosphere. She'd come to Valon expecting Palace Rhialden to be vicious, and it was, but the people here—

The people here hadn't spent a fifth of their entire family's fortune training their only daughter—purposely their only daughter so she would have no danger of competition or usurpation—to one day overthrow a kingdom. To one day, if she was successful, rule it.

She'd met the Seritarchus. He was petty and cruel and his own way, but he cared for Dressa. She saw that. She saw the slightest pinch between his brows when he seemed worried. He didn't have many visible emotional tells, but he certainly had a few.

And Dressa. Dressa was someone she hadn't expected at all. A pillar of sanity amidst all the subtleties. Dressa did her best to push back against the subtleties. When Dressa looked at her, Lesander saw oceans in Dressa's eyes.

Her inbox pinged.

Out of habit, she tapped the icon as it floated up, and a new window formed.

Lesander froze. The message was from one of her cousins, Nira Javieri, who stayed in the Javieri penthouse in Valon City. She'd seen Nira the day Dressa had been confirmed as Heir, in the greetings afterward in the Reception Hall. Nira had been the same Nira they always had been. All fake smiles and smarm. They were positioned in Valon, mainly, to reassure the nobility that the Javieris had dull teeth.

Lesander doubted anyone truly believed that.

But this message. This message contained one image, a smiling looping holo of Nira wearing dark sunglasses at a party, wine glass in hand, repeatedly toasting the camera.

But that wasn't what Lesander was staring at. Nira was wearing a red silk sari, embroidered in a pattern that Lesander's mother had made her draw again and again until she'd had it memorized and it had haunted her dreams. That pattern would show up when the Javieri family was ready to make their move.

Her heart was pounding in her throat. It was too soon. She'd thought she'd have until the public wedding, at least. Or after—she'd thought she'd have more time.

She hadn't truly, since the first night with Dressa, wanted to carry out her mission at all.

Her family had wanted all of the Rhialdens dead, but she'd persuaded them to try this first, to take the long road, to avoid a war. Let her marry the Truthspoken Heir. Let her, in time, become the Ruler Consort. Raise her half-Javieri children to one day rule themselves.

Her mother, Prince Yroikan Javieri, had never been overly patient. And her mama had never been overly good at persuading her wife the prince to take a different course than the one she was set on.

Her mother had told her, repeatedly, that they hadn't spent a fortune and taken the risks they had for Lesander to go marry a Truthspoken and live a happy and peaceful life. While the Javieris still were not in power.

Lesander rotated the holo with both hands, inspecting the pattern to be sure, absolutely sure, of what she was seeing.

But yes, it was there. The signal.

The handwritten caption under the holo, in her cousin's handwriting read, "Wish you colud be here!" Drunken spelling mistake and all.

Lesander dashed out an inane reply because it would be expected, and closed the holo.

Closed her inbox.

But another alert popped up, a keyword trigger she had on any urgent news regarding Rhialdens coming in-system. It was a rote keyword search—mostly everything having to do with the Rhialdens was in-system.

She frowned and tapped on the alert. It brought up a flurry of new windows, each tagged with the red timestamp of being from a comm drone which had arrived within the past fifteen minutes, its contents dumped and short-jumped around the system.

Contract Rhialden Manifests Magics, Suspected in the Deaths of Three.

Two Rogue Magickers Pursued Through Racha, Hestia, one a Rhialden.

Imorie Rhialden méron Quevedo, Arrested on Charges of Murder and Practicing Unsealed Magics.

Images, vids, and holos arrived as the comm drone's bandwidth was freed up from the first data dump.

Lesander leaned forward, tapping on one. It showed an androgynous person, very visibly resembling the Rhialdens, their hands in cuffs, looking angrily to one side. They were outlined in a vivid green aura.

"Fuck," Lesander whispered. There was no way, absolutely no way that could not be Arianna.

Was this why her family had pinged her now? To be ready. To watch for the second and final signal, or be ready for action with no second signal at all.

The kingdom was about to be in an uproar.

Lesander grabbed her comm and ran to go wake up Dressa.

Thanks so much for reading! I hope you enjoyed *The Shadow Rule*, and if you did, please consider leaving a review! The story continues in *Court of Magickers*.

Want to stay up to date on the latest books? Sign up for Novae Caelum's newsletter!
https://novaecaelum.com/pages/newsletter

THE CAST

Note: Because this future universe has full gender equality, binary gender characters (male, female) may be cis or may be trans. I've only stated if they're trans if it comes up within the story itself.

Ondressarie Rhialden (Dressa): The Truthspoken Heir of the Kingdom of Valoris, coming into her own. Former court socialite. Married to Lesander Javieri. Female, lesbian. she/her

Arianna Rhialden (Ari/Imorie): Second Truthspoken heir of the Kingdom of Valoris and would really like to change that. Hates when things are out of her control. Has a chronic illness. Agender, ace. she/her

Rhys Petrava méron Delor: Lieutenant in the Valoran Navy. Half-sibling to Arianna and Dressa. Has phosphorescent hair. Likes to research the alien Kidaa. Nonbinary, pan. they/them

Homaj Rhialden (Maja): The Seritarchus, aka the Truthspoken Ruler of the Kingdom of Valoris. Loves to control things even more than Ari. Might be coming unglued. Genderfluid, pan (mostly gay). he/him (usually)

Iata byr Rhialden (Yan): Bloodservant to Homaj. Acerbic, sharp, more than he seems. Male, hetero. he/him

Etienne Tanaka (Eti): Gardener on the resort world of Hestia. Loves plants, has lots of secrets. Trans male, pan. he/him

Lesander Javieri: Secret Heir Consort of the Kingdom of Valoris. Tall and gorgeous. Might be devious, who knows? Married to Dressa Rhialden. Female, bi. she/her

Vi Zhang: Captain of the Seritarchus's personal guard. One of the only people who can call him on his BS. Female, gray ace. she/her

Misha Moratu: Ensign in the Valoran Navy. Green Magicker. Has some secrets she's doing a good job of hiding. Has phosphorescent *green* hair. Female, pan. she/her

Kyran Koldari: Duke, royal PITA. Handsome and likely up to no good. Male, pan. he/him

Bettea byr Rhialden (Jis): Bloodservant to Arianna. Takes no BS. Genderfluid, aego. fae/faer

Ceorre Gatri: The Truthspeaker, aka the only person who can boss the Seritarchus around. Religious leader of Valoris. Takes no prisoners. Female, bi. she/her

Haneri ne Delor Rhialden: Seritarchus Consort, aka Arianna's, Dressa's, and Rhys's mother. Has seen some things, will see some more. Demigirl, pan. she/her

Count Badem: Proprietor of Windvale Estate on Hestia. Effusive and friendly, always the life of the party. Female, hetero. she/her

Ryam: Head gardener of Windvale Estate. Not generally a pleasant person. Male, pan. he/him

Dr. Lin: Physician at Windvale Estate. Expert in treating the Bruising Sleep. Male, hetero. he/him

Doryan Azer: Green Magicker. Healer. Will stand up to anyone for those in need. Nonbinary, pan. they/them

Mariyit Broden: First Magicker of the Green Magickers. Kindly, but doesn't take slack. Male, gay. he/him

Jalava: Commander of the Palace Guard. Harried, loyal, usually right. Genderqueer, pan. they/them

THE FACTIONS

Kingdom of Valoris: 187 worlds of theocratic goodness. Ruled by the Seritarchus. Bickered over by the high houses. Shares a border with Kidaa space.

The Kidaa: A species of quadruped sentients. Organized into clans, occupy a large portion of space. Far more technologically advanced than Humans. Hard to talk to. Pacifists (theoretically).

The Onabrii-Kast Dynasty: Former territory of Valoris, now their own empire. Also share the border with the Kidaa. Not super interested in sharing anything else.

Green Magickers: Organized sub-culture of people who manifest the ability to use Green Magics. Marginalized. Can't do violence.

The Adeium: Religion at the heart of Valoris. Genderfluid god. Oversees the Truthspeaker and the Truthspoken.

ACKNOWLEDGMENTS

For everyone who has cheered this serial on, has tried it out, binge read, bought or pre-ordered the books, read and shared it with a friend, and generally helped support me throughout the journey, thank you!

A huge thanks (always!) to Laterpress, who opened up so many doors for me. And many heartfelt thanks to my supporters on Laterpress and Patreon—you're directly funding dreams, folx! Lots of thanks and love to everyone at Robot Dinosaur Press, to the Vella folx who inhabit various Facebook groups and Discords, to my various friends who've listened to my ramblings and excitements, to my family who *have* to listen to my various ramblings and excitements, and to my pup who tells me when it is time to stop writing and get up and play.

This book would not be the same without all of you.

ABOUT THE AUTHOR

Novae Caelum is an author, illustrator, and designer with a love of spaceships and a tendency to quote Monty Python. Star is the author of *The Stars and Green Magics* (a winner of the 2022 Laterpress Genre Fiction Contest Fellowship), *The Emperor of Time* (a Wattpad Featured novel), *Good King Lyr*, and *Magnificent*. Stars short fiction has appeared in *Intergalactic Medicine Show*, *Escape Pod*, *Clockwork Phoenix 5*, and Lambda Award winning *Transcendent 2: The Year's Best Transgender Speculative Fiction*. Novae is nonbinary, starfluid, and uses star/stars/starself or they/them/their pronouns. Most days you can find Novae typing furiously away at stars queer serials, with which star hopes to take over the world. At least, that's the plan. You can find star online at novaecaelum.com

ALSO BY NOVAE CAELUM

The Stars and Green Magics

The Truthspoken Heir

The Shadow Rule

A Bid to Rule

Court of Magickers

The Nameless Storm (early access)

Lyr and Cavere

Good King Lyr: A Genderfluid Romance

Borrowed Wings (early access)

Shattered Self (early access)

The Space Roads

The Space Roads: Volume One

The Watered Worlds

The Watered Worlds (early access)

Standalone

Magnificent: A Nonbinary Superhero Novella

The Throne of Eleven

Lives on Other Worlds

Grim Birds: Five Tales of Cosmic Horror and Wonder (early access)

Sky and Dew

Visit Novae Caelum's website to find out where to read these titles on your favorite retailers or direct from the author!

https://novaecaelum.com

ALSO FROM ROBOT DINOSAUR PRESS

Terra Incognita by Mati Ocha
Hiking in the Peak District at the moment Earth is—accidentally—infused with magic and thrown into an indifferent and muddled system, Will returns to his Derbyshire village to find a ghost town.

Hollow King by Dante O. Greene
Barridur finds himself in Hell where he meets the fabled Hollow King. A cruel and capricious god, the Hollow King offers Barridur a chance to return alive to the living world. All Barridur has to do is defeat the Nine Champions of Hell. No pressure.

You Fed Us To the Roses: Short Stories by Carlie St. George
Final girls who team up. Dead boys still breathing. Ghosts who whisper secrets. Angels beyond the grave, yet not of heaven. Wolves who wear human skins. Ten disturbing, visceral, stories no horror fan will want to miss.

A Wreck of Witches by Nia Quinn
When you're a witch juggling a sentient house and a

magical plant nursery, you already think life is about as crazy as it can get. But scary things start happening in my mundane neighborhood when my friend goes missing. It's up to me and my ragtag group of witches—oh, and the ghost dogs—to get things under control before the Unawares figure out magic's real.

THESE IMPERFECT REFLECTIONS: SHORT STORIES BY MERC FENN WOLFMOOR
From living trains to space stations populated with monsters, these eleven fantasy and science fiction stories from Merc Fenn Wolfmoor will take you on otherworldly adventures that are tethered to the heart.

FLOTSAM BY R J THEODORE
A scrappy group of outsiders take a job to salvage some old ring from Peridot's gravity-caught garbage layer, and land squarely in the middle of a plot to take over (and possibly destroy) what's left of the already tormented planet.

THE MIDNIGHT GAMES: SIX STORIES ABOUT GAMES YOU PLAY ONCE ED. BY RHIANNON RASMUSSEN
An anthology featuring six frightening tales illustrated by Andrey Garin await you inside, with step by step instructions for those brave—or desperate—enough to play.

SANCTUARY BY ANDI C. BUCHANAN
Morgan's home is a sanctuary for ghosts. When it is threatened they must fight for the queer, neurodivergent found-family they love and the home they've created.

A STARBOUND SOLSTICE BY JULIET KEMP

Celebrations, aliens, mistletoe, and a dangerous incident in the depths of mid-space. A sweet festive season space story with a touch of (queer) romance.

Find these great titles and more at your favorite ebook retailer!

Visit us at: www.robotdinosaurpress.com

* 9 7 8 1 9 5 8 6 9 6 1 1 8 *
BV - #0038 - 120824 - C0 - 216/140/19 - PB - 9781958696118 - Matt Lamination